GOOD TO THE LAST KISS

GOOD TO
THE LAST KISS

Crimes of the Depraved Mind Series

Ronald Tierney

This first world edition published 2011
in Great Britain and the USA by
SEVERN HOUSE PUBLISHERS LTD of
9–15 High Street, Sutton, Surrey, England, SM1 1DF.

British Library Cataloguing in Publication Data

Tierney, Ronald.
  Good to the last kiss. – (Crimes of the depraved mind)
  1. Police – California – San Francisco – Fiction. 2. Serial
  murder investigation – California – San Francisco –
  Fiction. 3. Rape victims – Fiction. 4. Psychic trauma –
  Fiction. 5. Detective and mystery stories.
  I. Title II. Series
  813.5'4-dc22

ISBN-13: 978-0-7278-8030-7 (cased)

All Severn House titles are printed on acid-free paper.

Severn House Publishers support The Forest Stewardship Council [FSC],
the leading international forest certification organisation. All our titles that
are printed on Greenpeace-approved FSC-certified paper carry the FSC logo.

Typeset by Palimpsest Book Production Ltd.,
Falkirk, Stirlingshire, Scotland.
Printed and bound in Great Britain by the
MPG Books Group, Bodmin, Cornwall.

To John Fleener

With Appreciation

Though the entire work is fictional and no character, including the inspectors in the book, are based on anyone other than the author's imagination, James W. Bergstrom and Anthony J. Camilleri Jr., inspectors for the San Francisco Police Department at the time of my research, were instrumental in rendering police activities as realistic as fiction – and a heavy dose of artistic license – allowed.

Thanks also to Kirsten Jones, John Fleener, Karen Watt, David Anderson and brothers Richard, Robbin and Ryan for their reflections (though not necessarily approval) on the following pages. A special thanks to my good friend Mark Stevenson for helping me recreate the area in and around Iowa City.

*T*he kid knew it would be tonight. He could feel it taking
over, wrestling with his numb soul – a force out of nowhere,
taking him to a place he didn't want to go. Not a whole lot
he could do about it. He knew that too. He had tried to fight it
before. But this was the feeling. The beginning. He knew it. And
it would only get worse.

She had already flipped most of the contents of a childproof
bottle of Tylenol into the toilet during the act of getting it open.
Before that she discovered the dry cleaners had failed to replace
an essential clasp on her black evening dress.

Julia Bateman took a couple of deep breaths and – having
convinced herself that she had brought on a period of calm –
looked around her studio apartment for a couple of stray aspirins.
Nothing. Calm, she went back into the bathroom. Once her feet
touched the wet tile, they struck out on their own and her body
slapped against the floor. She got up slowly, checking to make
sure everything was still working.

Everything worked. 'See,' she said with a phony brightness.
'Every fucking thing is just delightful, isn't it?'

She couldn't find her face in the mirror. The old apartment
building had no bathroom exhausts. Steam still coated her reflection. When she took off her towel to clean the mirror it snapped
the bottle of Chanel No.19, shattering it in the tub, exploding
like radiation waves from the detonation of an atom bomb and
sending a cloying scent into her bathroom.

She cut a finger trying to pick up the little granules of glass
from the porcelain. As soon as she was convinced the visible
pieces of glass were retrieved, she ran the water forcefully to
draw the rest of the glass and the dregs of Chanel down the
drain. Afraid the smell would hang in her small studio, she ran
to the windows to open them, again to discover a small movement in the drapery across the alley.

What was it? Had there been someone there?

She decided not to care. She went back to the bathroom,

pulled out a tube of Ben Gay and applied it to the bristles of her toothbrush.

Inspector Vincente Gratelli was off duty, shoes off, a glass of Chianti in his hand, watching television.

He was not a pretty sight, even when he wasn't exhausted. He looked older than his fifty-five years and no one would mistake him for a retired fashion model even if his tie were tied and his shirt buttoned, and his hair combed.

This was the only TV he allowed himself – that and *60 Minutes*. The news. The national news ended. It was the local news now. The stylish mayor was talking about the murders. Gratelli switched off the set, went to the window. Darkness was overtaking the light. There was a pinkness down on the busy street. The color of the sunset, the influence of the neon. He heard a siren. It was beginning. He felt a little guilty. He should be doing something about the murders. When you know it's going to happen again, it seemed like you ought to just keep working – all day, all night. But there was nothing to go on. Absolutely nothing. So he finally gave up. Finally took a night. He'd eat. Go to bed early. Try to get some sleep. Get some energy so he could pile back in with a fresh mind and at least a mildly cooperating body.

None of them were easy. The homicides. These were particularly nasty. Some strange twists. The girls were young, too. The way they were left – that too was strange and sad and smarmy. Wasn't messy. Not bloody or anything. It was something more indefinable. Something less visceral, more unsettling in its sickness.

The kid knew it would be tonight. He could feel it taking over, wrestling his numb soul out of nowhere and taking it to a place he didn't want to be. Not a whole lot he could do about it. He knew that too. This was the feeling. The beginning. He knew it. And it would only get worse.

ONE

Julia Bateman couldn't help herself. She stole another glance. The object of her curiosity was Thaddeus Maldeaux. He sat across the table from her, down one seat. He was more striking in person than he was in the photographs published by the newspapers and magazines. She was not usually awed by celebrity or overwhelmed by the presence of another human being. It was a feeling that – at the moment – caused her discomfort.

David Seidman sat on her left chatting with matriarch Helen Maldeaux. Helen, most people in San Francisco knew, controlled the family who controlled large chunks of the nation's banks and investment institutions and media, not to mention a few powerful politicians, many of whom had already passed by the table and engaged her in flattering conversation.

It was impossible not to know about the Maldeaux family. Thaddeus – Teddy to his friends – was son of Helen. Someone less rich and less charming, who behaved as he did, would not have been allowed too near polite society. At thirty-eight, he'd been married four times – each to an innocent, young heiress or social celebrity. His extra-marital affairs were, however, the most tantalizing. The women were media savvy and rarely innocent. You would find Teddy's name in all the trendy magazines, often in *Vanity Fair* and *Interview* and *Tatler*. Occasionally in *Time* and *Newsweek*. Teddy's cast off girl friends often ended up as shooting stars themselves – bright and brief luminescences in the night sky – for all of the media mentions.

A few kissed and told.

'The frightening thing about Thad,' one said, 'is that he appears both masculine *and* intelligent.' She also said that he had perfected the 'dress-down' look – the slightly frayed cuffs on his slightly over-sized shirts and the slightly wrinkled fabric of his shirts. One would have easily recognized the names of those who designed his clothing, but these were not off the rack and you wouldn't see anything just like them on anyone else. 'He spends a great deal to look like a handsome peasant,' she told the magazine. 'A handsome stylish peasant of course.'

Julia already knew that Thaddeus and David Seidman were friends, though Julia had not met him before this evening. Julia sensed that David wanted to protect her from him – perhaps wisely so. David and Thaddeus graduated from Stanford and received law degrees from Harvard in the same years. They were fiercely competitive, though there was no real contest. Teddy outperformed David in sports, spending, womanizing and intellect. David was from a wealthy family as well, though one would never know it. Few knew that the Seidmans possessed even more wealth, perhaps because they wielded their power and influence less publicly and with considerably less flourish.

While neither of them *had* to work, David chose public service whereas Teddy seemed to choose public spectacles.

Julia wasn't comfortable. She wasn't comfortable last night at the opera and she wasn't comfortable here in the grand hotel. Sitting in its heavily chandeliered ballroom, a huge space filled with huge people – San Francisco's finest, oldest and most unreachable families – she felt as if she were Daisy Mae on a polo pony.

What brought them all together was the 2000 Maldeaux Dinner, a HIV/AIDS benefit. The others joining Julia, David, Thaddeus and Helen, were a famous cosmetic surgeon and his wife, a notorious designer and his friend, a *San Francisco Chronicle* columnist and the columnist's bored husband. Also at the table were a small intelligent looking man from Zurich and a novelist.

Robin Williams had just made an unsurprising guest appearance and had gone. Pavarotti had spoken. Eloquently and humorously.

Julia used the passing of speakers to excuse herself. She felt suffocated. The new speaker, another one of the famous San Francisco names, a member of an immensely rich oil family not usually known for generosity, climbed upon the dais to discuss the importance of contributing to an organization trying to create housing for those with HIV and reminding the audience that recent medical advances shouldn't mislead people into thinking there was nothing left to do.

'I thought women always traveled in pairs,' Thaddeus said, intercepting Julia's journey.

She couldn't help but stare back at the green eyes. His presence was nearly hypnotic. He moved close. His breath was on hers.

'David speaks of you often,' Thaddeus continued, 'but I'm guessing you give him only a little more than the time of day.'

Even in the dim light, she could see his eyes dance. His words weren't said to chastise, but meant as a spirited assault designed to both engage Julia and test her spirit.

'Then he's gotten a little more than you will,' Julia said without breaking stride.

The low-growling Camaro with the smoked windows cruised Taylor, Jones, Turk and Eddy streets.

The driver knew he was doing something wrong. Very wrong. If he'd believed his mother – what she'd said during those religion-infused moments between alcoholic binges – he was not just wrong. He was not just bad. He was evil. He was 'evil' before he'd done anything. And so maybe she was right. He didn't think about things that way. But if she was right and she didn't know the half of it, he was the devil incarnate. And there was absolutely nothing he could do about it now.

The pink lights of the gay strip joint's marquis and those of the liquor store reflected on the car's new wax job. The car slowed, pulled to the curb. A girl, who was making her own corridor through a teetering crowd of winos stopped, went to the passenger window of the Camaro. She shook her head 'no,' started to back away, but changed her mind and moved again to the window. She giggled. Her casual indecision was an obvious act. She looked in the window one more time, then got in the car.

Brushing him off had little effect on Thaddeus who kept glancing Julia's way, grinning.

'I think he's flirting with you,' David said.

'He's your friend,' Julia said. 'Can't you do something with him?' She thought she'd be more impressed with the guests than she was. On the other hand, in spite of herself, she was very taken with Thaddeus.

'Not Thaddeus. No one except Helen can do anything with him. And that's because her fingers are curled around a foun-tain pen which in turn is poised above the signature line of her will.'

'Constantly poised,' Julia said.

'Eternally poised, I suspect. Much to Teddy's chagrin.'

'Are you saying he wants her dead?'

'Julia!' Seidman said in mock shock. 'Oh, I don't know. He says he does, but I think he's just trying to be fashionably cynical and dark. She gives him whatever he wants, but he must ask each and every time. He's on a very short chain.'

'I have trouble imagining you two being friends.'

David smiled. 'Oh yes, I know. The dashing, swashbuckling Thaddeus Maldeaux and the old stick-in-the-mud David Seidman. Am I going to have to do something daring to win my lady's affections?'

'Maybe you already have. Looks as if you've just slain a fish of some sort,' Julia said, nodding toward a plate carrying a bug-eyed, fan-tailed fish gently, almost surreptitiously landing in front of David.

'Not exactly a dragon,' David said.

'We have to walk before we can run,' Julia said.

'He's not really as arrogant as he appears.'

'The fish?'

'Amusing. Teddy isn't really arrogant.'

'What would you call it, then?'

'Maybe an excess of confidence?' David said, smiling.

'I like that.'

'My charms are more subtle than Teddy's.'

She had been thinking the same thing, but also wondering if, at times, David's charms weren't a bit too subtle. 'Teddy is a childish name.' She glanced over the table. Thaddeus Maldeaux was looking at her. She couldn't make out the expression. She wondered if he could hear. Surely not.

'He is childish.' David produced a phony smile and nodded toward Thaddeus.

'Do we have to talk about him?'

'Certainly not,' David said. 'The less the better. I'd rather talk about us.' He put his hand on hers, kissed her ear.

'David,' she said softly, almost sadly.

'I know.'

'I know too. I don't feel good about this part of it. I'm just uncertain about things and I really don't like this feeling that I'm leading you on.'

'You're not. You've let me know where I stand. I'm leading me on. And I've been damn good at keeping me dangling. Why do you put up with me?'

'Because I like you. I enjoy being with you. I'm comfortable with you.'

'Mmmn hmmn. Comfortable. Like an old shoe.'

'We've had this talk, David.' Several times, she reminded herself. Was she leading him on? Was she being prudish? No, she didn't want him as a lover. And at this point in her life, she didn't want to have sex with someone unless it was a lover. Not out of prudery. She wasn't a virgin. She just didn't want to develop empty emotional baggage.

'Yes, we have.' He smiled, patted her hand and turned toward the conversation, dominated it seemed by the novelist. 'I know,' he said grudgingly. 'You've been honest with me. Friends?'

'Friends,' she said, turning her attention back to the table.

'The fact is if you are not in New York, you will not be taken seriously,' the novelist said.

'Time will determine who is a master of the craft,' said the little man from Zurich.

'You see, it's driven by the *Times*,' the novelist said. 'I don't mean the times we live in, but the *Times* we read. *The New York Times*. They seat and depose.'

'For now, perhaps. If it is fame you seek, then I understand.'

The novelist was quiet for a moment. 'Quite frankly it's readership. I want to be read.'

'You are published. I've heard of you,' the man from Zurich said.

'If he gets the *Times'* blessing, he will sell more books and make more money and people will grovel at his feet,' Thaddeus Maldeaux said.

'Ah, groveling,' the man from Zurich said. 'That is something different altogether.'

The novelist tossed his napkin down in disgust and picked up his wineglass, doing what had to be difficult – sneering and drinking simultaneously.

'Used to be just south of Market,' the designer said. 'Now, it's everywhere.'

'What?' asked the man from Zurich.

'Groveling,' said the designer. 'It's so wonderful. I'm so glad it's popular again.'

The main lights dimmed. There was a white spot on stage. Someone important had been introduced. Julia turned. A golden candle flickered strobe-like on Thaddeus Maldeaux's face. He turned toward her, his eyes catching hers.

The call came into room 450 of the Thomas J. Cahill Hall of Justice at Seventh and Bryant. A body had been found on San Gregorio Road not far from the General Store off Highway One. That wasn't SFPD business, but there were strong indications that the death of this girl was linked to the deaths of the others, most of whom had strong links to the city. This would interest inspectors Gratelli and McClellan. But it would wait until morning.

All but two of the fourteen paired, Formica-topped desks were empty. One of the two on-duty homicide detectives would relay the message.

The girl had been dead for a few days. The local authorities didn't know exactly how long. According to the message, the girl was found in a ditch, hidden in the tall grasses. A dog had discovered the corpse.

Julia was having difficulty shutting out the thoughts stealing uninvited into her brain. Each one was related to Thaddeus Maldeaux. Each one seemed to lend progress to a fantasy that was becoming more vivid, more dangerous.

'What are you thinking about?' David asked as the Wilkes-Bashford-dressed black mayor entered the tenth eloquent minute of his speech.

'Nothing,' Julia said, suppressing a grin.

'Oh, right,' David said. He looked over the table to see his friend's eyes dart away. 'Are you two flirting?' he asked Julia.

'What two?'

'You have this rather blissful grin on your face and he is spying on you every chance he gets.'

'He's a little too full of himself for my taste,' she said.

'Um hmmn,' David said.

Julia had a moment alone outside. David had gotten caught up with friends and Julia had artfully slipped away before introductions could be made and before she'd have to explain what she did for a living and that she lived in a little studio on Hayes Street, though no doubt they would all think that was quaint.

'Now, now,' she told herself. This was her own, private little game of insecurity. 'Grow up,' she told herself.

She walked further out toward the sidewalk. The huge, dark private club was before her. Then the delicate little park. Behind it was Grace Cathedral. She looked around. The hotels – the Fairmount, the Mark Hopkins, the Huntington. Up here was where the power was, well before the turn of the century. The titans of banking and railroads. Even Levi Strauss – a single, shy man who smoked cigars and invented blue jeans – had been one of the kings of the hill.

Down the hill meant that you descended into the glittering edifice complexes of the financial district; or the swarms of touts and tourists at the piers; or the Peking duck and ginger scents of Chinatown; or back down into the Tenderloin, the tattered bottom of the safety net, where the more base acts of humanity were committed less privately.

'Where have you been?' David asked, coming out and finding her staring at the cathedral.

'I was thinking about getting away.'

'Are you going up to the river tomorrow?'

'No. Friday.'

'Why not go early? I could meet you there – for one day anyway.'

'I've got an investigation to complete,' she said.

'Let Paul do it, that's why you have an assistant.'

'Paul has to help as it is. Stakeout. And two of us aren't really enough.'

'What is it this time?'

'A guy is suing my client over some on-the-job back injury. Says he can't walk. He may be telling the truth, but the insurance company wants to be sure before they cut the check. The guy stands to collect a bundle.'

'So you are standing in the way of this poor man and happily ever after?'

Julia ignored what might have been a deeper insinuation.

'How about I come up Saturday afternoon?' David asked.

'Why do I always end up having to say "no"? I want to escape everything.'

Thaddeus Maldeaux and his mother brushed by them on their way to a waiting car.

'David? Handball?'

'Sure,' Seidman said.

He had ignored Julia. Her stomach pitched. She was shamed by her schoolgirl reaction.

The Camaro was parked on the right, facing down the hill. It was the girl's idea to come up there. It was her idea to get out of the car. She stood in front, her back to him. The entire city of San Francisco – pulsating with light and energy – unfolded below them. She was more than willing and had even suggested that they could make out up there, way above the Haight. She told him he reminded her of someone.

'Eminem?' he asked. He'd been told that before. But he had a better build than the rap star and resented the comparison.

'No, someone darker.'

'Darker?'

'Inside darker.' She liked him. She would make him happy, she told him. She was so glad to be away from the city. Here, there was electricity in the air. 'I forgot how beautiful the world could be,' she said.

He moved closer. She leaned back pressing her body against him. It was quick. She didn't really have time to resist. He was so quick and so strong.

He lifted the limp body and carried it down the other side of the hill, the vast ocean down there, out there somewhere. Fewer lights dotted the far hillsides. It was lonelier here. Even so, this was the most daring he had ever been. He could see well. It was as if he had a special night vision. He coldly scanned the area for joggers or lovers. No one. He found a spot down the hill, a small plateau on the gradually sloping earth.

He calmly and expertly undid the buttons of her dress. It wasn't until she was fully naked, that the cold, sharp perception gave way to a deep melancholy – a rich, sad ecstasy.

He undressed, carefully folding his jeans and tee shirt as he had done her clothing. He looked at the unreal shadows and the paleness the moonlight cast upon her body and on his. He dropped to his knees. He felt the blades of grass against his calves. He felt the chilled air on his flesh. He looked up at the sky. There was no way to determine if the moment were real or a dream. Yet, it was the way it was. And he never felt more alive.

There was nothing about him now. Not the ground, not the sky. So calm, he thought. She was so at peace. He let his hands glide feather-like over her body. He was so at peace. There was just the two of them. Naked. Quiet. Still.

When the ritual was complete, he kissed her gently on the lips, dressed, gathered the small stack of clothing and shoes, and left. He drove around until it was light. Barely light. He put her clothing in a Goodwill box.

TWO

G ratelli was awakened early by the phone. Soon after he shook some semblance of morning into his head and plugged in the electric percolator. He retrieved his morning *Chronicle* from the hallway, then called McClellan. After that, he called Albert Sendak in the medical examiner's office. Not one, but two bodies had been found, both linked to each other and to the rest of them.

One body was decomposing south of San Francisco on Highway One near San Gregorio. Not SFPD territory but the local police were sure the body would be of special interest to them. The local police wouldn't touch anything if someone could start down immediately. The medical examiner would oblige them.

The other body was a fresh kill up on Twin Peaks. A jogger found the body just as dawn broke. That's where the two San Francisco inspectors would go first – where the trail was the freshest – before heading south down Highway One. If the two slayings were connected, Gratelli thought even in his groggy state of consciousness, then the killer was getting anxious. The deaths were coming closer and closer together.

Gratelli rummaged through the stacks of operas – works by Rossini, Donizetti, Bellini, Verdi and Puccini. He was searching for something comedic. He picked a Donizetti to listen to while he sat at the small table in his tiny kitchen. He sipped his coffee and unfolded the newspaper. He'd been in Homicide enough years not to let a few dead bodies disturb his routine.

His thoughts were on the opera – the one playing and the one he would see this week. Because of a duty roster switch, he thought it wise to switch his tickets. It was some German

composer – and not even Mozart – which lowered the priority.
He could even miss it if he had to. He did not enjoy the Germans,
or the French for that matter. But the Germans were the worst.
He endured, rather than enjoyed, the endless and pompous Ring
Cycle. He remembered the season when the opera house was
infested with fleas and even that was more enjoyable than
Wagner.

After the sports section, he got up, refilled his cup and sat
again. He sighed as everyone does when faced with something
unpleasant and inevitable.

The morning paper had three separate stories on the killings
– and the media didn't know about this new one. He and
McClellan would likely spend as much time with the news guys
as with the investigation.

Julia Bateman and Paul Chang split the day's watch. A video
camera nearby if they should suddenly see their suspect doing
cartwheels on the street. So far, they hadn't seen Samuel Baskins
at all. He hadn't even ventured out to limp and stumble to the
corner grocer.

So she started the watch at six a.m. She would observe Samuel
from the entrance to Mr Baskins' building. Baskins, whose
earnings probably placed him near the poverty level, was now
a potential millionaire several times over – that is if he lived
long enough to collect it – because his employer failed to have
the machinery checked on schedule. A few hundred pounds
dropped on Sam's shoulder. X-rays revealed nothing. Exams
revealed nothing except deep and what ought to be temporary
bruises.

That he didn't have something vital smashed or broken was
miraculous. The insurance company claimed the miracle for
their own. Sam contended that there were no miracles only the
sad fact that medical science failed to explain why he couldn't
walk without a great deal of pain. He claimed to have neck and
back pain so horrendous that he could not work, that he could
just barely get through the day attending to his pain. Before
Baskins found a lawyer, he had injudiciously sent several,
hysterical, violence-threatening letters to the company and after
that to the insurance company.

Julia sipped from a cup of coffee she got at McDonald's on
Van Ness and watched the building near Leavenworth and Turk.

What made her look up as the dark Camaro cruised by in the gloom, Julia Bateman didn't know. All she knew was that in the darkened, smoked glass window, penetrated only briefly by the morning light coming through the buildings, there was an eerie stare; enough to make her shiver and encourage her to grab another sip of coffee to offset the sudden cold.

It was below the back half of a Victorian on Stanyan – a basement really, a cave – where the driver of the Camaro lived. Once inside it could still be night. Soon he would be asleep. He would miss a day of working out. And a day of work. That happened on the days following the nights of the kill.

He felt as he usually did. His mind was nearly blank. His eyes were tired. Very tired. But his body was still alive, feeling everything that touched it – the tee shirt against his chest, against his nipples. The denim against his thighs, his buttocks, his sex. He lit the candles. The CD he had just picked up at Tower Records was in place. He pushed the button.

He undressed.

He positioned his shaved, oiled naked body on the bed so he could glimpse at his flickering, golden reflection in the mirror beside him. He would relive every moment of the evening. It would arouse him. He would satisfy himself. He would be calm for a few days. He would be sad, but it was the only time he felt anything other than anger.

He fell back into the bed. His head was slightly raised on the pillow so he could look down at the body he had so carefully constructed. He admired its firmness, its smoothness, now letting his palm glide over his chest, down his flat, firm belly, sliding over and inside his thighs.

He closed his eyes, the vision of the young woman, her pale flesh lit by the moon on the dark grass. At once he felt her flesh and his own. He could feel himself drift into the place. A secret place. All the time in the world to caress her soft and pliant body.

Instead of falling further back into the vision, he was oddly and disagreeably startled by the image suddenly, seemingly projected on the inside of his cranium. It was the woman in the Miata – a convertible with the top up, bright blue and shining in the morning fog, the car on Leavenworth and Turk he saw as he returned from the kill. The car demanded to be seen. The face in the window drew him to it. It startled him then. Startled him now. The stare she gave him had flashed in his mind without warning. It jerked him rudely from his sexual reverie.

He remained in bed trying to recreate the mood. He closed his eyes, ran his palms over his smooth, firm flesh, trying to recreate the moment on the hill. When he couldn't urge it into the dark frame, he tried recreating others. Another night. The San Gregorio beach. The ocean. The sand. The sound of the waves. The salt breeze. Nothing would come to him, or if it did, not for long. Instead of sweet, sad melancholy he felt a rising anger. It was that woman in the car. Why had she done this to him?

He climbed out of bed, stood under water as hot as he could bear. He would go work out. He would go to the gym. It was the only way he could work it off. All this meant he would be sucked up again into the cycle. Sooner because of her. He would have to do it again in just a few days.

The full-length mirror in the bathroom was all steamed. Usually he'd wipe it clear first so that he could inspect his body. He wasn't in the mood. He was pissed. He dried quickly.

The door to Julia Bateman's Miata opened with such suddenness that it jolted her. But it was merely an interruption of bland thought by a smiling, always energetic, teasing Paul Chang.

'Hi toots,' he said to his boss.

'Go toots yourself!' she said. 'You scared the hell out of me. What are you doing here?'

'I couldn't sleep. Bradley stayed over. I don't know. By morning, I was ready to throw him out of bed, out of my apartment and out of my life. But I left instead.'

'Why?'

'Who knows? You know how blonds are.' He smiled.

'No I don't know how blonds are or how anyone is. He must have something. Good in bed?'

'Yes,' Paul smiled. 'You want the details?'

'Absolutely not.' She paused. 'Not all of them.'

They both laughed.

'How was last night?' Paul asked.

'Boring. Sort of.'

'What wasn't boring?'

'It felt a little like Hard Copy meets PBS.'

'Who?'

'The usual San Francisco celebrities – those with talent and those with money.'

'Who was at your table?'

'I don't remember most of them.'

'Jules! What good are you?'

'Some writer. A plastic surgeon . . . oh, Maldeaux.'

'You met him? Christ.'

'It's no big hairy deal,' Julia said.

'Oh right. "Oh", she says casually, "Maldeaux". And the way you said it. One word. Maldeaux. God. Maybe Picasso. Or Brad Pitt, when he's blond.'

'Brad Pitt is two words.'

'Yes, but you can't just say "Pitt". "Maldeaux" you said. Sort of like, what? He's an institution or something. A Lincoln. A Getty, a Rockefeller, a Rothschild. A Maldeaux. Thaddeus Maldeaux. Just the sound of it.'

'David calls him Teddy.'

'Is he as dangerously exciting as we are led to believe or is he four-foot-eight with a toupée?'

'Definitely bigger than life.'

'Mmmmn,' Paul said, trying to figure out what she was thinking.

'Is he gay?' he asked then thought for a moment. 'Could he be bisexual?'

'Don't know. And it's not my world anyway. I'm sounding pouty, aren't I? What I mean is trying to become genuinely a part of that world would be like my trying to become a Hasidic Jew. I sprang from another culture altogether.'

'Who says? People change their worlds all the time. Look at Whoopi. Look at the guy who married Martha Raye. Look at me, by all appearances you'd think I was Chinese or something.'

'You are Chinese,' she grinned.

'Ah, but I'm not, I'm a Christian Reformed kid from Grand Rapids and that is the state of mind, far removed from China. I'm John Boy trapped in Charlie Chan's body.'

'Not really Chinese?'

'Well, I'm not particularly reformed, but Bradley says I'm about as Chinese as potato salad. It's true. Now tell me you don't want to be famous, have the world buzzing about Julia

Bateman? Your picture in *Vanity Fair* like Madonna or Sharon Stone or Heidi Fleiss?'

'No, I'm afraid I'm not going to be your brush with fame.'

'You never, never know. So have you seen our guy?'

'What guy?' Julia asked.

'Why are you here? You enjoy staring at dilapidated brick buildings while the poor and indigent crawl from their Maytag box homes and greet the day with all the gusto of a slug? The reason you are here is one Samuel Baskins, victim or malingerer. Any sign of him?'

'No.'

'You want me to take over?'

'I'm fine.'

'You were up late last night, I can tell.'

'Do I look horrible?'

'A little. I've brought a pad and I plan to do some sketches.'

'A little romantic poverty?'

Thaddeus Maldeaux had breakfast with his mother. The grand old house was dusty and unkempt. The furniture was worn, frayed. The oils in their thick, ornate gold frames were dark from decades of neglect. Mother and son talked about the decline and death of afternoon papers. She also fretted about the Internet and how it was destroying journalism in general and newspapers in particular. Thaddeus tried to soothe her. Their company was prepared for the changes.

'We'll do fine,' he said.

'That's not the point,' she said. 'Where will people get the truth? Now, just anybody with a computer can say whatever they like. Where will the truth be when this plague has completely swept over the world?'

Mrs Maldeaux was not a pretty woman. The thought had crossed Thaddeus' mind that she was not even a handsome woman. She was short, stout and bosomless. The wattle under her chin seemed to match the waddle under her arms. Her rear end looked as if it had been flattened by the backside of a coal shovel.

Her husband, Andre Maldeaux, on the other hand, had killer looks and empty bank accounts. He wouldn't have left Helen of his own accord. She was as devoted and possessive of him as she was of their son, Thaddeus. Andre was killed in an auto race in Europe. Fortunately, he didn't injure his handsome face. He did, as the old line goes, make a great looking corpse. Thaddeus was terrified he'd have a daughter who favored his mother. Then again, he would rather have a daughter or a son who had her intelligence, her resolve, her ethics. She was truly a good woman despite what he said about her and often to her. He wished he were half as good. Like all true beauty, her kind of beauty only surfaces when people can see below the surface.

He showered, shaved. Living with his mother at his age! He smiled at the thought. He wiped a bit of steam from the mirror. There were things to do today – legal matters on Sansome, a board of directors meeting at the Transamerica building and property inspection south of Market. He would lunch there. Great little places, he thought, though he had only sampled a few.

Thaddeus looked in the mirror closely, examining the wrinkles around his eyes. He'd look twenty-eight if it weren't for those little buggers, the spider webs around the eyes. The wind and weather he thought, then forgot about the wrinkles as he tried to determine which cologne he would use. The Prospera? The Romeo Gigli? Or his own, the plain bottle with his name and assigned number – the scent created for him in Paris. He chose the latter.

Other things to do? Perhaps the club. If he had time, he'd do some handball or tennis, get a rub down. There were times he played hard and long just to get the massage. Then, of course, there was Julia Bateman. He wasn't sure what the attraction was. Was it simply because she was with David? No, he thought. He'd never found David's choices in anything appealing before. He would see her again. Today, perhaps. He'd find a way.

Being the only one of the fourteen San Francisco homicide cops to actually live in the city, Gratelli easily got to the Twin Peaks hillside before McClellan. He had to pass a gaggle of joggers held fifty feet away from another crowd of cops and medics.

'Anything?' he asked the cop from General Works, the guy who called in.

'Murder,' the cop said. 'That's why we called you – thought you needed the overtime. And what do we have . . .' He glanced at his notebook. 'Neck broken. Sometime last night probably.

So far, seems to fit with the others. No I.D. Pretty girl, looks a little rough around the edges. Not likely a society bimbo. But who knows? That's why we have experts like you. You wanna see?'

The cop didn't wait. He pulled the fabric down to reveal the entirety of the bluish, slender body, including the odd angle of the neck and head.

'M.E. and Photo on their way.'

There was a little shuffling in the crowd and some cursing that Gratelli recognized as McClellan's.

'Cover the fucking thing up,' McClellan said. 'Jesus fucking Christ, I haven't even had breakfast yet.'

'Looks like she's another pearl on your string,' the cop said as he covered the face. 'How many now?'

'Who's counting?'

'They found another down on Highway One, San Gregorio,' Gratelli told his partner McClellan.

'Let's see what we can get here,' McClellan said. 'Then let's go to the beach.' He looked around at the people. 'What in the hell are we all doing walking on the fucking grass?' He raised his hands to the sky as if only God could understand his frustration with mortals. 'No fucking wonder we can't cage this slime ball. We got people walking all over the fucking evidence.'

'Watch your mouth,' came a voice from the back. It was Lieutenant Broderick from General Works. 'There are kids over there.'

'Get the fucking kids outta here,' McClellan said very quietly. 'Then they won't hear me say "fucking" all the time.' He looked around. 'What the hell are they doing here anyway? This isn't the fucking Donna Reed Show, you know.'

'And the press. Come on, McClellan. You're a natural asshole, you don't need to work so hard at it.'

'I put a hundred percent into everything I do,' McClellan said.

'Eating, drinking . . .' said the cop from General Works.

'My belt size is my fucking business.' McClellan grinned evilly. 'Hell you check out homicide sometime. Not a belt under thirty-eight inches except for Gratelli and that fruit, Bushman.'

The cop shook his head, looked at Gratelli. 'One of these days, they're gonna change the rules and homicide cops won't have lifetime appointments. You'd think you were the fucking Supreme Court or something.'

'Watch your mouth,' McClellan said. 'There are children here. Gratelli's only fourteen.'

'Yeah, he looks fourteen.'

'Drinks a lot. Women, you know.'

Gratelli said nothing to the lieutenant. 'Leave your car here,' he told McClellan. 'We'll pick it up on the way back in.'

The medical examiner had sent an investigator. They had their own uniform, one that looked halfway between Navy officer and doorman. He was heading toward the body, when McClellan and Gratelli broke from the crowd.

'Fresh kill, they better get something this time,' McClellan said. 'But a smart guy wouldn't lay down any bets.'

McClellan was silent all the way down to San Gregorio. Gratelli played his opera and Mickey didn't utter one nasty remark about opera fairies or make some remark about how it might make much more sense if it were in English.

The smell of death is sweet, but not pleasant. Fortunately there is often something unreal about the sight of a corpse. When whatever it is that gives life – a soul, an electrical impulse, a chord of celestial music – is gone, the corpse seems less human. Perhaps not human at all. Seeing murder victims usually pissed off McClellan, made him especially ugly and difficult. Something about this body for McClellan was different. The body had been ravaged. The face hadn't. The face held something much too human and much too innocent to look at. McClellan didn't get angry this time.

His lower lip quivered. He shook his head. 'Oh shit,' he said, low and quiet.

'What?' Gratelli asked.

'I used to see her in the streets. We talked.'

McClellan walked up the side of the gully. The tall grasses bent under the wind. He stared out at the ocean. He didn't move again until they were ready to leave.

The neck had been broken and the body had been placed, not thrown in a ditch. It was probably at night, probably very late at night or early in the morning, when the back roads were unlikely to have many travelers.

Coming back to the city, McClellan was quiet. Sullen. Finally

as the skyline appeared before them, he broke: 'So, we gonna
have a whole season of baseball this year or are we all
gonna switch to football?'

'I don't know.'

'Don't know why I ask you. Damn Italians. All you guys
ever do is sing. Not one of you could ever swing a stick.'

'DiMaggio,' Gratelli said.

'What's that supposed to mean?'

'Sells coffee pots, marries Monroe. Somebody told me he
played baseball.' Gratelli turned to look out of the window.

'Up yours!'

After a long period of silence, McClellan started again.

'What kind of guy would break a girl's neck, get her naked
and dump her in a ditch? Nothing else, not even rape as far as
we can tell.'

McClellan had worked himself up. He was breathing heavily,
irregularly.

'In a zoo,' he continued, 'you can tell what the animals are
and what they're likely to do. Here, no way. We got guys blowin'
off their kids for the insurance money. Somebody else dumping
body parts in dumpsters in an alley. This guy decides to pick
up chicks, break their necks and leave 'em around the city,
seems about par for the fucking course.'

McClellan dabbed his forehead with a handkerchief as the
afternoon sun pounded his side of the car.

Julia had relieved Paul at noon and Paul returned the favor at
five, allowing Julia to meet Sammie at the gym. For the most
part, they were just gym buddies. Their worlds didn't overlap
much – save an occasional dinner after the workout. But for
Julia, Sammie was great at the gym. She encouraged and chal-
lenged Julia to put her heart into the routines, not letting her
give up or glide through the three-times-a-week workout. And,
perhaps sadly, Julia thought, aside from Paul, Sammie was her
only other friend.

'How did you know where I live?' Julia asked Thaddeus
Maldeaux. She wanted to be indignant. She wanted to be angry.
Instead it was difficult to hide a smile. But she did.

He stood just behind the driver's door of the two-year-old
black Toyota Camry parked at the curb. The unpretentious auto
was blocking a lane of one-way evening rush hour traffic heading

west on Hayes Street. And Thaddeus himself was in danger of
being side swiped by drivers anxious to get home.

'You're in the phone book. Page one of the private detective's
primer.' He smiled. 'But you know all about that, being a detective and all.'

'An insurance investigator. Though I like the sound of detective. It makes me more interesting.'

He noticed her staring at the car. 'My mother's. I don't own
one.' He smiled again. 'What's a spoiled rich boy doing driving
such a mundane car?'

'I didn't . . .'

'My mother's truly rich, Julia. And whether you believe it
or not, this was an extravagance. I think she really wanted a
Chevy Cavalier. She was going to splurge and get the four-door.
She used to try to beat the paperboy out of a week's delivery.
The truly rich are truly tight.'

Julia found herself grinning. 'I'll take your word for it.'

'She wouldn't really cheat the paperboy. I made that up. She
is frugal, but she's a wonderful woman. A wonderful mother.
And I don't deserve her. I don't deserve you either, but I've
come to take you to dinner.'

'I have plans.'

'You do?'

'Don't I?'

'David is tied up tonight.'

'Oh. He sent you in as a replacement.'

'I'm the understudy. When he's unable to fulfill his oblig-
ations, I get my big chance.'

'Not a chance.'

'Now, now. It won't be bad. I promise. We can go across the
street. Caffe Delle Stelle. Delle Stelle,' he said relishing the
sound. 'Love it.'

'Thanks, but . . .'

'You don't have plans. You have to eat. I'll park, check out
the galleries and ring your buzzer about seven thirty, then we'll
eat. I'll walk you back. I won't come up. I'll be very, very
good.'

'Why are you doing this?'

'I feel it's my moral obligation to eliminate prejudice when
I can.'

'Prejudice?'

'I know. You think you don't have any. But you do. Toward the deprivation deprived you have deep-seated animosity.'

'I see,' Julia said. In addition to money and looks, he also had a sense of humor.

'You will. You will.'

THREE

'What are the disadvantages of extreme wealth?' Julia asked Thaddeus Maldeaux inside the bright little Italian restaurant on Gough Street.

'We get kidnapped a lot.'

She smiled. 'Patty Hearst.'

'Yes. The Getty kid, remember. The kidnappers sent back the boy's ear. These were my peers. Nearly. There were others who didn't make the papers.'

'OK, being rich is dangerous.'

'People are always hitting us up for money – and if we don't cough it up then we're selfish. People are starving all over and we don't care.'

'Bad press.'

'And speaking of press, no privacy,' he said.

'The evidence is mounting up. You have terrible lives.'

'But most of all we don't know if people who seem to love us, or even profess to like us, actually do. They may be interested in what we can do for them. Money, fame . . .'

'And power.'

'And power.'

'And glamour.'

'And glamour sometimes. That's why I like you.'

'Because I don't like you.'

'There's not a chance you could put that in the past tense?'

'Maybe.'

'I thought my charming . . .'

'And humble,' she said.

'. . . and humble nature would have . . .'

'This is delicious,' she said.

'The food, you mean.'

'Yes. The food.' It was more than the food, more than the
candle-lit decor, more than the smells of garlic and olive oil
and the scent of the handsome waiter. No question it was
Thaddeus. He was irresistible. What it was about him remained
a puzzle. The waiter was as handsome as Thaddeus. The garlic
and olive oil that permeated the air was more appealing than
any cologne. She looked back into the eyes of Thaddeus. Not
sad. Not bright or deep. No sign that behind his eyes, there was
extraordinary wisdom or unique understanding. Not the eyes of
a saint. What was it? Chemical? Energy maybe from a being . . .

'The worst thing about being rich and spoiled is that nothing
means a whole lot.'

. . . not like anything she'd seen. Control, sureness, knowing
itself.

'It's so drab climbing all those mountains, zipping off to
Paris for lunch and Morocco for dinner,' Julia said, wondering
how she could be so foolish, but wondering also how she could
keep herself from tumbling into the . . .

'Mmmmn, yes.'

. . . force field. 'Well, you've certainly straightened me out.
The next time I see some guy on the street begging for a quarter
so he can put a down payment on some cheap wine to warm
him up and send him back into oblivion, I'll reconsider where
I put my sympathies. I'll ask him if he truly understands how
badly the Maldeaux family has it.'

'Oh Julia,' Thaddeus said as if he were exhausted. 'David
said you are a challenge.'

'You two have some sort of wager or something?'

'No. And to be completely honest, he doesn't know I'm here.'

'That's nice.'

'What?'

'Your having the consideration to tell me when you're being
honest.'

'Truce? Just through dinner. Incidentally, I'm not looking for
sympathy. Just understanding. I know I am a spoiled rich kid.
I know how lucky I am. I know that one, highly motivated
famous man's sperm made it to that one receptive rich woman's
egg. And here I am, not only did my little tadpole beat out
thousands of other little tadpoles but it found the golden egg.
If it had been a couple of Somalians doing it, I'd be counting
grains of rice, but it wasn't. I've done what most spoiled rich

kids have done plus some. Let me give you the stuff that
impresses most people.'

'Sure.'

'I've sailed the Cape – not Cod – trekked the mountains near
Tibet, witnessed camels like beads on the horizon of the Sahara
and attended the brothels of Bangkok satisfying urges I never
knew I had . . .'

'I get the point.'

Thaddeus shook his head. 'No you don't. It impresses people
for the wrong reason.' He leaned across the table. 'Do you think
this is bragging, me telling you this?'

'Isn't it?'

'On Kilimanjaro, there are places – part of the way up – if
you stay there for twenty-four hours you will experience deep,
deadly winter and lush, heavy summer every day. Every day,
for as long as you stood there – the rest of your life perhaps
– it won't change. All four seasons in twenty-four hours. The
plants have adapted to both arctic and the tropics. Do you
understand?'

'I understand what you say. It makes sense. I'm not sure I
understand it in the way you'd like me to understand it.'

'Precisely. You need to experience it. It's like nothing you
know or can imagine. Everyone delights in a sunset.' He shook
his head again, this time at his own inability to convey his
thoughts. 'This isn't sunsets, Hallmark's version of Mother
Nature's charming palette of colors. To go to Africa and see it
for what it is, or Peru, or Tibet, do you understand is not to
say you've been, but it is to have your existence transformed.
To live. Do you understand?'

'Let me tell you something,' she said. She took another sip
of the wine to clear her throat. It certainly wasn't clearing her
brain. 'When I was a child, back in Iowa, seven or eight
maybe, in the winter I used to put my wool nightgown over
the heat duct. Then I'd undress in the dark and stand there
cold in my cold upstairs room. When the nightgown was really
warm, I'd pull it on and climb in bed as quickly as I could,
cover myself up and try to go to sleep while it was still warm.
Those first warm moments were as close to heaven as I could
get. I looked forward to them every winter's night. Do you
understand?'

'I do,' he said. 'That was a long time ago.'

'Not so long. And there are other things that mean something to me.'

'What?'

'A good book. Looking at the fog come in. I'm glad to be alive,' Julia said. 'Don't try to make my small life seem worthless.'

'Believe me, I'm not. You are very worthwhile.'

It had been light when they entered the restaurant. Now, as they departed, it was dark and cool and damp. At the corner of Hayes and Gough they went left instead of right and walked into a neighborhood of galleries, restaurants and cafes. They agreed on another cup of coffee but didn't know which to choose. Arbitrarily, they chose Mad Magna's.

Oddly, to Julia's mind, Thaddeus Maldeaux seemed to fit into the strange collection of San Franciscans who patronized the place. It was loud, boisterous, filled with folks you wouldn't find in the audience of the 700 Club.

'The Hindus have a phrase,' Maldeaux said, as they sat at the little table near the bar. 'I think it's *neti, neti*. It means "not this, not that."'

'I know I'm being egotistical here, but what does all of this have to do with me?'

'That's what I want to know. I've never spent much time with a middle class girl from the Middle West, especially one who doesn't appear to have an axe to grind. I'm tired and bored with everyone I know and seem destined to meet. For some unexplainable reason, you are different.' He waited for her response. She gave none. He shrugged, gave her a hopeless smile.

'I'm just opposite fashion, opposite fame, opposite . . . I don't know. I'm not making much sense. I'm just me. I don't need to have a make over. I'm not looking to be someone else. I don't like all of these questions.'

'What was life like, what were you like when you were growing up?'

'Usual growing up,' she said, blushing. She hadn't been prepared for the change in focus.

'What is that?'

'I don't know. I was a tomboy. A tough little girl.'

'What did you do. For fun, I mean?'

'I don't want to talk about me. It's boring.'

'So let's talk about me,' he said, grinning.

'OK, you're right. Let's talk about me. I used to go to the river. Get a ride out to the Cedar River. A bunch of us. Mostly boys.' She laughed. 'All boys, but me. We'd do make believe, pretend we were lost in a jungle or something. We'd make our own bow and arrows, swing from vines. Dare each other.'

'You and a bunch of guys?'

'Yeah,' she smiled. 'Donnie Patton . . . mmmnn and the others.

'So who was this Donnie Patton. You liked him?'

'I did then,' she said. He was like Thaddeus in some ways. Handsome, curious, unrelenting. Staring straight into her eyes. Wanting something. Determined to get it.

'Was the river beautiful?'

'We thought it was. So far away from other people. A little wild. Odd flowers and leaves. I'm sure it doesn't compare to the Amazon rainforest.'

'And what happened to Donnie?'

'Don't know. After awhile, we grew up, I guess. No time to go out and play.'

'I really want you to come out and play with me.'

'You really think I am an adequate antidote to your malaise? Maybe you just need to find someone richer, more bored than you are.'

'What if I don't like rich people?'

'I'm not sure that I do either,' Julia said, unable to suppress a grin.

'Let me tell you a little secret. I'm not sure I like the vast middle class. Boring. Cows. Maybe some day you'll have to show me the Cedar River. Change my mind.'

'You think I could change your mind? About anything.'

'Do something,' he said.

'I'm happy,' she said.

'What's going on? How many years do we have on this earth? Doesn't matter. We're content with cable TV. It's unfathomable. Worse, there are millions of homo sapiens who are more excited by virtual reality than reality. What are they saying? "I want to live in a world that looks like the one I can control." Aren't they saying, "I don't want to have a relationship with a real, live, breathing human being?" Christ, breathe. Live! There is a real world out there to experience. Do everything once.'

Maldeaux looked around, noticed others were staring. 'We've already covered that, right? Tomorrow? One more opportunity to get to know one another?'

'I'm going out of town. I have a little cabin up around Russian River. My escape.'

'Another river, right?' he smiled. 'You like rivers.'

'I guess,' she said.

'Maybe I'll go with you.'

'No. I think you've just missed the point.'

At the door to the Estrella apartments they stood quietly.

'I'm not going to invite you up,' Julia said.

'OK. Despite what you might think I wasn't trying to work my way into your bed.'

'Good.'

'I'm not sure I'm looking for romance.'

'Just a pal, huh?'

'I don't know. I don't know why I expect you to understand me. Do you have a yearning?'

'A yearning?'

'Yes. A word we don't use anymore. It is a want you want so bad it's painful. Do you?'

'What about you?' She didn't want to think about it.

'There doesn't seem to be much left. That's pretty frightening.'

'I don't know what you mean,' Julia said.

'I know. I know you don't. I'm babbling. I guess I don't want to leave you just yet.'

'No, tell me what you mean about being frightened.'

'Maybe . . .' He shook his head. 'Never mind. You've got your key?'

Julia nodded.

'I'm gone.' Thaddeus Maldeaux said, disappearing around the corner.

That night two things were on her mind. A bit of guilt about David Seidman. No matter how much she tried to justify her rightness of action and no matter how many times he said he understood, Seidman seemed to stoke her guilt.

Number two was obvious: Thaddeus Maldeaux. Julia tried to think of something else. It didn't work. The more she tried to get her thoughts away from him, the more they were tugged back to Thaddeus. It had been a long time since she had these kinds of feelings. Frightened, hopeful, elated – all simultaneously or at least in rapid succession.

These were schoolgirl feelings. 'Get a grip on it Julia,' she told herself. 'He'll take you for a little ride out to the middle of nowhere and you'll have to walk back.'

She remembered when she was fifteen. Donnie Patton. She remembered how he made her feel all rubbery. She remembered the walk by the muddy Cedar River – a dozen or more miles outside of Iowa City – out in the middle of nowhere. She remembered her dog, the white German Shepherd romping along the shore. She remembered the brown water, the dragonflies, the kissing on the sultry summer day – his body pressing up against hers, his moist lips, softly pressing at first, until her heart began to beat rapidly. Julia remembered it clearly. He pressed harder, sucking her breath from her.

She remembered his hand slipping inside her blouse, underneath the bra. He took her hand brought it down, past the waist, pressed her palm against the hardness beneath the coarse denim of his jeans.

Julia pulled away. She allowed her hand to go back, to be guided inside. She let him remove her blouse, then finally the rest. His palms were sticky and he smelled of oranges. Funny, she thought. Funny what you remember. She remembered her white blouse waving like a flag, stuck on the limbs of a dead tree.

The next day Donnie ignored her.

Julia didn't want to think of Donnie anymore, or of any of the others, including the one she married. She climbed out of bed, went to the window and looked down on Ivy Street, little more than an alley two floors beneath her window.

She felt alone and lonely. When she realized at least she hadn't been thinking of Thaddeus, she smiled. But, there she was. Thinking of Thaddeus. She was too old for this, she thought. Too old. It wasn't pleasant. It wasn't sensible. It was frightening.

Her choices in men had never been too wise. Despite the enormous pull he already had upon her, she was sure she needed to resist.

Julia climbed back into bed. She felt safer in the little alcove. She thought about calling Paul. It was too late.

She closed her eyes. Did she have a yearning? Yes. She did.

The Camaro rumbled first down Dolores, then swung over to Mission Street. The car and its *basso profundo* engine and the familiar rap repetition didn't cause much of a stir. Mean, loud cars weren't rare in the neighborhood.

There were a lot of people still on the street despite the lateness of the hour. The night didn't feel right. Too many people. Somebody would see her get into the car. A brother, maybe. A friend. He looked at his gas gauge. He was maybe twenty miles until empty. It wouldn't do to have someone in the car while he stopped for gas.

If this sexual freakiness welled up in some dark part of his brain, as it seemed to, young Earl Falwell sensed he was still in the half-light, still in control, though barely. He could get through the night. Surely he could. He wanted to. He didn't like what was going to happen. He never did. This was the worst time in the cycle. He was being torn apart. It always tore him apart until he gave into it.

What if he just locked himself up in a room somewhere? He'd even thought about going to a head doctor. He thought about going to the police. But he couldn't bring himself to do it. He only thought about turning himself in when the urge was early up on him. By the time it got a grip, he could tell himself – convince himself – this would be the last time – and he could convince himself it was just this once. Just this one time. One more time.

Once he found the right person, there were no thoughts about what he would or wouldn't do. He would be in the middle of doing it. Afterward, after the ritual, after his tension was relieved and the obsession released its hold, the next morning he'd be so disgusted he couldn't imagine himself ever doing it again. He always thought it was over. But it never was. Maybe he could chain himself to the wall and go cold turkey, rid himself of these relentless urges altogether. Be free. Live a life.

He could get through the night, he thought. He'd just pick up a bottle of tequila or gin and drink himself silly. When he was drunk he only thought about doing it. Sober, it was hell.

He swung back around the block on his third pass at 24th

Street and headed back toward Market. He took Van Ness north to Lombard Street and Lombard west until he found a gas station. He pulled in.

He looked around. He kind of liked Lombard. Though he was born in rural Tennessee, Lombard reminded him of a lot of streets in a lot of cities he'd passed through. It was comfortable in a way. It was an everywhere street, with its gas stations and motels. Could have been Dallas or Kansas City or Nashville. Certain parts of any city were all the same. The street was still busy – a stream of cars headed west to get on the Golden Gate.

At the pump, as he put the nozzle in the hole, he saw a girl get out of her car. Once she passed to the pumps and the green fluorescent light shown on her, he thought she might be the one. She had that look. Somewhere between pain and death. A strange nervousness that made for a familiar sadness. A long, delicate neck. This was irresistible.

He felt it all come back. If only that one chick hadn't spoiled it all the other night. If that woman's face hadn't spoiled his ritual, he could have gone for awhile without him getting caught up in it. It was coming on altogether too quick. Now, dammit. It was going to happen now. With this girl. Damn!

He pushed the little gadget on the hose that let the gas flow on its own and walked over to the chick that got out of her Mazda. It was an old Mazda, the one with the aluminum, rotary engine. A wonder it was still running, he thought.

'Need help?' he asked her.

She kind of jerked her head up in surprise. 'Oh' slipped from her lips almost accidentally.

'Didn't mean to scare you,' he said, looking from her eyes to her long, graceful neck.

'It's all right,' she said. But it was obvious she didn't mean it. 'I don't need help.'

She was definitely scared. Her eyes darted about like a bird's. She was in her twenties, late twenties. Older than he normally found to be right.

'I can check the oil for you.' He noticed movement in the backseat of her car. It was a child. The child was in a car seat. It wouldn't be a problem.

'I'm in a hurry.' She said it hurriedly.

It would be tough for him to let her go.

One more, he thought. 'Then I'll stop it. If I have to kill myself to do it, I'll stop it. After this one.'

He had miscalculated. When next he looked up she was paying for her gas. He shut off his pump immediately; but she was on her way back to her car. He had to pay. Pay quickly. Just as he got to the register the guy behind the counter got a phone call. He chatted. She was in her car. For a moment he thought about making a break, leaving a twenty and a ten dollar bill on the counter to cover the twenty-one on the pump. No. Damn. Fuck. She was driving away. She peeled out of the station as if she knew of her specific and immediate peril.

Damn, he was getting too desperate, too careless. He'd have to make it through tonight.

He didn't understand these mood swings. How quickly fear would overtake his confidence or – as quick as the flick of a switch – how suddenly he could see so clearly the object of his desire and know how to obtain it.

The steroids, probably, he thought. Cool it, he told himself.

The next day seemed especially long for Julia Bateman. Because Paul was to pull eight hours on Saturday and Sunday, Julia took Friday by herself. There wasn't much of a point. The subject of her investigation hadn't budged from the house.

She discovered Thaddeus standing in front of the entrance to the Estrella when she returned home.

'No,' she said, simply.

'Why don't I go with you?' he asked.

'No,' she said again.

'We can go to Mexico.'

'That's not the point. The point is that I need a rest. A little solitude. And there's no point at all in the two of us doing much of anything together.'

'You're terrible,' he said, smiling.

'I do mean it.'

'Look, what's wrong with Mexico?'

'Nothing. Go. Enjoy yourself.' Julia turned, took the keys from her purse and moved into the small entryway before the locked doors.

He followed.

'The only thing about the lovely middle class is that they put such limits upon themselves. They can't allow someone to do something nice for them. They can't do anything on the spur of the moment. Let me show you an extraordinary place in Costa Rica. Really. It's not the least bit decadent.' He smiled. 'It's wholesome and everything.

She had to acknowledge that part of her, the 'I don't want to be indebted' part of her personality. She might also have to agree that she lacked real spontaneity.

'Thanks,' she said, putting the key into the lock. 'But I don't want to go.'

'Do it for me, please. I am so bored. Everybody I know is so cynical about all the things one shouldn't be cynical about and not the least bit cynical of the things they should. I want to show you this absolutely incredible jungle in Costa Rica. You won't regret it. We'll be like brother and sister or two five-year-olds on a hike into the woods. We won't even play doctor. It will be fun. Innocent. An adventure.'

'Please take no for an answer,' she said. She knew she was being stubborn. She also felt her resolve slip. She was more than tempted to accept. And what would be wrong with that? Nothing, except that she didn't want things to move as fast as they would if the two of them were to spend that kind of time in that kind of place – just the two of them.

She didn't want to feel what she was feeling. There was no way the two of them would be forever. And she didn't want a short-term emotional investment with someone who was improbably but definitely appealing. 'No.' She stared at him before going in.

'You must let me help you experience what it means to be alive.' Thaddeus was speaking to no one now.

The next morning Thaddeus tried calling her. The answering machine picked up. He decided not to leave a message. She was on her way to the river, apparently.

He called David Seidman. And Seidman agreed to meet him at the club. An hour of handball. A quick lunch. David could squeeze it in, he said.

Seidman picked up a surprising win. He hadn't been skillful, but he was full of determination. Thaddeus called it 'heart' and was pleased. Winning wasn't the objective for Maldeaux. Never was. Keeping fit, challenging himself was. For Seidman winning was the purpose of the game. It was the purpose of life.

Seidman smiled through the perspiration. He had stopped to talk to someone in the hall that led to the locker room. Maldeaux had showered and was nearly dressed when David came in still wearing a smile.

'Good work,' Maldeaux said.

'Thanks Teddy,' David said. 'Why don't you grab a drink and I'll catch up with you in the lounge. Don't order me one, though. I've got an appearance at three.'

'Fine,' Thaddeus said, giving his friend a friendly punch to the shoulder before heading for the door.

'Oh Teddy!' Seidman said.

'What?'

'I'm out of toothpaste.'

Teddy came back, opened his locker. 'Take what you need.'

'So how serious are you? About Julia, I mean?' Maldeaux asked his friend at the bar.

'She's not your type Teddy. Simple. Sometimes a little goofy.'

'Goofy?' Maldeaux smiled.

'Yes. I'm not saying she's dumb. Sometimes a little scattered. She's smart, runs her own business . . . but . . .' Seidman was flustered, having trouble finding the words. 'Very independent, not the type who is content to hang on the arm of a man.'

'We've gotten off the track here. I just asked if you were serious?'

'Right.'

'You're not saying?'

'No. It's none of your business.'

'You're serious. She's not.'

'Dammit, Teddy!' He looked around. He'd said it too loud. But the crowd was too courteous to stare. 'I love her. It's just not going to happen.'

'Then why hang on?'

The table was ready. Once seated, the lunches arrived. A salad for Maldeaux. A steak for Seidman.

'We're just friends now,' Seidman said. He was still nervous. The bright energy he exuded after the win was now a dark, brooding silence. After several moments, he blurted: 'Go for it!'

'I sort of . . . have,' Thaddeus said. 'I mean I don't know where it's going. What I find attractive . . .'

'I don't want to hear it. I don't want to hear about your sexual Olympics. It's disgusting.'

'No, no. The attraction is not sexual. That's what I'm trying to say. You say she's bright. She's truly bright. Her mind is like a blossom, ready to bloom.'

'Her mind, you say?' Seidman said with disgust.

'I know. Maybe I'm changing a little . . .'

'Let's talk about something else.'

'What?'

'You didn't have any toothpaste.'

Maldeaux laughed. 'I'm deeply sorry. Actually, I do. It's in a tin. Powder.'

'You're so fucking weird,' Seidman said. 'Who has tooth powder these days?'

'I was somewhere in Europe when I ran out.'

'And that bottle of cologne. That was cologne wasn't it, the one with the handwritten number?'

'I had it made.'

'You don't do anything the usual way, do you. You have to try everything that comes along. You can't leave anything untouched.'

'David, I'm sorry. Next time I'll leave a bottle of Old Spice in there in case you need it.'

'I used some of it. I smell terrible.' Maldeaux leaned over to smell. Seidman pulled back. 'Stop it. What will people think?'

'Two young people in love.'

'Stop it.' Seidman laughed. 'You always get the better of me.'

'Not today, my friend. You whipped my ass. And so far, I haven't gotten anywhere with your charming Julia.'

FOUR

She heard voices. Perhaps a radio somewhere. Why would someone be playing a radio in a graveyard? Where was it? She tried to look. She could not turn her head. In front of her was a large, rose-faced, granite tombstone.

JULIA CARVER Bateman
BORN: DECEMBER 12, 19
DIED

All the dates were there, but tall grass obliterated some of the numbers. The voices were closer, clearer. There was conversation. She heard her name. Then again.

'Ms Bateman?'

Why would someone be using her name on the radio?

'Can you hear me, Ms Bateman?'

The tombstone was bathed in a soft and eerie luminescence. The light became more intense. The stone, the name, the dates – all disappeared in bright light much like an over-exposed photograph.

There was only one voice now. And it was near. In the same room. What room?

'Ms Bateman, there are some people here who would like to ask you some questions.'

Julia Bateman heard that. For a moment she was able to distinguish between the two worlds. She tried to open her eyes. It hurt.

'Ms Bateman?'

She tried to speak. It hurt. Too much. There were forms in the white light now. Dark, shadowy figures around her. For a moment she thought she might be in a casket.

'I think we'd better wait until tomorrow, Inspector,' a voice said.

'Maybe later this evening?' another voice said, this one deep and gravelly.

'Tomorrow maybe. Call us first.'

Julia heard the same gravelly voice, now at a distance. 'Does she have tomorrow?' She couldn't hear the answer. Sudden quiet. The light dimmed. There was a moment of darkness, then, as if someone flipped the switch in her brain, the inside of her head lit up.

On the highway now. Highway One. Up the coast from San Francisco. The ocean on her left. Salt smells in the air. Happy. The sun was out, the breeze was cool. She was relaxed, on the highway now, the top down on her cobalt blue Miata. Adrift on the highway.

Outside the door men were talking. She couldn't hear them above the sound of the wind and the purr of the engine.

*   *   *

'She might be ready tomorrow, Inspector Gratelli,' the doctor said, wanting to keep discussions of this kind out of Julia Bateman's earshot. 'She may appear unconscious, but the heavy hit of morphine doesn't necessarily prevent her from hearing the conversation. Do you understand?'

Gratelli nodded. 'I'm sorry.'

'She's strong,' the doctor continued. 'You can talk to her tomorrow, I think.'

'I hope so,' Gratelli said, a voice so deep yet so strained, it sounded as if it was painful to speak. 'She's all we've got.'

'On second thought, make it Monday. Give her the weekend.'

Gratelli wore a black raincoat over a black suit over hunched shoulders. Everything about him seemed carelessly put together. His hair was long, but not stylishly so. He needed a hair cut. His bushy eyebrows were black and there were enough bags under his eyes to check into the St Francis. Wild hairs sprouted from his elephantine ears. His hands, too, were huge and the hair on his wrists curled over his watch.

Gratelli was thinking. He was thinking about the girl, wired, tubed, tied, drugged – and that was part of her recovery. Who would want to do this kind of thing to anyone? You could find just about whatever you want in this world. Problem is that something you don't want can find you.

'Number what?' the doctor asked.

'What?'

'How many so far?'

'Not sure it's connected. Eight if we count this as one. Two in the last couple of days.' Gratelli shook his head to acknowledge the futility of keeping it a secret.

Outside, in the morning Inspector Vincente Gratelli appeared to be a gargoyle — escaping from the imposing but not quite Gothic San Francisco General, near Potrero Hill.

Two men approached him. An Asian man in his late twenties, probably, and an athletic-looking, dark-haired executive type pushing forty-five. They looked at Gratelli, expecting an answer to a question they hadn't yet asked.

'What do we know about Julia?' the guy in the suit asked.

'Nothing,' Gratelli said, shrugging.

They walked on without further comment. Gratelli headed for his car. The Asian, he didn't know. The one with the expensive suit was an assistant D.A., David Seidman.

Gratelli was glad there was no press. This one had been quiet, happening up in the woods as it did. Because the details had been withheld, no one had yet publicly connected Julia Bateman to the others.

Gratelli had already talked to the house appraiser who found her. They talked by phone. Apparently, Julia was considering putting the cabin on the market and wanted to know its value. The front door had been left open. After knocking and calling out and not getting a response, the woman ventured in. Without the appointment, Julia would likely be dead.

Julia was taken to the hospital in Santa Rosa, where she lay unconscious for three days, then transferred down in the morning. Gratelli guessed this one had slipped by the dozens of reporters who had been covering the string of victims over the last dozen or so weeks as if it were World War Three. The newspaper folks were probably still feeding on the body on the hill.

It made Gratelli's life easier if reporters weren't shadowing him every step of the way. This one was the odd pearl on the strand. For one thing, she was alive. Or nearly so. And she had been beaten. None of the others had. And he damned well didn't know what to make of it.

There were other differences: Julia Bateman was older. She was found inside. Alive. And beaten. Nothing that the reporters knew would lead them to believe Bateman was another victim. Nothing that would lead the police to connect them either – except for the mark.

The Doc had promised to be quiet. It was bound to leak sooner or later, but later was definitely better than sooner.

'You got a live one,' the medical examiner said looking at the photographs laying on his desk.

'Looks that way for now,' Inspector Mickey McClellan was always surprised at the old man's cheery nature. To the paunchy inspector having a constant smile on your face and a lilt in your voice was too weird in light of his job description which, among other things, included the cutting of flesh and the sawing of bone. 'What do you think?'

'I think the mark is the same, roughly the same place.'

McClellan looked at the photo again. The lights were brighter there than in his office – sterile, light and bright. He could see the picture more clearly. There was a mark on the inside and upper part of the thigh. A crudely carved rosebud, two, maybe three inches long.

'A movie fan, you think?' the examiner said.

'What?'

'Rosebud,' he said.

'So?'

'Nothing,' the examiner said, joke gone unnoticed. 'That makes it like the others.'

'Exactly?'

'The guy's no artist. They all vary a little; but I'd say it's the same guy.'

'The doctor in Santa Rosa said no semen,' McClellan said.

'Like the others. You find anything?'

'Nothing. No pubic hair. No hair, period. No threads. No prints. That's all we know until we get up there and talk with the locals.'

'The immaculate deception,' the examiner said. 'How old this time?'

'Mid to late thirties.'

'Why the hell is that, I wonder.'

'That's what Gratelli wants to know. Me, I think our little engraver just wanted a real woman for a change.'

'Yeah,' the examiner said more to bring the conversation to a close than to agree.

'Busy day?' McClellan asked.

'They're all busy.'

The heat, the sun, both went away. Julia felt cool as her little convertible swept inland. Darker, too, was the highway, as the sky was suddenly hidden by giant pines interspersed with equally tall deciduous trees. The scent of the ocean gave way to the scent of eucalyptus.

'Julia? It's Paul. David's here with me too.'

She heard the voices and she tried to form the word 'Paul,' but her lips wouldn't cooperate. She tasted metal. It was the same taste, she remembered, when she was little and wore braces.

God, it was colder. It was darker. Julia couldn't see the road. Lost.

'Nurse! Something's wrong!'

Julia heard that. She thought she recognized the voice. It was Paul's voice. She remembered Paul, thought she did, thought she should. The sound seemed so far away, far away in the future. The inside of her brain exploded in light. She was eleven. She was in the hallway of a strange house. She called for her mother. The hall went on forever. There were no doors. She turned back. Darkness in front of her, darkness behind her. Was she going in the right direction?

Now there were voices. One voice in particular, one she didn't recognize.

'V-fib. Code blue.'

Indistinct voices, scurrying sounds now.

'Another line of saline. Epi. Now!'

Julia wasn't sure where she was anymore. There seemed to be some commotion about her in the hollow darkness.

'Now!' someone shouted.

Something struck her. Jolted her. The pain. The hallway came back. 'Oh God, not again,' she said somewhere inside of her head and now the hallway went away and there were only harsh splashes of light – like lightning – inside her. She wanted it to stop. She would gladly die if it would stop the pain.

'What happened?' Paul Chang, the young Asian man asked the doctor.

The doctor didn't seem to be worried. 'Ventricular fibrillation. A little shock, epiniphrine. We have her back.' He seemed distracted for a moment. 'She's been through a lot.'

'A little statement of the obvious,' David Seidman said, his anger barely contained. 'Is she going to make it?'

'I was much surer about that an hour ago,' the doctor said almost whispering. 'I don't know the extent of brain damage if any. Without going into details, her body suffered immense trauma.'

'I'm going to want the details,' Chang said to the doctor.

'No, you're not, Paul,' David said, putting his hand on the young man's shoulder. 'Look, I understand how you feel. I feel the same way. But let the doctors handle it here and let the police handle the rest of it. You guys aren't equipped for this kind of thing. I'll have my eyes on the case every step of the way. And I'll keep you informed. No criminal experience. Don't mess things up for the professionals.'

Paul glared.

'Listen, I promise, Paul. They'll find the bastard, I'll see to that.'

Paul just stared at the assistant district attorney. David removed his hand. The doctor left.

Earl Falwell had the bass up so loud the car shook. His fingers tapped the steering wheel of his black '88 Camaro more out of impatience than trying to keep the beat. The traffic was snarled on the interstate between Daly City and San Francisco. And he was steamed.

It was his day off. He'd had his morning workout at the gym and sometimes, even after getting juiced, he'd be a little calmer after a bout with the weights. All through the workout, he hadn't had those thoughts, that feeling. But he knew when it was coming and it was coming now. It was like that kid in grade school who knew when he was going to have a seizure and he could tell the teacher and they'd know what to do. But this wasn't exactly like that and there was nothing to do about this. There was no one to tell. No one to lock him in a room or tie him to a bed until the sensation went away.

The traffic snarl was getting to him. Maybe he'd swing off this pike and hit the mall. Maybe he wouldn't have to do it today. Yeah, right. It would take him over by evening. It was all so predictable. He'd do it. He'd feel better. He'd get depressed. He'd kind of go down, like a submarine, into some other part of him. Then there was nothing he could do about it. Then he'd feel good. Then he'd feel terrible and it would start all over again.

He probably should have worked. Earl didn't mind loading the trucks. He wasn't too fond of his coworkers, but most of the time he could just tune in on himself and work up a decent sweat, eventually tiring out his body. The boxes were filled with paper products, computer paper mostly, and they were heavy. He did more work than the others. They didn't mind. Neither did he. The time passed faster. He put more strain on his body and that was good. Sometimes his mind would follow and he could resist the urges.

He should have worked. If he were stuck in traffic much longer, the day would be a waste anyway.

The car ahead of him, a silver Honda Prelude, moved a few

feet and Earl pushed the Camaro almost close enough to nudge
this immediate barrier to speed. His left foot on the clutch, he
revved the engine threateningly a few times, looked up, caught
the reflection of his eyes in the rearview mirror.

He pulled the mirror down so that it showed his face. Zits.
At twenty-two, Earl Falwell still had zits. Maybe it was the
steroids. He inched the mirror down so that it gave him a look
at his chest. The pecs were starting to look real good. Somebody
at the gym told him he looked like Eminem. Was it at the gym
or somewhere else? Someone else? Eminem. That wasn't too
bad. But he wanted to look mean and Earl didn't think the
rapper looked all that tough wearing those loose jeans and
showing his shorts and all that.

Earl weighed one hundred ninety pounds. Six months ago,
he was at one hundred forty-five. Six foot, two inches, and a
lousy, puny one hundred forty-five pounds. Not any more. He
was on his way to two hundred and twenty-five.

Nobody would fuck with him anymore. Not like they did in
the Army. Not like they did in Leavenworth. He'd already put
the scare of God into his stepdad. No more messin' around
from him.

Earl pushed the mirror back up, noticed the Honda had
advanced a few feet. This time Earl let the Camaro tap the
fender as he closed the gap. The Honda driver turned and
scowled. Earl gave him the finger.

The little scene was played again as the guy ahead inched
forward. Earl tapped harder this time. Earl couldn't tell what
the guy was screamin' at him, the ugly face all wrenched around
over the seat. Now, shit, the guy was putting the Honda in
reverse. Banged back.

It had been a game. Now it wasn't. Suddenly, it wasn't fun.
Earl didn't really know where the anger was coming from. It
seemed as if it just welled up out of his chest and into his head,
into his breathing or something and he was ready to explode.

Earl put the Camaro in neutral, jerked on the hand brake and
was out of his car in one movement. The guy in a gray suit
was getting out of his car, but Earl helped him a bit by grabbing the suit and jerking him out. The kid had pummeled the
guy's head three times before the guy even knew what was
going on.

Earl slammed the guy back down on the hood of the Honda,

his knuckles coming down hard on the guy's forehead, right over the eyebrow. Blood was coming from somewhere. Now horns were honking. Earl and this guy were the only ones out of their cars. There were screams in the midst of the smell of auto exhaust.

People were telling Earl to stop. The guy was trying to say something, but all he could manage was the gurgle of bloody spittle.

Earl could see himself in the reflection of the hood of the Honda. He could see splatters of blood there too. And that just seemed to make him angrier.

FIVE

Gratelli, on his second visit, guessed the woman who left Julia Bateman's room as he came in was a social worker, some kind of rape therapist. He couldn't be sure. His dominion the last eight years was homicide and a lot of things had changed in the way the police handled sex crimes.

When he saw Bateman, she was sitting up in bed staring down at her hands. Her head was still swollen. Hard to tell whether the condition was a result of the surgery or the beating. Beside her, in a chair pulled up close to the bed, was David Seidman, the assistant D.A.

David was telling her that he didn't know what to say. She didn't offer to write his lines.

Gratelli had seen Seidman in court. Seidman, in front of a judge, was a sharp, confident prosecutor. Jurors were impressed with his courtroom demeanor, his conservative good taste in clothes, and the handsome head of dark hair with gray temples almost too perfect to be anything other than hair salon magic.

His prosecutions were flawless. Since Seidman often took the capital offenses, the big cases, Gratelli witnessed the smooth and simple way the young prosecutor laid out difficult and complex cases. Unlike many, he had a full grasp of every, intimate detail. He'd always done his homework. The police liked him. The media respected him. The public was beginning to hear of him. There were rumors he would be mayor, perhaps governor some day, despite his surprising lack of charisma.

This was a different guy altogether, hunched over, embarrassed.

'Professional visit?' Gratelli asked, startling Seidman.

'Not exactly.'

'Miss Bateman,' Gratelli said to Julia. She didn't look up.

'She's been like this,' Seidman said. He reached down and touched her hand.

She didn't respond.

'I thought you were homicide, Inspector. This is sex crimes or General Works, right?'

Gratelli shrugged noncommittally. He wasn't in the mood to explain anything – let alone the serial homicide connection – to Seidman. He'd know sooner or later. But like the press, it was better later.

'I want to talk with her,' he said to Seidman in a tone that couldn't be mistaken for anything but official.

There was an awkward moment when it appeared Seidman would insist on staying for the conversation. But Gratelli's disapproving look must have changed the lawyer's mind. Seidman got up slowly and went to the door.

'If there's anything I can help you with, let me know.'

'You and I probably need to have a little chat too,' Gratelli said.

'Inspector Gratelli?' Seidman said at the door.

Gratelli turned.

'She didn't know, I think.'

'Know what?'

'What happened to her. The woman told her.'

'What did happen to her?' Gratelli asked, wanting to know what the assistant D.A. knew.

'That she'd been raped,' Seidman said, a puzzled look on his face.

'Was she?' Gratelli asked.

'Wasn't she?'

Gratelli shrugged.

'What in the hell do you mean?' Earl said, staring across the table at the little red-headed lawyer who unburdened his tattered briefcase of a half dozen manila folders.

'What I said,' the guy replied. 'They won't do your bail.'

'You talked with them?'

'Yes, I talked with them.'

'What did they say? Exactly.' Earl asked, pushing the anger down. He'd already screwed up by letting his temper get the best of him. That's why he was sitting here.

The lawyer rolled his eyes. 'Exactly, your father said . . .'

'My fucking stepfather!'

'Your fucking stepfather said . . . *exactly*, he said: "Let the little asshole rot."'

'Was she there? My mother?'

'Yes.'

'What did she say?'

'She said exactly nothing.'

Earl looked away, then up. His eyes locked on a corner where the walls met the ceiling.

'That guy's gonna live isn't he?'

'Appears so.'

'You don't like me, do you?'

'I have to defend you. I don't have to like you. Now, tell me again, who got out of the car first?'

Inspector Mickey McClellan sat at the Formica topped table in the Stockton Street noodle joint when Gratelli came in. Chinatown used to be McClellan's beat when he first came on the force and he hung out there whenever he had the chance.

'So what'd she say?' Mickey asked.

'Nothin'.' Gratelli sat down. Though it would make his bladder work overtime for a few hours, the police officer ordered tea. The coffee was lousy there.

'Couldn't, wouldn't, what?'

'Dunno,' Gratelli replied. There was a long pause while Mickey slurped some noodles off the chopsticks. 'Maybe in shock. Maybe brain damage,' Gratelli continued. 'Mouth wired shut, vacant stare and I doubt if she could hold a pen even if she knew what the hell was going on.'

'A zombie,' Mickey said. The Inspector's insensitivity was legendary. He called blacks 'jungle bunnies' and gays, 'those little winged creatures.' Women were 'babes' unless they possessed the qualities he imagined all female police officers had. Then they were members of the 'lesbo squad.'

Gratelli took very little notice of Mickey's apparent prejudices. The balding, potbellied Inspector McClellan held everyone at the same level of disgust. It was equal opportunity bigotry. His prejudice was universal. Vietnam, years of vice, drugs and homicide brought him into contact with the baser elements of every category of humankind. The only difference between Mickey and a good percentage of the other cops who felt a kind of generalized hate as personal defense, is that he never bothered putting on a public face.

His hate, however, was no longer full of passion, no longer malevolent. Calling Chinese 'slants' was a way to keep people at a distance, keeping them as lifeless objects so he wouldn't puke or have nightmares when he saw some Asian kid floating in the bay.

'We get a victim who could tell us something and the lights are out on the top floor,' McClellan said.

'Yeah,' Gratelli said looking out of the corner window seeing the stream of Chinese faces flowing by.

'Bateman's a P.I., right?' Mickey asked. 'Maybe she made some nasty enemies if I can guess what you're thinking.'

'That wasn't what I was thinking.'

'You don't seem to buy into the idea that this Bateman gal gets a serial number like the others. Copycat maybe?' McClellan asked.

'Dunno. She was beat up. None of the others were.'

'Same guy,' McClellan said. 'Something goes wrong. Maybe she freaks out. Asshole loses his nerve, beats her up, but not so fucked up he leaves without the tattoo.'

'What makes you think so?'

'I don't know. Same kind of chick.'

'Julia Bateman is not the same kind of 'chick',' Gratelli said. 'She's not poor. She's not helpless . . .'

'She is now . . .'

'She's not that young.'

'Well, Bateman was within the drive time. Two hours from the city. Old or young, beat up or not, she's got the mark. Nobody knows about the mark.'

'A lot of people know about the mark.'

'Who? Nothin' in the papers, nothin' on TV about the mark,' Mickey said, deftly trapping some noodles in the grip of the two little wooden sticks.

'Thirteen sets of cops, fourteen sets of coroners, maybe even ambulance drivers and who knows who else. And no doubt a couple of ambitious prosecutors.'

'So you're sayin' we got two cases, not one.'

'No.'

'What are you sayin'?'

'Nothin'.'

'Well, here's the skinny. They want us to stay on the Bateman thing.' Mickey used the word 'they' for anything that came down from the Lieutenant or higher. For him, everybody above him was some vast 'they' bureaucracy. Some gray machine. He'd accepted them as he did everybody else, putting them in a specific category of the general category – 'asshole' – and keeping them at arm's length.

'What about the task force?' Gratelli asked.

'If you look at the organization chart on this thing we are connected to those folks by a little dotted line. We talk to them. They talk to us. But you and me bub, we are by ourselves from now on. Just Bateman and only Bateman so help us God.' He smiled. 'That suits me.'

'You're not saying that like you mean it.'

'Yeah, well, what the fuck?'

'I don't like it either.'

'It's like we're not doing the job,' McClellan said. 'I'd like to know who the fuck would've done it better. You ever heard of this? Takin' us out like this? Shit.'

'Political,' Gratelli said. 'Too hot. There'll be another news conference.'

McClellan was quiet, except for the slurping sound the noodles made as they disappeared between his lips. An incredibly mild explosion, Gratelli thought. He was taking it too well. McClellan's life wasn't about acceptance, but that seemed to be what he was doing, gradually slipping from nearly uncontrollable anger to indifference.

'So what do we do now?' Gratelli asked, sipping his tea.

'I think we take in a little baseball or take a little drive up to Gurneville. Your choice, kiddo.'

'Julia?'

She didn't hear Thaddeus Maldeaux come. Nor did she hear him speak. A nurse had taken two dozen cream colored French tulips from him. She would find a vase and return. He pulled a chair up, beside her bed.

'I don't know if you can hear me,' he said touching her hand. 'I should have gone with you. Or better yet, you should have run away with me.'

He waited. The nurse came back in, put the vase on the rollaway table. 'They're beautiful,' she said and left again.

'It's tough,' Maldeaux said softly. 'The world is a strange place, Julia. Sometimes it is so beautiful it takes your breath away. Sometimes it is so horrid . . .' he said, voice trailing off. He looked at her. There wasn't much to recognize. Swollen, blue, distorted face. 'And you never know when something dark and foreign and deadly will strike. You know, under the sea there are wondrous things we've never seen, most of us. Colors and shapes of living things that would amaze us, take us away from our normal daily lives. There is a turtle I saw that looks like a leaf. A harmless leaf. But it is hungry. Like all of us, we do what we must to survive. And so a fish goes by, thinking it is a beautiful day in its vast watery neighborhood and the fish does not see what it is who lies in wait.'

He leaned over the bed, whispered in her ear.

'You'll survive, Julia. Then you need someone who can help, who can tell the difference between turtles and leaves.'

SIX

It was all so real. Julia Bateman could smell home – the place where she grew up. There was a crispness in the morning air. It carried the scent of the sun burning dew off the grass. She stood behind her aunt's white frame farmhouse.

She was on the highway now, the rolling blacktop that rose and fell between the Amish farms. They waved to her. The women in their long dresses waved as if they knew her, loved her. The men too, in their dark clothes, waved, welcomed her.

She could feel the breeze in her hair. She was gliding across the ribbon of highway in the sun. How was she moving? She didn't know. She looked down. There, in her blue Miata convertible. She didn't have that car in Iowa. Then, as if by magic, the landscape changed. She was on the highway along the ocean now.

She'd done this before. Repeatedly. Even asleep, she knew it would be the same as it was before. Driving up Highway One along the California coast. It was all too familiar now. The carefree feeling she had was giving way now to a sense of anxiety. Into the pines. Getting darker. She was frightened. There was her Aunt's house, only it wasn't white anymore. It was dark and dingy looking. What was it doing there, half hidden, lurking in the trees?

Julia Bateman was in the house. There were pictures. Her sister, her father. She didn't have a sister. It was a picture of Julia. A picture that was supposed to be her mother; but it wasn't. It was Julia Bateman staring back through the dusty glass. In the hall now. A long hall. Thin, wind blown drapery drifted in like ghosts from doorways she hadn't known were there. Something was going to happen there. She knew it. It was terrible. She couldn't look. She put her hands over her eyes.

'Oh God, no!'

She smelled something like ammonia. Julia Bateman opened her eyes to see her legs stretched out under a white blanket. Beside her were machines with tubes that stretched out and into her. She remembered now. She was in the hospital. She took small comfort in the knowledge that she was alive.

'We thought we lost you yesterday.'

Julia looked over by the window. It was Paul Chang.

'You're going to be OK, Jules.' He came to her, sat on the bed. 'I'd hug you but I think it might hurt right now.' He patted her hand. 'Don't try to talk. We'll have plenty of time for that.'

A woman came in. About Julia's age. A sturdy woman with dark, short-cropped hair.

'Jules?' she said, edging to the bed. She seemed almost frightened and the emotion seemed not to suit her.

Julia's eyes seemed to show recognition for a moment. Then the eyes went dull again.

'Hey Sammie, how ya doin'?' Paul said quietly.

'Paul.' She responded warmly, but her eyes were on the patient.

'How's she doin'?'

The answer was in the silence.

Too much time to think. Earl unbuttoned his jail shirt and looked down at his chest, hoping they wouldn't keep him in too long because he'd be missing his weights. It took less time to lose muscle than it took to gain it.

So his lawyer didn't like him. Stand in line, he thought. If there were things about Earl Falwell people didn't like, Earl was the first to learn them. Hell, his dad didn't like him well enough to stick around or to contact him once he left. And that pissed his mother off, because, if the truth be known, she sure as hell wished the old man would have taken Earl with him.

His stepfather wanted Earl out of the house the moment the toad moved in.

People didn't like him when he was a little, pimply mouse of a kid. Now that he was strong, they didn't like him any better. Now they were scared of him. He could see it in their eyes.

Outside, in the world, he could fool people sometimes. When he first met them, he could act all nice and shit, like he cared about what was going on in their lives. Give them something.

That's how he did it. That's how he got the girls to go with him. Meet them at the mall, maybe the beach at San Gregorio or somewhere on the streets in San Francisco. Down around Turk Street they were kinda scuzzy, but they weren't all that bad when they were young. They'd talk to him. He was always shy with women. Came in handy. Made them feel comfortable. Then he'd find out what they're into. Rock bands mostly. Then he'd say he had these tickets to this or another concert. Whatever was in town or coming to town, some group they'd die to see.

Only he didn't have the tickets with him, he'd tell them. He'd have to go get them. That would always work. And they'd go with him. He'd get them out somewhere. Always somewhere different. Hell, he didn't even remember where a couple of them happened. He remembered it would be someplace in the middle of nowhere. And that'd be it.

What he really wanted was a woman, not some girl who barely had her pubes; but the young ones were easier. He didn't feel so awkward around them. And they trusted him. Most of the time, they didn't even see it coming.

McClelland and Gratelli met with Judge Wharton the next morning to get the warrant to search Julia Bateman's San

Francisco residence. However they decided to go to the cabin in the woods first.

McClellan drove. Gratelli, this time, rode shotgun, the unmarked Taurus making them look like a couple of hardware conventioneers in a rental.

They drove without conversation, up Highway 101, choosing speed over the beautiful but tortuously slow Highway One. They bypassed Mill Valley, Novato and Petaluma before having to exit at Cotati, where still another bypass would get them around thriving and trendy Sebastopol.

Gratelli would have preferred the scenic route. McClellan seemed immune to anything aesthetic. Once out of San Francisco, it didn't matter that much to Gratelli. The sky was a cloudless, hazeless blue and the sun through the glass warmed him, enticed him to relax. He allowed Puccini's 'Un bel di' to creep in and sweep out the debris that littered his mind. It was as good a way as any to spend a Friday afternoon, a fine way indeed to reduce the tension before gliding into a weekend.

Gurneville, the closest town to the crime scene, was one dot on the map beyond Forestville. It wasn't until then that McClellan spoke.

'You know where I can find a cheap apartment?'

'The Tenderloin,' Gratelli offered as a joke.

'Too expensive. I checked.'

'Who's interested?'

'Me,' McClellan said, eyes still on the road.

'Yeah, why is that?'

McClellan didn't answer. He didn't need to. Gratelli regretted asking. He had pieced together the signs. It was the breakup of a twenty-five-year marriage. That many years was a near record in the police department, where male officers, and now female officers, accumulated multiple spouses. But when a marriage lasted beyond the second decade, there was another dangerous time. When the kids left. When they were on their own. Nothing to hold the shaky partnership together. The years of late hours, mediocre pay, lack of communication, pent-up anger, disillusionment took its toll on the most well-intentioned, devoted families.

Even now, McClellan couldn't talk about it.

'Why in the hell would that dink want to move way up here?

Christ, a woman alone in a cabin in the boonies, she's asking
for trouble.'

'Un bel di' was irretrievable. Fitting for Julia Bateman,
Gratelli thought. The aria from *Madama Butterfly* was the song
of innocence and the prelude to the grim, ironic realities of life
and death. And Gratelli's quiet afternoon escape was over. They
neared the cabin.

As Inspector Mickey McClellan went with cops from Santa
Rosa and Gurneville inside Julia Bateman's cabin, Gratelli
wandered the outside perimeter of her property. There wasn't
much of it. The cabin itself was set into the hill, the front jutting
out, leaving only a modest yard in front before it was cut off
by the gravel road.

Even so, the cabin was almost invisible from the road, hidden
by pines of various heights which canopied a wilderness of
ferns and other greenery below he couldn't identify. If the lights
were on inside, then perhaps someone could detect human
existence. Otherwise it was doubtful, especially doubtful in the
dark. The drive might give it away, though it was narrow and
was slightly overgrown from disuse.

An automobile parked in the drive might call attention to
itself by reflecting a headlight. However, Julia Bateman's blue
Miata was parked around the curve and in a space under the
house. Had it been moved since the crime?

The doors and windows to the cabin had not been jimmied.
There were no footprints, no broken twigs or squashed plants.
No sign anyone had tried to peek in the windows. If the brush
had been beaten down, it wouldn't have surprised him. In fact,
he was surprised that the local police hadn't tromped around
the grounds.

How did the rapist get in? Not likely through the windows
and not likely through either door unless they were left unlocked
or Julia Bateman had let him or them in herself. Possible. She
hadn't yet spoken a word on the subject. What was also possible
was a climb up the hill to the roof. Stones had been embedded
along one side of the incline toward the back of the cabin to
inhibit erosion.

It was possible to climb that way and return by that route
without leaving much if any imprint.

Gratelli took a deep breath and went inside the cabin. The

question of the rapist's access was immediately answered once Gratelli got beyond the living room and headed toward the bedrooms where the police officers who had agreed to meet the two big city cops were engaged in a heated discussion, punctuated by nervous laughter.

Consciousness seemed more accessible to Julia Bateman, though not necessarily more desirable. She was now able to mentally separate the two worlds, the one lit inside her mind, the other outside. And to some extent, now, she was able to choose which one to inhabit.

Earlier, she had heard the nurses talk about a reduction in morphine and was able to conclude that was what accounted for her rise into the real world. She had also heard them tell the doctor that 'the patient's heart beat and blood pressure were nearly normal and continuing to improve.' Julia was, however, indifferent to the news.

At the moment she was being given a sponge bath. They'd begun by gently dabbing her face with warm water sending periodic needle pricks of pain that spread like tentacles into her brain. It was less painful when they gently swathed the warmth on her chest and belly. Then the warmth disappeared as the moisture evaporated and she would chill in one spot and become warm in another.

She chose not to open her eyes, but merely to feel the not altogether unpleasant sensation. Whoever it was worked in silence. And when the bath was completed, Julia felt the cool sheet again cover her. Then another layer – a cotton blanket – was tucked up under her chin.

Julia could feel herself drift again, her body tingling against the cool sheets. She was sure she could hang on to consciousness, but allowed herself to drift, feeling a comfortable warming of her body.

As a child, in the early summer, she'd play all day, forgetting how the weak sun could still sting her skin with a light pink blush. She would shower and climb naked into her bed. This is how her flesh was now – warm and cool, safe and secret. She was completely aware of every inch of her body.

In those adolescent days, she discovered the strange pleasure her nakedness gave her – the slight swell of her breasts and the electricity of her nipples against the starched sheets, the secret touching.

Dark now. Heavy quilt over her. Sounds. Sounds overhead awakened her. She opened her eyes, but couldn't see in the darkness. At first Julia Bateman was frightened, but she was sure it was a raccoon, perhaps a possum. The area was full of nocturnal creatures. She closed her eyes. The sound again.

The cabin had a flat roof, so the sound was not far away nor was there much in between her and the sound to buffer it. Couldn't be raccoons, she thought. It was a heavy sound. A bear? Surely not. There were brown bears in California, but weren't they in parks?

Her .32 revolver was in the desk drawer. The telephone was on the desk. The desk was in the living room. She decided not to turn on the light. If it were a bear, it probably didn't matter. If it were a burglar, the light would let him know her whereabouts.

This wasn't the first time she'd been in danger. Hang around Turk and Eddy Streets in the city for a few years. Anybody who could do that would be able to stay cool in a volatile situation. Her bare feet touched the cool wooden floor. Her arm went out to feel for the doorway. She moved slowly into the hall.

A patch of starry night showed itself in the skylight. Suddenly her naked body was bathed in light. She looked up again, but was blinded by the light. There was a creaking sound, then a loud crack. The light went crazy and something huge was sucked into the cabin. Nearly on top of her. She heard breathing. The light came at her and she saw nothing else.

Inspector Mickey McClellan was holding the long suction tube of a portable vacuum cleaner as Gratelli came into Julia Bateman's bedroom.

'I see a broken skylight. I don't see any glass,' Gratelli said.

'This is why.' Mickey waved the tube. 'This is why we got no evidence,' McClellan said.

'He cleaned up afterward,' one of the Gurneville deputies said.

'This guy was thorough,' McClellan continued. 'He took the bedclothes, vacuumed the mattress and carpet and probably the body.'

'What about the bag?' Gratelli asked, nodding toward the little red vacuum.

'This is priceless Gratelli, tell 'em.' McClellan nodded to the deputy who spoke earlier.

'Best we can tell Inspector, the perpetrator not only stole the bag but he sucked water through the tube there and dumped it in the commode. Then damn if he didn't wash the commode.'

'Nobody searched outside?'

'No, Inspector. We waited. We saw the tattoo there and well, you know, we had that other kid, that other homicide up here earlier. We waited for you.'

McClellan pushed the switch on the vacuum with his foot. 'Me,' he said over the whir, 'I figure the maid did it.'

Everybody but Gratelli started laughing.

SEVEN

David Seidman spent Saturday and Sunday mornings at Julia Bateman's bedside. Paul Chang did the same in the afternoons. Sammie stopped by both days, stood awkwardly for fifteen minutes or so and excused herself. She didn't so much leave the room as escape it. Otherwise, nothing changed. The nurses had cranked up the bed, putting its inhabitant in a sitting position. Julia's eyes were open. She didn't speak.

Sometimes she looked in Paul's direction, but with little interest. Either she didn't know him or wasn't much interested in his being there. Not knowing which, Paul assumed it was the former.

'I called your father,' Paul said Sunday afternoon. He waited. No response. 'He's coming out. He'll be here around ten in the morning.' No response.

'I'm watering your plants,' he continued, 'checking the mail, things like that at the apartment and things are going OK at work. I can handle it for awhile. Keep things going. So don't worry, Jules.'

Julia Bateman didn't appear to be worrying.

'I checked your cabin Saturday morning. Tried to, anyway. The cops wouldn't let me in.'

Paul was sorry he mentioned the cabin. He hadn't intended to bring up what had happened, even indirectly.

'I told your father he could stay at your place, but he decided to stay downtown somewhere. I told him he could reach me at the office on Monday.'

Paul felt silly just babbling on when he couldn't be sure she heard or understood a single word he was saying. He sat the rest of the afternoon in silence, his hand touching hers.

Pauli Vincente Gratelli awoke Monday morning as he always awoke, eyes sealed shut by the too plentiful secretion of some chemical or another. There were mornings he would have to pull the lids apart and brush away the grit to be able to see.

It was as if nature intended his slumber to be more permanent. This morning, the seal required intervention and though he didn't remember dreaming – he never remembered – his unusually tired body suggested the night had been restless.

He imagined that it had something to do with the killings. Gratelli was usually able to shed the more gruesome aspects of his work when he was off duty – something he'd learned to do only in the last five years or so. Perhaps it was the age of most of the victims. These weren't exactly children, but they were young. That made things more difficult. Perhaps it was Julia Bateman's battered body and shocked numbed mind that made it worse. In homicide, the victims are usually dead and beyond pain. Not alive, suffering.

He closed his eyes to redirect his thoughts and get a fresh start on the morning. Official police work began after his morning coffee and the *Chronicle*.

His bed occupied a small, windowed alcove in the smaller of the two bedrooms in his small apartment. He knew the temperature outside was probably around fifty degrees; but the sun was warm on his face and bare arms.

He wiped at his eyes one more time, threw the covers back and slid a bony leg over the side, eventually bringing himself to a sitting position, where he'd turn off the alarm he'd beaten by at least fifteen minutes and where he'd remain until he felt his blood circulating to his feet.

When he was satisfied that his feet were ready to support him, Gratelli reached down and aligned his slippers, then slipped his feet into them. The bedroom was carpeted, the bath and kitchen weren't. He pushed himself off the bed, moved to the closet where he grabbed his robe from the hook on the back of the door and headed to the kitchen.

He ground the coffee beans, drew water from the faucet into the ancient percolator, started the gas burner with a match – all in the morning ritual. Next he went to his wall of shelves in the living room selecting Rossini's *L'Italiana in Algeri*, letting the music begin while he went to the front door for his morning paper, a continuation of his ritual – a ritual only slightly modified by the loss of his wife to ovarian cancer ten years ago. His family suggested he move to a new place, even if it was just down the hall. Find a nice widow somewhere and start a new life. He liked it the way it was. He didn't want a new life. Anna was his wife. She was still his wife. He liked being where he was. He liked the memories the apartment, the furniture, even the percolator gave him.

The memories were not sad. They gave his life meaning, a richness it might not otherwise have.

Gratelli usually chose comic opera to start the day. The days were often tragic enough. He sat at the small chrome table with the black top in the tiny kitchen and went methodically through the paper. It seemed an emptier paper without Herb Caen – another break in the rhythm. He read the back of the style page next. He'd begun to like the columnist who resided there. A little wit, humor and intelligence before he went back to the front page.

The story was a few pages in and small which meant the reporters had not yet tied Julia Bateman with the others. It didn't mention her name, but did mention a San Francisco business woman was raped and beaten at a weekend cabin three miles outside of Gurneville.

'Oops,' he thought. The last sentence read: 'Gurneville police said they would not comment about any possible connection between this and the recent spate of savage murder-rapes in the greater Bay area.'

Gratelli took another sip of coffee, letting the music take his mind off it for the moment.

Aerosmith's *Love in an Elevator* was abruptly cut off by a hand crushing the snooze button on the digital clock radio. Paul Chang turned back to the center of the bed where he saw the body of his blond-headed friend.

'Come on, wake up Bradley,' Paul said, nudging the bare shoulder.

'What?' the head turned slowly, groggily toward Paul.

'Wake up. You've got two hours to get home, get ready and get to work.'

'What day is it?'

'Monday.'

'What time is it?'

'Seven,' Paul said, trying to figure out whether he loved Bradley or merely loved Bradley's blond hair. It didn't matter now. For now all he wanted was Bradley to get out of bed, get dressed and be gone. There was still an hour before Paul would have to get ready. And he wanted to fill that time with sleep.

'Go back to sleep,' Bradley said, crawling out of bed, standing, disoriented for a moment. 'I'll call you Wednesday or something.'

Paul watched as this handsome specimen of naked humanity moved across the room then disappeared into the hallway. Paul was glad that Bradley wasn't the type requiring polite chatter over a cup of coffee the morning after. The last things that Paul remembered were hearing the water run in the bathroom and feeling Chat, his Burmese cat, hop on the bed to steal the warmth of the former occupant.

When he woke again, Julia was on his mind. He must have dreamt about her, but he couldn't remember. He thought about her trips to Russian River, thought about the time he spent with her at the cabin. How wonderfully relaxed she became, reading and looking at the river. Julia's eyes always made her seem open and vulnerable no matter what she said or how she acted while working. At the cabin, she was a kid again – laughing, joking – and between the two of them they were able to erase a couple of decades of existence.

The cabin wouldn't be the same. And now, Julia's eyes seemed more empty than innocent.

'You are doing fine. You're over the hump.'

Julia Bateman recognized the voice and now saw the face of the doctor, a face that seemed too young to belong to a doctor. It didn't seem serious enough. Dark curly hair and big white teeth showing in a wide smile – a look more appropriate to an aerobics instructor or an activities director for a cruise ship.

'I'm making my rounds,' the doctor continued. 'I'll be back
in a little while.' He patted her forearm. 'Listen, you're going
to have a heavy day. A couple of police officers will be up this
morning. And I understand from one of the nurses that your
father will be here too. If all this gets to be too much let us
know. OK?'

She felt herself nodding as if someone else were controlling
the movement.

'Good,' the doctor smiled. 'See you in a little bit.'

Early in Gratelli's career he would spend an hour or so at Caffe
Trieste before duty. He'd smoke several unfiltered cigarettes
and down a cup of espresso, the small china cup rattling on its
small china saucer as he replaced it on the false marble-topped
table in front of him.

He no longer smoked, could no longer take that strong a dose
of caffeine and no longer desired the company of people that
early in the morning. He now took his coffee to go.

Gratelli stood on the sidewalk. His building – the one with
a few storefronts and a few apartments above them that he'd
inherited from his father – was behind him. He waited for
Mickey McClellan. They took turns with the city-owned car.
Last night was McClellan's.

It was a morning cool that had a little bite to it. It wasn't
raining and you couldn't really call it a fog, but there was
dampness in the air. The people on Grant Street walked briskly,
shoulders hunched, defending the body against the cold.

He wished he'd put on his raincoat. Gratelli had only a few
moments to tap his feet and jingle the change in his pocket
before he saw the Taurus rounding the corner and heading his
way. He had hoped they'd be issued a Caprice, one of those
monster comfort cars. Some of the cops had Caprices. The
Caprice reminded him of the big, old round Buick his Uncle
Frank had back in the late forties.

McClellan's eyes were puffy and pink. There was a sleep
crease on the side of his cheek. His flesh had the look of having
had a fresh and rough scrubbing. Mickey hadn't been up long,
nor was it likely he'd gotten much sleep before that. It was also
likely that McClellan had remained in the city over the weekend
rather than going home. The tell-tale signs would have disappeared during the hour drive in.

'You have the papers?' Gratelli asked, choosing to avoid any question about his partner's condition and the causes thereof. Mickey didn't take too kindly to kidding, especially in the morning.

'On the way,' McClellan said, glancing over his left shoulder and pulling away from the curb. 'I was running late.'

Gratelli thought about asking Mickey to stop by the Opera House to pick up his tickets for Thursday's performance, but wasn't sure if the office opened that early or if it opened at all on Mondays.

'No hurry,' Gratelli said, rubbing his hands and settling into the warmth.

Julia Bateman sipped orange juice through a clear plastic straw. There was another container filled with something gelatinous on the shelf-like table that had been rolled up to her bed.

She felt less groggy. She seemed to be able to trace the internal route of the juice as it entered her system and seemed to activate her body as it passed through her. It startled her consciousness to the next higher level.

'Are you feeling better,' asked the redheaded nurse cheerlessly.

Julia nodded. She figured if she lied the nurse would leave sooner. The fact was that she was sore all over. Muscles. Bones. There were organs in her body she couldn't recall ever being aware of. She was aware of them now. And they hurt.

The nurse checked the clear plastic bags suspended above Julia's bed. The liquid drained down through plastic tubes, one of which went through a little machine that had a small, slowly blinking red light. The nurse adjusted something on the machine.

'Can I get you something?' the nurse asked.

Julia shook her head 'no.'

McClellan pulled to the curb on Hayes Street in front of a bookstore advertising rare books and across from Bateman's apartment house. He pulled the official papers from the breast pocket of his gray suit.

'Wait,' Gratelli said. 'That's the kid who was with Bateman's D.A. friend.'

McClellan looked at the person exiting the apartment house. 'The slant?'

'The young fellow from the hospital.' Gratelli rarely chastised his partner for the ethnic slurs but he'd be damned if he'd just agree with terms like 'the slant.'

'That's what I said, the slant.'

'Is there anybody in this world you do like, Mickey?'

McClellan thought awhile.

'Dogs,' he said.

'Any human beings?'

'No.'

They waited a moment for the guy to turn and walk into the little parking lot beside the building. He got into a mint VW Bug with tinted windows. As he backed out of his spot to head on to Ivy Street, a little alley behind the building, Gratelli wrote down the license plate.

'You wanna run it now?' McClellan said.

'Might as well.'

Gratelli and McClellan sat quietly and waited. Some young, well built guys went into the gym next to the parking lot. Some other guys left, looking fresh and pink.

'Makes you sick, doesn't it?' McClellan asked.

'What now?'

'People spending so much time trying to make themselves pretty.'

'Doesn't bother me.'

'Every damned one of them is a jock sniffer, bet you my next paycheck. Jesus.'

'You let way too many things bother you,' Gratelli said.

'Whaddya mean? I don't let nothin' bother me. Just observin' the fuckin' human condition, that's all.'

The radio told them that the car was registered to Paul S. Chang, that Chang was clean and that he lived in the building he was coming out of.

'A neighbor,' Gratelli said. 'Knows Bateman, knows the assistant D.A. through Bateman because he is a neighbor.'

'Well now that you got everything all figured out, let's go have a look.'

'What's the matter, the elevator don't work?' McClellan asked the apartment manager who headed up the stairs.

'We're only going up one flight,' the older gentleman said.

Gratelli noticed the old guy had twenty years on McClellan,

but McClellan had sixty unwanted pounds on the manager. And the way the old guy said how it was only 'one flight' was clearly intended to take McClellan down a peg or two on the wise guy chart.

The manager knew why the police stopped by. Paul Chang had told him at least the assault part of it. And he inquired on the way up about her condition. He never asked for the papers but unlocked the door to Julia's apartment and, after telling the two cops to make sure the door was pulled to when they were done, left them.

The first thing Gratelli noticed when he turned from the hall and went into the main room was a small bank of windows. He headed toward them. The second thing he noticed was a shade being pulled down in the apartment across the narrow alley – Ivy Street.

McClellan came into the room, having taken a detour into the kitchen. He was eating a banana.

'Couple a more days, it woulda been inedible,' he said by way of explanation.

'Make yourself at home,' Gratelli said.

The main room was pretty small. Maybe twelve feet wide and perhaps a foot longer than that the other way. There was a bed stuffed into an alcove that was once, judging by the marks of now absent hardware, a Murphy Bed.

The bed acted as a kind of large, built-in sofa since the opening faced into the room. Beside the bed were stacks of books, mostly paperbacks and mostly by women – several of them by Margaret Atwood, L.C. Wright and P.D. James. There were stacks of CDs – Cole Porter, Gershwin.

Along one wall was a long, desk-like structure. It appeared to be a door on top of two filing cabinets. On it was an expensive looking lamp, several neat stacks of paper, a computer and printer, a small copying machine, a telephone that doubled as a fax machine, plus a stapler, stamp dispenser.

There were two high-back chairs of similar style but different material and a small, low bookcase under the window that held a few plants and below that a stereo unit.

McClellan began sifting through the papers. 'I wonder how much a place like this goes for.'

Gratelli looked around the small space thinking it was no wonder she went to a cabin on the weekends. He couldn't imagine being cooped up in this place all day long – working here, eating here, sleeping here.

'I figure she's billing four thou a month,' McClellan said. Mickey was rummaging through a stack of billing statements not yet mailed. 'Wait a minute, here. There's a check made out to our Paul Chang. Why is she paying him?'

Gratelli looked at the check. 'The kid works for her, see the withholding.'

'Oh yeah, well . . . it's interesting nonetheless, don't you think? The kid is a little private dick.'

'She's an insurance investigator,' Gratelli said.

'So?'

Gratelli shrugged, headed toward the window. The shade in the apartment across the alley was still drawn, but on one side, the vertical line, the edge of the shade was broken. Whoever it was didn't want to be seen, but certainly wanted to see.

McClellan headed back toward the kitchen. Gratelli looked over the desk. There were two stacks of unopened mail. A quick look showed that one pile was personal, addressed to Julia Bateman at her Hayes Street address. The other was more official looking, addressed to Bateman Investigations at a post office box.

He looked around for an appointment calendar and finding none figured that it was either in her purse, at the cabin or perhaps it was on the computer. Inaccessible at the moment, in any event.

'Look what I got,' McClellan said, coming back into the main area, having raided the refrigerator.

'A glass of milk. That's nice Mickey.'

'Nah, nah, nah. The other hand nimrod.'

'Why Mickey, it is a key. What a wonderful day in the neighborhood.'

'On a hook. Above the hook was the name "Paul." And Paul's key has a number on it. A two hundred number. Right on this floor. And he's off somewhere.'

'First you steal a banana, then the lady's milk and now you are gonna break and enter. Whose side you on?'

'Look, the date on the carton? Two days from now. She won't be back, OK? Second, I didn't ask for no key. It's there. A gift. Fate.' McClellan looked up at the ceiling, extending his hands to the heavens beyond, then glanced back down at Gratelli who'd dropped to his knees to look through the filing cabinets. 'A judgment from the ultimate Supreme Court, huh?'

'Since when did you become so religious?' Gratelli asked pulling out a battered, bent and at one time manila file folder.

'Since he shined his grace on thee . . . and thine . . . and whoever. You coming?'

'No,' Gratelli said, finding something intriguing inside the folder. 'I don't even know you're gone.'

EIGHT

There was a man standing at the foot of Julia's bed. He wore dark clothes. She opened her eyes because she felt someone's gaze. He moved to her bed, sat down on the edge.

'Jiggles, you are the ugliest old thing to come down the pike in a long time,' he said touching her forehead with a kiss.

It was like the whole goddamn dam burst. As she raised up, arms outstretched, she chilled, her stomach dropped, her throat tightened and she exploded in tears.

He hugged her. 'Now, now baby,' he said.

A moan came from inside her. She felt the wire cut into her mouth as she tried to catch her breath. No air could pass through her nostrils. They were filled and running on her father's coat. Her body convulsed in sputtering sobs.

'It's all gonna be all right, I promise you.' He held her to him, palm caressing the back of her neck.

'Come back here you son of a bitch!'

Gratelli recognized McClellan's voice. The sound came from the hall. He dropped the files and lurched awkwardly to his feet, reaching for his .38 in the same motion. In the hall, he pressed his ear to the door. He heard the thumping sounds of someone running. Gratelli, holding the gun straight up, close to his face, eased the door open, moved quickly into the hall, leveling his gun in the direction of the sound.

McClellan, his back to Gratelli, had dropped to his knees facing the wall. 'You bastard,' he said.

Gratelli's eyes scanned the hall. He saw nothing. Then he saw a small furry burst of brown race away from the huddled body.

'Son of a bitch,' McClellan said, standing, out of breath. He turned back to Gratelli and seeing his partner holding his gun, 'You're not planning to shoot the little bastard are you?'

Gratelli laughed.

'How the fuck was I supposed to know there was a cat in there?' McClellan was red-faced.

Gratelli put his pistol away, walked down the hallway to the brown cat, who sat looking at him as if all of this had been a game.

'Hey you,' Gratelli said in a soft, gravelly whisper. Gratelli lowered himself to a squat. 'How 'bout you and me going back home, partner?'

The cat seemed agreeable. Gratelli's big hands scooped him up and the three of them went to Paul Chang's apartment.

Having been snookered into McClellan's breaking and entering, Gratelli decided he might as well look around.

Chang's place had the same layout as Bateman's, only reverse. Unlike Bateman's, Chang's didn't so much double as an office as an artist's studio.

The bed was in the middle of the room. On the wall opposite the bed was one huge bookcase with big, heavy books – Matisse, de Chirico, Ruscha, Rauchenberg, O'Keefe. Most of the names he recognized, though that was about all he knew about them. There were also books on photography. Some names Gratelli recognized. However, there were two books laying on top of the rows he didn't recognize.

He pulled them out. One was called *Teenage Lust* and thumbing through it noticed they were all photographs of street kids, male and female, caught, it seemed candidly, in some mix of sex and violence.

McClellan came over to get an eyeful of the second book – photographs of some guy named Witkin who seemed to specialize in women with penises and snakes and rotting vegetables.

'Christ,' McClellan said. 'We got a sick boy here.'

Gratelli shut the book and carefully put it back where he had found it.

'He's an artist.'

'Yeah, well . . .' he shook his head. 'Our boy's also got some leather threads in the closet. Some kind of harness, leather pants, jacket.' McClellan examined the pants. 'Buttless,' McClellan said.

The alcove where Bateman had her bed in the other apartment, Chang had a large artist's table. On it was a huge piece of cardboard, on which ripped photographs of body parts were being assembled into some larger, more abstract picture.

'The kid's kinda kinky, don't you think?' McClellan asked. 'Maybe we got a candidate.'

'Come on, she knows the guy.'

'Gay boy too.' McClellan pointed to a greeting card with a male nude smiling back. Inside were the handwritten words, 'Keep your Wednesdays open, Bradley.'

'That pretty much rules him out, don't you think?' Gratelli suggested.

'It's a question of how bent is bent. You been around long enough to know these things.' McClellan picked up a book with no cover. There were sketches and some notes scribbled in pencil.

'. . . to examine the edges of existence,' McClellan read out loud. 'How far one steps out, not knowing if you've gone too far, if there's a way back, is the distinguishing characteristic that separates art from craft.'

McClellan's face twisted into a caricature, mocking sophistication. 'Some pretty highbrow words. Just an excuse to be kinky. The boy is bent. Bent enough?'

'Can't see him breaking a girl's neck.'

'I can.' McClellan said, going through the bureau drawers next to the alcove. 'Pretty stuff.' McClellan said it with disgust, holding up a pair of leather shorts. Then he extracted a book from loose underwear and socks.

He opened it to the first page. 'Chapbook #23,' it said.

McClellan flipped through it. There were ragged and torn pieces of photos and incomplete sketches, some as innocuous as a photo of Barbie and Ken dolls. Others were naked bodies and body parts. There were words inscribed at random it seemed. Some were in poetry form. Some were narratives.

McClellan started to read from the top of a left-hand page.

'Get this,' McClellan said, reading a sentence. "Just as pain is less desirable than joy, pain is more desirable than numbness.

Feeling something – anything – is better than the anesthesia, a state of nonexistence." The guy's into some serious shit.'

McClellan flipped a few more pages.

'Clippings,' he said. 'Dahmer. And here's some on that guy who cut off his son's head on the highway in New Mexico. The kid in the alley off Polk. Christ, this guy is. . . .'

He didn't finish the sentence. Then he picked it up again.

'Listen to this: "Dahmer had been left alone too long. Absent a world in which to belong, he created his own and was unable to escape it. He juggled two worlds. Successfully for a while. Then they collided." What the hell does that mean?'

'I don't know,' Gratelli said. 'You are pondering the imponderable.'

'What?'

'Nothing.'

'OK, you tell me what this means. He's still writing about Dahmer,' McClellan said, reading another page, '"the sickness in our hearts comes from hate and the hate from fear. And when the fear becomes too much, we are left with our sickness, alone with our sickness. We feel powerless. We feel we are dying. We seek whatever it is that will make us feel alive again. If necessary we create new worlds, one in which we become God, if necessary, to make sense of it."'

Gratelli waited for another comment from McClellan. But he grew silent. He turned away. Then, as if he'd decided something he came back and began to look at the book.

Gratelli didn't say anything.

McClellan continued leafing through the little book.

'This collection of body parts Chang has and lots of tattoos in his photos and this killer's engraving of flowers on girls' legs . . . I mean, maybe this is all connected.'

'These are his thoughts, McClellan. You see anything in there that resembles a rose tattoo?'

'Not yet.'

'You can't arrest a man for his thoughts. You don't even know what he means by it all. Maybe he's writing a story.'

'What do the lawyers say on TV? Goes to state of mind.'

'Can't use anything in here anyhow. No warrant.'

'No, but we'll have a warrant next time and we'll know just where to look if I need one.' He carefully put the book where he found it. 'That was Chapbook number twenty-three,'

McClellan said. 'Where's the other twenty-two? Or number twenty-four? Maybe we got a rose tattoo in there somewhere.'

They went back to Julia's apartment. Gratelli noticed the curtain across the alley shift again.

McClellan followed Gratelli back down the stairs, then out through the first floor garage and on to Ivy Street. Gratelli looked up at the back of the apartment house where he'd seen the drapery move, trying to make sure he could get the right place once he was inside. There was no way through though. The two cops went to Franklin, then to the front of the apartment.

A woman was leaving as they hit the front door, allowing them entry without having to talk to the super. It was a frame building. The hallways were dark, narrow and musty.

'Who is it?' came a voice after McClellan pounded his big fist against the door.

'Police.'

'Just a minute.'

'Now!' McClellan bellowed.

There was a click. The door opened, caught itself on a chain. A relatively young black face peered through the narrow divide.

'What is it?'

'We'd like to talk to you,' Gratelli said.

'What about?' the face replied.

'May we come in?'

'I'd rather you didn't,' the voice said.

'What's your name?'

'Anthony.'

'Anthony, I suppose you got a last name,' McClellan said.

'Jones.'

'Jones?'

'Jones,' Anthony responded.

'Mr Jones, Inspector Gratelli and I would like to talk to you and we'd like to talk to you inside.'

'Why can't we talk like this. What's this about?'

'It's about somebody across the alley over there who nearly died,' McClellan said.

'We'd like to talk to you about that,' Gratelli said, keeping his voice calm. 'We'd like to be able to see what you can see from your window. You know what I mean?'

'Can you come back please?'

'All this just makes us want to come in and talk with you all the more.'

The face backed away. The two cops could hear the kid take a deep breath. The chain dropped and the door opened.

The guy was maybe twenty, wiry and wearing a towel around his waist. The shine on his body suggested it had been oiled. In the small bay window, there was a chair facing out – though the draperies had been pulled and the room dark, there was a strange sacredness about it. Perhaps a dark and evil one. On the floor by the chair was a pool of clothing. On the table beside the chair were a pair of binoculars and a bottle of almond oil.

McClellan went to the window, peeked through the part. In a few moments, he turned back. Shrugged. 'Come take a look . . . second floor, to the left.'

Gratelli looked. There was a man lying naked on a bed and a woman dressed in leather doing the deed.

Gratelli looked back. Anthony Jones stared at the floor.

'So fucking early in the morning,' McClellan said. 'And we got ourselves a little peeping Anthony.'

'Am I under arrest?'

'Who the fuck knows?' McClellan said, shaking his head. 'She could pull the goddamn blinds.'

Gratelli laughed.

'What's so funny?'

'Nothing.'

'Yeah nothing. Hey, Jones, you shouldn't be looking at that crap.'

'They look back. They watch me,' he said defensively.

'I didn't want to know that,' McClellan said.

'They want me to look,' Jones pleaded.

'OK, OK,' McClellan said. 'Give it a break. You're only issued one of those. You wear it out, you go without.'

Gratelli pulled McClellan into the kitchen. 'Go run our Mr Jones. I'll ask a few questions.'

Back in the car, heading toward the hospital, they rode in their usual silence. Gratelli was surprised that McClellan hadn't gotten a little physical with the peeping Tom. He usually liked to push these guys around, scare them and vent some of his own anger. Instead, McClellan went a little soft.

The information on Jones wasn't much. There had been some previous complaints about him exposing himself in the window of a previous residence, but nothing else. What Gratelli discovered was that the Jones boy had plane ticket stubs that showed he'd been in East Chicago during several of the murders. They'd verify it, of course. They'd put him on the list. It almost wasn't worth it. But he did have a view of Julia Bateman's studio apartment, though not much of one. If they put everybody who had some sort of sex kink on their list, they might as well just substitute the San Francisco phone book, the lieutenant told them. Still, who knows what a quiet little guy like the Jones kid would do in the middle of the night?

Just as they pulled into park, McClellan said. 'You know you never think of homosexual slants you know? I mean, I know there is. I seen 'em. Used to be a place called the Rendezvous downtown some years ago. But it don't seem natural. None of it seems natural. Gay Vietnamese. Gay Mexicans. Isn't there one fuckin' country that don't have homos? You think there's gotta be. Yet there's a whole fuckin' city full of homos, all sizes, all colors speaking ninety-seven different languages.' He shook his head. 'How you suppose it happens? What turns a guy?'

Gratelli shrugged.

'I mean, fuck, you ever think about that shit?'

'I don't know,' Gratelli said. 'You being a good Irish Catholic boy, you probably messed around . . .'

'You're ass, Gratelli.' McClellan pulled into the hospital lot, and pulled into the space in front of the fire hydrant.

'When I was a kid, maybe thirteen, me and my cousin Joey sat in back of Uncle Frank's black Buick looking at magazines . . .'

'I don't want to hear it,' McClellan said.

Gratelli shrugged, repressed a smile that would have been rare in any event and got out of the car and followed McClellan into the big old building.

The humor of McClellan's sudden priggishness slipped away quickly as he thought about Julia Bateman. Few people besides other cops would understand how he felt about questioning a rape victim – especially one as brutalized as Bateman. He would have rather have spent an afternoon on a bed of nails than cause her the agony of reliving any part of that experience.

*   *   *

Julia saw the two men come in. She didn't recognize either of them until Gratelli spoke.

'Ms Bateman, I'm Inspector Gratelli, San Francisco police.'

Her father got up from the edge of the bed.

'I'm Royal Bateman.'

'Her father?'

'Yes sir.'

'This is Inspector McClellan.'

'Nice to meet you both. Is there any news?'

'No,' Gratelli said. 'Too early. We need to get some information from your daughter. You might want to grab a cup of coffee or something, stretch your legs. We might be a while.'

'I'd like to stay.'

Royal Bateman said it in a way that wasn't a request.

Gratelli looked at Julia. She nodded.

'All right. As long as you understand we might be getting pretty graphic here.'

The senior Bateman stepped aside, moving toward the window as Gratelli pulled a chair beside Julia's bed. McClellan hung back by the door.

'Ms Bateman, I'm going to try to ask questions in such a way that you can answer yes or no. Don't try to speak, OK?'

She nodded.

'Did you know your assailant?'

She shook her head no.

Early in the questioning, Julia Bateman didn't feel the strain. Perhaps, she thought, she had vented everything crying in her father's arms. She felt little emotion. The events seemed so distant, so unconnected to her, she felt as if she were remembering some movie she had seen or book she had read.

But eventually the darkness seemed to be creeping back. As she nodded to one question and shook her head at another, her thoughts became more vivid.

'Were his hands coarse, rough?'

She shook her head 'no,' but could feel them now, wet, slippery hands. Julia could smell him.

'Did he say anything . . .?'

She shook her head 'no.' But she could hear him breathing as if he were next to her. Now.

She could no longer understand the questions.

'Ms Bateman?' It was the gravelly voice.

She put her hands over her eyes, but it did no good. What she saw was inside her head. There was a sweaty body over her.

'You got any ideas about lunch?' McClellan asked as the red Taurus pulled out of the hospital parking lot.

'I'm not hungry.' Gratelli was exhausted and his stomach churned like he'd just gulped down a cup or two of sulfuric acid.

'You'll be hungry. You need to eat.'

'Why is it I always need to eat when you're hungry?'

McClellan laughed. 'You're skinny.'

'I'm healthy.'

'You look dead.'

Gratelli knew he did. He looked like his father, dark hair, pale skin, bony features. Couldn't gain weight if he tried. His brother Marcello got the mother's genes. Those were the fat genes. Marcello looked more alive than Vincente for the entire forty-eight years of his life, before he died of a heart attack.

'My brother looked very healthy when he died,' Gratelli said. 'Better just to look dead than be dead.'

'I'm not so sure about that,' McClellan said. 'You upset about what we talked about earlier?'

'What?'

'About messin' 'round in the back seat of your Uncle Frank's Buick?'

'Mickey, listen . . .'

'Shut your fuckin' trap a minute, will ya? I'm trying' to tell you something. Kids do it. Curiosity. OK?' McClellan took a deep breath, let it out. What he was about to say wasn't easy. 'Once. I was fuckin' twelve years old, ragin' hormones, and all that, you know,' McClellan said, gritting his teeth and staring straight ahead. 'We went skinny dippin' and were just laying there dryin' out and hell the sun and the hormones and talking about things . . . hell we were just showing each other what we had, you know, and how big it could get. And well things got outta hand.'

'You played with his . . .'

'Don't make a federal case out of it, all right? I just figured to set the record straight. We're even now. You messed around. I messed around. Once. End of story.'

'I never messed around,' Gratelli said.

'What do you mean?' McClellan blurted, turning toward Gratelli.

'I mean I never messed around.'

'No, no, no. You and what's his name with the magazines in the back seat of the Buick, right?'

'Joey. My cousin. We didn't mess around.'

'You said . . .'

'I said the two of us were in the back seat of my Uncle Frank's black Buick looking through some magazines. You didn't let me finish. He was telling me about looking in the window of this apartment house and seeing two guys going at it. That's all. First I knew about that sort of thing.'

'You never . . .'

'Not me,' Gratelli said. 'I don't mind you like guys, though.'

'That was thirty fuckin' years ago!'

'All right, I don't mind that you used to like guys. Listen, this is San Francisco. We got gays on the force.'

'Cut it out, Gratelli.'

'You're right. It's none of my business. But you brought it up, remember. And I think that's great, healthy, you know. Developing a little sensitivity.'

NINE

The best part of having McClellan as a partner was that Gratelli wasn't obligated to be the cop's friend off-duty. Gratelli had never met his partner's wife and McClellan had never set foot in Gratelli's apartment. Both of them, unlike most police officers, clocked off the force and off each other at the end of their shift.

No bowling, no shared drinks before heading home, no weekend barbecues. Gratelli had no idea how McClellan spent his off hours except for the rumors that he was a boozer. For all Gratelli knew, McClellan made birdhouses on Saturday mornings or coached little league. He did know that McClellan had a wife and a couple of kids who had to have some expensive dental work and now were going the college route; and he knew now that the marriage was in trouble.

The lack of a deep, personal friendship didn't seem to bother either one of them.

The worst part of the partnership was lunch. McClellan's palate was accustomed to Denny's. Even preferred it. Or maybe one of the tasteless noodle joints in Chinatown. McClellan liked his food cheap and filling.

Food for Gratelli was, like opera, one of life's few celebrations. He could wear cheap suits, get by with a barber rather than a hair stylist, could even endure an inexpensive but decent Chianti; but he was willing to lay out real money for his opera seats, a fine old LP recording and a really good meal. Food for McClellan wasn't a celebration, it was like pulling up to a gas station and pushing the hose in the hole and pumping it in until the tank couldn't take any more.

Even so, he'd given up the lunch fight years ago. He'd rather chew on a cheap hamburger than listen to McClellan complain for three hours that he'd spent seven dollars for lunch. Of course, Gratelli knew McClellan would complain about something anyway. That way Gratelli wouldn't have to bear the guilt.

McClellan made one exception – once a week at Original Joe's. The neighborhood wasn't great, but the restaurant was. But that was only once a week. Fridays, usually. The stew was the best. Both Gratelli and McClellan said it was just like the stew their mothers made. Gratelli's mother was Italian. McClellan's Irish. Stew had somehow crossed ethnic lines.

This time, they sat in the McDonald's at the end of Haight Street on Stanyan across from the entrance to Golden Gate Park. Gratelli had managed to get through his fish sandwich and about half his fries. McClellan was on his second Big Mac.

'You remember the fight they had trying to get a McDonald's in here?'

Gratelli nodded. The neighbors fought it. He was sorry they'd lost. He hated seeing the chains invade his city.

'You remember what this neighborhood was at the time, practically burnt out? Still ain't much. Shit,' McClellan said. 'City's out of fuckin' control. The Castro was an Irish neighborhood, Gratelli. Now the queers own it. Look at your neighborhood, for Chrissakes. Hell, you Italians used to run this city. Now look at you. The Chinese are runnin' you out. The Japs and Chinks have all the money. The queers run City Hall.'

'Why don't you move to Ohio or something?' Gratelli said.

'I ain't being run out,' McClellan said. 'Bunch of fuckin' weirdoes have taken over the city.'

'The city was founded by prostitutes, gamblers and con men, remember?'

'Well they were whores, gamblers and con men who learned the fuckin' English language. Now we got Salvadorans, Mexicans, Colombians, Chinese, Cambodian, Vietnamese. What was it Bateman said? The guy who did her had brown eyes?'

'She said she thought he might have had brown eyes. It was dark, remember, and she wasn't sure why she thought that. Hell, I have brown eyes.' He shook his head. He didn't know why he was being so short tempered. Maybe he didn't like being second guessed by a task force either. It was like he and McClellan were being sawed off – no longer part of the department. No doubt it was because they didn't want McClellan's big mouth open when the press was around. 'You believe all this crap you spout?'

McClellan put down his sandwich. He shook his head. 'I don't know, Gratelli. Everything's so fuckin' outta control. There's gotta be some reason for it.'

All the other times Gratelli called him on his litany of hate, McClellan would respond, 'You bet your sweet ass I do.' Now he saw his partner quiet, sad. McClellan took a bite of his burger but seemed to have trouble swallowing it.

'Are we gonna make this fuckin' meeting?' McClellan asked.

Gratelli looked at his watch. 'We got time. Finish your burger.'

'Live life, love and be happy,' was what Paul Chang wanted to tell her as he sat on the edge of her bed, his fingers gently and affectionately trailing up her forearm. This was an expression they shared often, especially when times were rough. But seeing Julia's bruised face, her lost and frightened eyes staring at her hands, this was clearly not the time.

He did not know what to say. They knew each other well enough to be comfortable during long silences, but words were all he could offer by way of support and he didn't have any.

Julia's father and her doctor were engaged in conversation near the door and not out of Julia and Paul's earshot.

'I don't advise it, not for a few days.'

'There are fine doctors in Iowa City,' Mr Bateman said.

'I don't doubt that there are, not for a minute. And I'm

sure that being in warm and familiar surroundings will encourage recovery. My concern at the moment is the time between here and there. She's very steady and she's doing well, but I'd like to have her here for a few more days anyway. Then we can talk about it.'

Paul got up and went to Julia's father as the doctor retreated into the hall. 'Mr Bateman, I'm going to be able to watch over her.'

Royal Bateman turned as if he'd been struck. 'I want Julia out of this loony bin. For good!' He seemed to recognize his overreaction. 'Paul, I'm sorry. I'm so thankful you called. But this isn't the place for her. You're a young man, you're tough, looking for the excitement this kind of city can offer. I understand that. But it's not for Julia.'

'Julia's tough,' Paul said, then realized how bizarre that sounded while the woman remained in shock, a physical and emotional wreck. 'She'll come around.'

He believed he knew her and he believed this to be true. More to the point, he didn't want her to leave – to be hauled back like a prisoner to a place she had once escaped.

'She'll come around. At home. Where she belongs.' The voice was calm, firm and seemed to make Julia's trip back to Iowa not only certain, but permanent. 'I know,' Bateman continued, 'that leaves your job up in the air . . .'

'I don't give a damn about the job, Julia lives here.'

'I don't think you could call this much of a life.'

Paul Chang turned toward Julia. If she had heard a word of the conversation, it didn't show.

The news conference was over. The mayor had announced the task force as Gratelli had guessed he would. The mayor gave the media background on the members of the team, emphasizing the level of professional expertise. 'Whatever is necessary,' the mayor told the media. The task force was meeting now, the mayor said sternly, looking out at the cameras, eyes unwavering, unblinking.

Gratelli and McClellan were definitely the odd men out in the meeting called by Police Lieutenant James Lee Thompson. Not only were they the only members not on the larger task force and not introduced to the others until now, but they were older than all the others except Lieutenant Thompson.

It was also evident these were the 'new' police officers. The room wasn't smoke-filled. The pre-meeting conversation was polite and professional. Everybody seemed freshly scrubbed and crisply and conservatively dressed. If Gratelli and McClellan didn't know who they were, they would have guessed the group had just popped over from their high-rise offices on Montgomery in the financial district. Among the fifteen or so new police, there were two women, two blacks and one Asian.

If the politically correct preppie cop crowd gave Gratelli a pause for reflection, it made McClellan squeamish. Gratelli noticed his partner's darting eyes and sour grin. Change didn't come easily to McClellan. While they'd both seen these folks before – and had worked with some of them – seeing them all together like this was enlightening and frightening for McClellan. Gratelli was amazed. There was McClellan, an old bull moose with scruffy hair and a couple of tips missing from the antlers fighting for his life, a noble fight for plain speech and tradition, and a dumb, ignoble fight against education and tolerance.

To the young professional cops seated on folding chairs in the small room, McClellan – with his potbelly, nicotine-stained fingers, brash mannerisms and insensitive commentary on the world in general – must have been seen as a figure in sepia tones. There were fewer and fewer McClellan types in the department.

And those others with their hearts half in the old guard, didn't mind cloaking their personalities some when the new breed was around. They talked the talk and would even walk the walk when they had to. McClellan was certainly not a career role model and associating with him wasn't the wisest of political moves. As insensitive as McClellan appeared to be, he'd no doubt picked up the vibrations. He sat as far removed from the others as the walls would allow.

Lieutenant Thompson, on the other hand, was the quintessential police model. He adapted. He'd stopped smoking several years ago, jogged, kept his suits conservatively current, stayed mentally clear. He was always pleasant but never aligned himself politically, certainly not aligning with or against anyone.

The San Francisco office of the chief of police had become a revolving door. Chiefs were hired and fired much faster than mayors. Thompson took his work seriously enough and was content being a lieutenant rather than the mayor's chief and primary lightening rod. As far as Gratelli was concerned, Thompson – walking to the front of the room with his short silver hair and gray eyes – was quietly and patiently or perhaps just cautiously ambitious; the kind of guy who was happy to stay out of the newspapers and not be subject to the turbulently political whims of the San Francisco Board of Supervisors and a hungry alternative press. He would be happy to retire just short of chiefdom.

Next to the mayor, the chief of police was the most high-profile city job. And right now, with the string of sexual killings, the current chief probably wished the spotlight were shining on someone else too.

'OK,' Thompson said, 'most of you know each other. The other thirty or so officers on the task force will be informed by memorandum of what is discussed here. I just wanted to make sure you know Inspector McClellan and Inspector Gratelli who are working the Bateman angle specifically.' He looked, as everyone in the room did, at the two interlopers. 'Since she's the only live witness we know, what can she tell us?'

McClellan folded his arms across his chest. 'Not much,' he said.

'I don't know how much you all know, exactly,' Gratelli said. 'Miss Bateman is a licensed private investigator who drove from her main residence in San Francisco Friday afternoon to spend the weekend in her cabin near Gurneville. She was subsequently raped and brutally beaten at about eleven that night in her cabin. The perpetrator appears to have entered through the skylight in the hall of the cabin – actually dropping through the glass – striking Miss Bateman with a heavy object that at the moment we believe to be a flashlight. We believe he took her to the bedroom, raped and beat her repeatedly.'

Gratelli took a breath.

'What do we know about the attacker?' asked a woman in her late 30s.

'The intruder wore a ski-mask, gloves, his body was completely covered,' Gratelli said. 'We think he is on the young side – that is probably under forty – and relatively fit because of the way he got in. The drop from the roof to the floor through the skylight is probably twelve feet. There is no indication that he was injured in the process.'

Heads nodded.

'Is there anything she can tell about him?'

'Brown eyes,' McClellan volunteered, grinning at Gratelli.

'Ms Bateman can't be sure,' Gratelli said. 'She's in shock still. Her mouth is wired shut. Our interview was a series of nods and headshakes and an occasional written answer. Actually, we can't even be sure it was a he.'

'Could be a lezzie,' McClellan said. He grinned, a look that suggested he knew exactly what their opinion was of him and he was rubbing their faces in it.

'As you do know,' Thompson said, unfazed, 'there's nothing at the scene. Apparently our guy – assuming it was a guy, and I do – cleaned up afterward and was damned efficient in doing so.'

'That's right,' Gratelli said.

'Was she actually raped?' asked the woman who had asked the question earlier. 'I mean, was the guy getting off on it?'

Gratelli remembered she was the civilian psychologist brought into the case with much fanfare after the third victim was found and the incidents linked together.

'As far as Miss Bateman could tell . . . uh . . . something was inserted. But, according to the medical report, there was no semen.'

'And we don't know how big it was,' McClellan said. The room was quiet. McClellan sought to retrieve his remark by suggesting it had been serious, after all. 'I mean, I suppose that could be a way to identify him or something.' McClellan's face went beet red and he squirmed in his seat.

'It was difficult talking with her,' Gratelli said quickly. 'We need to give her a few days to rest.'

'With a little rest perhaps her memory will be more vivid,' Thompson said dryly, looking at McClellan.

Everyone laughed except McClellan – whose embarrassment seemed terminal – and Gratelli.

The FBI criminologist offered a profile.

'I know we've gone over this, but for the benefit of the inspectors on the Bateman end, let me repeat. Because the victims were young and disadvantaged – excluding Bateman for now – we believe the perpetrator to be shy, under twenty-five, anti-social, probably abused as a child. VW bugs used to be the popular vehicle for a serial killer. Don't ask me why. Now, he is likely to own a van. He may very well stutter or otherwise have a communication problem, not to mention serious problems with sex.'

'How do you know all that?' McClellan asked.

'What he's done fits the pattern established by other serial killers who have left these kinds of victims.'

'What color is the van?' McClellan asked, arms folded. Gratelli wished he would just shut up and listen.

'Probably black, dark gray or dark blue. Dark in any event. Or at least plain.'

McClellan shook his head.

'None of this works for Bateman,' she continued. 'He's either changing his target which is possible, or something has changed in his life. Perhaps he has built some confidence. She could have been some sort of accident, a miscalculation on his part. Could be just that the opportunity was so right, he couldn't resist.'

'Our perpetrator could have done Bateman. I believe he did,' McClellan said.

'Yes,' she said. 'Like I said, a change or insight on his part, a graduation of sorts based on increased confidence, an opportunistic decision. Any of those would explain what amounts to a modest modification of his behavior. She was the most recent victim, right?'

'Yes,' Gratelli said. 'As far as we know.'

'Since this one was somewhat different, perhaps this signifies a change in pattern.'

'Any other possibilities?' Lieutenant Thompson asked.

McClellan and Gratelli were dismissed. The meeting, however, continued.

TEN

'What more can I say?' Paul asked his two visitors, Inspectors Gratelli and McClellan as he handed them an inch-thick manila folder. 'These are a few of the recent cases, the nastier ones. There's also a little file on a Darvy McWilliams. She testified against him in a parole hearing. And I've put in a little profile of Ezra Blackburn, her former employer who might have a grudge. Might not.'

Gratelli and McClellan had been all but banished from the serial killings. The task force and new homicide detectives were following up on what was becoming increasingly cold leads in deaths of the others – the girls. No new deaths that fit the pattern. No new leads.

Bateman's case remained on the fringe. Gratelli and McClellan still had it, though it was clear what Gratelli and McClellan were doing was now little more than clerical as it related to Julia's possible connection. They were to build files to show the police had followed all the leads. 'Cover your ass' was the operative philosophy. The task force was divided on the Bateman connection. On one hand, it really didn't fit. On the other, there was the tiny detail – the rose tattoo. For Gratelli and McClellan, Bateman was the only link to the deaths worth pursuing. So despite the short shrift the department gave the investigation, Gratelli and McClellan continued to pursue it.

'You've been very thorough,' Gratelli said to Paul Chang. 'Appreciate it. But could you tell us a little more about her?' Gratelli sat on the edge of the day bed. McClellan leaned against the windowsill. Paul was in his adjustable chair. He swiveled away from the drafting table.

'Like what?'

'How about, where were you the night this happened?' McClellan asked.

'How about here. My apartment. Here.'

'By yourself?'

'Um. Uh. Yes. Working.'

'Anyone with you?' McClellan continued.

'I just said I was by myself.'

'Well you didn't seem too sure.'

'I was trying to remember if Bradley was here. He wasn't.'

'Bradley being your close buddy?' McClellan's question was punctuated with a nasty grin.

'You could say that.'

'I could say a lot of things,' McClellan said.

'Problem there is that not much of it would make much sense,' Paul said.

Gratelli looked around the apartment. Nothing had changed since he and McClellan did a little illegal search. He felt a little awkward knowing so much intimate stuff about Paul Chang. He knew it was unfair. If only cats could talk.

'What about friends?' McClellan said.

'Mine?'

'Hers, dummy,' McClellan said.

'Sammie Cassidy. She works at DRP Insurance, one of the companies we work with. They're not real close, but have lunch, hang out every once in a while. Workouts at the gym. That sort of thing.'

'Surely there is someone else,' McClellan said, turning back. Gratelli scribbled Sammie's name in his notebook.

'Me,' Paul said, seemingly having trouble thinking of another. 'We spend a lot of time together. Otherwise she was pretty reclusive. Nobody special.'

'You and her get together outside of working hours?' McClellan asked.

'Sure. Shopping. Movies. Plays sometimes. Galleries.'

'David Seidman. I guess he's nothing special,' Gratelli said.

'Yes, of course, I forgot David,' Paul said.

'Why did you forget David Seidman?' Gratelli asked.

'I don't know. He's forgettable.' There, he had said it.

'Maybe I could take your little smart ass down to the rubber room sometime,' McClellan said.

'Not into rubber.'

McClellan's laugh was filled with disgust. He turned, looked out of the window, down across Hayes Street. The peeper was on the other side, the alley side of the building.

'But Julia Bateman likes Seidman,' Gratelli said.

'Yes, she does, but not as much as David would like.'

'Oh?' McClellan turned back around. He seemed interested in the conversation again.

'I don't think so,' Paul said, answering McClellan's cryptic suggestion.

'Don't think so, what?' McClellan asked.

'David Seidman did not attack Jules. No way.'

'Why not?' the overweight detective said, coming toward Paul, nearly tripping over the little brown cat.

McClellan let out a string of obscenities and the cat went toward Gratelli, unfazed by it all, hopping on Gratelli's lap.

'It's like Chat knows you guys,' Paul said.

'People make that mistake all the time,' Gratelli said. 'Nobody knows Mickey. Not even Mickey.'

'Makes sense to me,' Paul said. He turned to McClellan, answering his question. 'Because David loved Jules.'

'She didn't love him is what you're saying,' Gratelli said.

'She liked him,' Paul said. 'They spent time together.'

'Did that bother you?' McClellan asked.

'No,' Paul said. He laughed.

'Because he wasn't a threat to you?' the heavier cop continued.

'This is weird,' Paul said, standing up. 'I have a life. Jules has a life. I hope she has, anyway. I was neither threatened or unthreatened. I wanted . . . want her to be happy.'

'She couldn't be happy with this David guy?' McClellan said.

Paul shook his head. 'Listen carefully. David is a nice man. Jules is a nice woman. But no bells. No magic. No symphonies. No tingling sensation. You getting any of this?'

'You're coming about this close,' McClellan said putting finger and thumb about an inch apart, 'to being on my enemies list. And that's not a place to be.'

'Part of our job is to ask questions other people think are stupid,' Gratelli said. 'Any other boyfriends? Maybe the recent past?'

'No. The only guy she goes out with is David. Aside from me, that is.'

'That doesn't count for much in the man-woman department, does it?' McClellan asked.

'No.'

'So, c'mon now, anybody make her bells ring lately?' McClellan asked, his face up next to Paul's.

'I don't know if I'd tell you anyway.'

'Go sit down, Mickey,' Gratelli said.

'She had dinner with Thaddeus Maldeaux,' Paul said. 'Just dinner. A little magic, I think.'

'But you don't think he buried the sausage? Is that what you're saying?'

'I'm sorry, I was unable to put it so poetically,' Paul said.

Gratelli was fortunate enough to arrange to meet Seidman at his house. He preferred not having the man feeling the full power of the D.A.'s office while they talked. Also, Gratelli believed that a person's home was far more revealing than an office; even more revealing in the case of a single man.

McClellan agreed to split up and go talk to Ezra Blackburn. This too was a bit of luck. McClellan's confrontational attitude and dislike of authority would make Seidman a more difficult interview than it had to be. McClellan's sledgehammer approach was far better suited to a man like Blackburn.

Gratelli knew where Seidman's house was. The rising star in politics lived on that long, steep slope that rose from the back of Levi's Plaza up to Coit Tower. One either parked on top and walked down or parked at the bottom and walked up, depending where on the hill you lived. Seidman, as it turned out, lived midway – a trek, no way around it. Gratelli decided to get the painful part of the walk done first. He parked below and went up.

A couple of wild cats scampered in front of Gratelli, then darted off the path. It wasn't dark yet, but it was evening. A light fog drifted in, presumably on little cats' feet. It would be dark when he left.

'Mr Seidman,' Gratelli said, breathless.

'Hello Inspector. Come in.' Seidman smiled.

The place was larger than it looked from outside. The main room was warm and masculine. Woods, brown leathers, a big, bright piece of contemporary art. Through the window, one could make out a bit of the city between the trees.

David Seidman picked up a plastic remote, turning the volume down on a classical piece of music Gratelli didn't recognize. German, probably, he thought. Or contemporary.

'Thank you for seeing me,' Gratelli said. He had paced himself, but was breathing hard just the same.

'Anything to help Julia. Sit down.'

The leather chair seemed to fit itself around Gratelli's bony frame. Comfortable. Even more comfortable because of the long walk. He could have just put his head back and slept.

'You've got your own built-in Stepmaster out there,' the inspector said.

Seidman smiled again. No doubt he was used to the complaint and, perhaps, took some mild sadistic pleasure in the efforts people had to make to see him.

Gratelli took a deep breath. 'What do you know about all this?'

'What I hear. Rape. Possible connection to the tattoo artist.

Unsolved.' The last word he said, pointedly. 'Do you have anything?'

'You are friends with Ms Bateman? That's established.'

'Yes, that's why I'm following it. The case.'

'And uh, what is the nature of your friendship.'

Seidman cocked his head to one side, now understanding Gratelli was there for more than courtesy or to seek advice.

'Friendly,' Seidman said.

The sheepish quality present on the attorney's face in Julia's room shortly after her arrival from Gurneville, was no longer visible.

'Could you be a little more descriptive.'

'We dated, inspector.'

'Engaged?'

'No.'

'Is this a romantic relationship?'

'Undecided, I think.'

Gratelli searched his pocket for a pen and notebook, not so much because he needed them for notes, but to give him some reason not to look at Seidman while he formulated how to put the next question.

'It's been suggested that it was not a romantic affair on her part.'

'Who told you that?' Seidman asked. After a long silence in which it became evident Gratelli was not going to answer, Seidman answered his own question. 'Paul Chang.'

'What makes you say that?'

Seidman smiled. 'I'm not used to being cross-examined.' He took a breath. Smiled. 'Because Paul is about the only person who would know that sort of thing.'

'Why would he know that?'

'Because they're friends. Girlfriends as far as I can tell.'

'True then?'

'What?'

'That you and Ms Bateman were friends, not lovers?'

'Yes.'

'Did that bother you?'

'Yes, it did. And where was I the night she was attacked? I was at a fund-raiser for the Mayor. About seven hundred people, give or take fifty, can vouch for my whereabouts. I was on the dais for two hours. Then I went to a more intimate party.'

'And how long were you there?'

'Two, maybe three hours. That would put me out at two or three a.m.'

'Pretty late.'

'It was a Friday night.'

'Julia's attack could have happened almost anytime between late night and early morning.'

'I understand the implication,' Seidman said, unconcerned. 'You might ask my dog.'

It was obvious the assistant D.A. was trying to keep the mood light and the interview as friendly and unofficial as possible.

'Might you have been upset with Ms Bateman because she was seeing Thaddeus Maldeaux.'

'She wasn't seeing Teddy.'

'You know Mr Maldeaux?'

'We're very close. From Stanford. Who told you she was seeing him?'

Again, Gratelli was quiet.

'Paul Chang. Why do I ask?' Seidman answered, breaking the silence.

'Mr Chang just happened to mention that Ms Bateman had dinner with Mr Maldeaux a night or so before she left for her cabin.'

'So?'

'Actually, you sound bothered by Mr Maldeaux's relationship with Ms Bateman.'

'It hadn't progressed to a relationship stage – in a romantic way, I mean. Teddy and I have discussed it. I don't think she was interested in him.'

'You also seem a little put off by Paul Chang's relationship with Ms Bateman. Are you generally a possessive sort of person.'

'Jealous of Paul? Heavens no. Paul and I would not have had the same kind of relationship with Julia. Ours would have been one between a man and a woman.'

'Your close friend, Mr Maldeaux, didn't tell you that he asked her out and that she was quite attracted to him.'

'She thought he was immature, childish. She saw through him.'

'And you two are friends?'

'Yes. I would tell him the same thing I've told you. And my friend, Teddy, would tell you I'm an old stick in the mud who never does anything adventurous, never takes chances. Still, we're good friends.'

Seidman was smiling, but Gratelli sensed a little seething underneath.

Gratelli waited. Seidman had worked up some anger. When people get angry, they get careless.

Instead David Seidman suddenly laughed. 'You are good. I could use you in court.'

'As I understand it. Mr Maldeaux is handsome, charming and very rich.'

Seidman tried to cover the displeasure Gratelli's remarks gave him.

'And he usually gets what he wants. But he wasn't about to get Julia.'

ELEVEN

E zra Blackburn lived on Sanchez, a few blocks south of Market. The white framed house hinted at Victorian, but it had been dressed plainly, and treated without affection. A dozen rail-less steps led up from the sidewalk to the white door.

A dark-haired man with exaggerated facial features sat in a wheelchair. He was halfway visible in the narrow opening. He was a big man – all fat.

'Don't want any.'

'Don't have any,' McClellan said. 'Ezra Blackburn?'

'Mother made only one.'

'My name's McClellan, Inspector McClellan.'

'What do you inspect, Mr McClellan?' Blackburn asked, widening the gap between door and doorframe and giving the inspector a whiff of stale air. 'Is it termites, building permits, spoiled food?'

'Murder,' McClellan said, flashing his badge.

'In that case, come in,' Blackburn said, rolling back to allow the large police detective entry. 'Inspect all you want. I've removed all the asbestos, radon and rotting corpses.'

The small entranceway and the two rooms immediately visible

from it were cluttered with mail, magazines, newspapers, plates, glasses and various wrappers. McClellan followed Blackburn into a room that had a sofa and TV, virtual islands among the stacks in a surprisingly large room. The pathways, most of them, were wide enough for a wheelchair. Some of the stacks, farther back toward the walls, got narrow. There was no filth, merely stacks in an order that could only have made sense to Blackburn.

'My cleaning lady has called in sick for couple of years. If you can find a place to sit, by all means sit.'

'I'll stand.' McClellan noticed a giant bag of potato chips, half empty.

'You're here about a murder?'

'Julia Bateman.'

'The bitch is dead?' he blurted.

'Not quite.'

'Really?' It seemed as if it were just now sinking in.

'Really. I guess she's not in your will.'

'I gave her a start, helped her get established. I run into a little trouble and while I am sorting it all out, she runs away with my business.'

'That's reason enough to kill the bitch. Hey man, I'm on your side.'

'Hey, hey, hey.'

'Hey yourself.'

'I'm not a killing kind of guy, you know?'

'Could have fooled me. Checked your files, fella. You kind of like pushing women around.'

'C'mon, that's domestic. Wife shit. Different altogether. What happened to Julia?'

'It's different because you got a marriage license. That it?' McClellan didn't like the guy. 'Somebody beat the living holy hell out of her.'

'When?'

'You don't know?' McClellan said.

'Stop it.'

'So how did that happen?' McClellan asked, gesturing toward the wheelchair. 'Fall through a skylight or something?'

'Got hit by a bus.'

'When?'

'Year ago.'

'You suing them, Blackburn?'

'Trying to get a little compensation. Out of work, you know. Pain. Medical bills.'

'Well you sure as hell know the insurance business. Know what buttons to push. What works, what doesn't. Right?'

'Life's full of irony,' Blackburn said. 'Is Julia all right?'

McClellan walked down one of the narrow aisles. He noticed a copy of a girlie magazine next to the wall. He retrieved it, opened it. He glanced at the air brushed 'Babes of Toyland.'

'She all right?' Blackburn asked impatiently.

'The bitch will live, Blackburn.'

'I didn't mean it like that,' Blackburn said. 'I don't mean to call her that. Just comes out. I'm sorry about it. I liked her. I was gone for five years. There was no business for me to come back to. But she could have offered to help. Is she all right?'

'Don't know,' McClellan said, flipping through a few more pages. Then he closed the magazine and looked at the cover. 'Better stop before I get some bad ideas. Current issue, huh? You're a bit of a magician getting down an aisle like that in your wheelchair.'

Blackburn laughed nervously. 'Yeah the phone rang and I just tossed it. I didn't realize I'd have to move all this shit to get back to it.' He held out his hand for McClellan to give him the magazine.

'Funny, isn't it?' McClellan said. 'Irony or something, right? So how much money are you going to get before you make a miraculous recovery?'

'I don't need this kind of accusation. Check with the doctor.'

'I will. Let's talk about some dates and times, and where you were and who you were with, OK?' He tossed the magazine on the farthest stack back.

TWELVE

The next day, McClellan jockeyed the desk and tried to connect with Julia Bateman's friend, Sammie Cassidy, while Gratelli visited Maldeaux. There was no need to rankle anyone in the Maldeaux family. No one wants to piss off a media empire.

It was early. Thaddeus Maldeaux was half dressed. He was barefoot, wearing slacks and a summer t-shirt. His hair was still wet from the shower and slicked back, making him look like a forties movie star.

'Glad to meet you,' he said to Gratelli at the front door. Gratelli had expected a butler or at least a maid, but got the superstar himself. 'I appreciate your coming over here. It's a little early in the morning to face bureaucracy. Or maybe I should say reality.' Maldeaux smiled his charming smile and nodded for the investigator to come in. 'Listen, I'm getting some breakfast together. Let me fix you something.'

'Thanks,' Gratelli said. 'I've eaten.'

'I'm so hungry. Do you mind hanging around the kitchen while we talk?'

'No, that's fine.' On one hand the home was less than he would have imagined. There seemed to be a lack of gold and crystal. The decor was restrained. Worn. The oils he passed as they went through the dining room to the kitchen, were dark, brooding scenes of wars fought by soldiers armed with swords, their naked bodies draped with transparent swaths of cloth. Not a lot of protection in those days, he thought.

'Coffee at least,' Maldeaux said. He put water on to boil, found bowls, pans and utensils with the ease of someone who had done it many, many times before.

'Sure,' Gratelli said. 'How well did you know Julia Bateman?'

'Not well enough,' Maldeaux said. 'Listen, it's just as easy to cook for two as it is for one.'

'No thanks. What do you mean "Not well enough?"'

'I liked her.'

'She's not really in your circle of friends, is she?'

'I don't have a circle of friends, Inspector. I have friends.'

'You know what I mean.'

'Yes, but you don't know what I mean,' he said without hostility. 'Aside from the old friends and the usual circle of opportunists that forms around a silver-spooned *enfant terrible* like me, are people who are impressed with celebrity or money or power or something or the spectacle of it all. Julia didn't care about that stuff. She didn't even want to like me.'

Maldeaux was working on a large onion. He talked as he

brought the large knife down in a chopping motion, getting the pieces smaller and smaller.

'Did she?'

'Like me? I think so.' Maldeaux put coffee beans in the grinder, pushed a button. Over the harsh whir of blades cutting through the hard beans, Maldeaux shouted, 'Inspector, I do wonderful things with artichokes and peppers and eggs and stuff.'

'I'm sure you do.' Gratelli shouted, then waited for the grinding to stop. 'You liked Julia because she wasn't easily impressed? According to the stories, you are attracted to the beautiful people, people in the limelight, people who want to be in the limelight. She's not like that.'

'No, she's not like that. She's not even beautiful.'

'You are attracted to her; but in your eyes she's not beautiful?'

'Not in the conventional sense. She's not beautiful in the way the others are beautiful.'

'No. A different beautiful.'

'Exactly a different beautiful. One that exists without make up. A beauty that doesn't vanish with age. One that doesn't depend on the right lighting. From the inside. My mother,' he added in what seemed to be an afterthought, 'is not a beautiful woman in a conventional sense. Yet she is most beautiful by what she is – and I don't mean a wealthy dowager. I mean because of her principles, I suppose. Because she cares and protects, sometimes incredibly innocently.'

'You and Ms Bateman have a lot to talk about?'

'You want to know if this is the first time I found a commoner attractive?' He laughed. 'What were my intentions? When was the last time I saw her? Did I see anything suspicious?'

'OK,' Gratelli said. 'Add an alibi to that and we will have covered a lot of ground.'

'OK. Orange juice. Can I talk you into orange juice?'

'No.'

'In the event you haven't noticed, I'm pretty vain. I'm also getting older. I'd like a child. Or two. But only in a real marriage. Long term. Grow old together. Be grandparents. I want someone who is bright and interesting, a challenge in those areas, but not someone who wants to be on the pages of *Vanity Fair*. I don't want someone who wants to have a fling for a few years, then divorce me so she can have enough money to live well and buy her own boytoys while my sperm dries up.'

Maldeaux smiled. Nodded. Waited for Gratelli to give some indication he understood, perhaps sympathized. Getting none, he continued. 'I saw Julia as someone who could have been the kind of wife I wanted. Bright, tough. To put it less than romantically – a different, more hardy stock. We had dinner. That was about it. Nothing torrid or unseemly. A first step. She was pretty hesitant about step two. Then that happened.'

'You know about that?'

'Of course. David Seidman and I are friends.'

'Interesting. She was seeing him, right?'

'Yes.'

'You weren't being very loyal to Mr Seidman. Your intentions weren't, as they say, honorable, were they?'

'David didn't . . . doesn't have a chance. For David, Julia is the kind of girl who would tell him how much he reminded her of her brother. Oddly enough, an affair between Julia and me would have been the best thing to have happened to David. He might have realized he needed to move on, get on with his life.'

'He doesn't understand what you understand about living?'

'Yes, I think he does. I apologize for my lack of humility. Otherwise, I suppose I might be flawless.' He grinned.

'Go on.'

'I didn't see or talk to her after that evening. We had dinner, coffee. I left her at the apartment house door. I didn't go up. I saw nothing suspicious. She didn't say anything about being stalked or being afraid of anything. She said she was going up to her cabin, somewhere up near Santa Rosa. She looked forward to it. She anticipated and wanted to be alone. At least that's my take.'

'All right.'

'Let's have our coffee out here,' Maldeaux said, pouring two cups from the glass pot that held the recently plunged coffee. They headed for a rear door that opened to a balcony garden.

On the short trek from kitchen to surprisingly sun-drenched foliage, Gratelli asked him where he had been that night.

'Wow, what a day,' Maldeaux said. 'Isn't it beautiful.'

When Gratelli arrived and entered through the front door, the sky had been gray and the air filled with a light mist. Outside it might have been in La Jolla, or Santa Barbara rather than

Pacific Heights. Gratelli wondered if the sun always shined on the rich and handsome.

They sat at one of three marble-topped tables on a large balcony that was six or seven feet above the ground and over-looked a park-like, meticulously kept lawn. The balustrade was only partially visible because it was lined with sensuous color, dripping with exotic, flowering plants.

'My alibi is feeble. I was here. In this house. You'd be surprised how many nights I spend alone, in my room, reading a book.'

'And how do you know what day I was referring to?'

'I know it clearly. David called. Frantic. I thought about it. Wondered if only she had accepted my invitation or perhaps invited me to go with her.'

Maldeaux shook his head. His eyes were sad. 'You know, you're so close. One small, seemingly insignificant decision can change your whole life.' He looked at Gratelli. 'It can kill you. In some ways, existence is so fragile. Was the man seated there in the restaurant where we ate that night the one? Was he stalking her then? Making up his mind. You wonder how often you've stood next to a murderer on the elevator or passed him on the street. I'm rambling. I'm sorry.'

'And who might be able to say where you were that night besides you?'

'My mother,' Maldeaux said. He smiled. 'I know, I know. It should strike you as funny that I'm still living with my mother. I'm really a big baby.'

'I wasn't laughing.'

'Your eyes were,' Maldeaux said. 'It's all right. Really. I marvel at it, myself. I have other places, but I live here when I'm in San Francisco. There's no point at all in my taking up some other space when there's so much of it here. I've seen smaller hotels. So much space. Much more than my dear mother could ever make use of.'

'Anybody else? Hired help?'

'Mother has someone here most days. Most of the time she's out here in the garden pretending she is doing some-thing constructive. Sometimes she goes out to some board meeting to write checks to foundations. A good woman. Too good. Spoiled my father. Spoiled me. The last of the innocents.'

'That's it?'

'The other person, I mentioned. Mrs Havel. She cleans mostly. Helps mother. She really doesn't do much. And what she does do, she doesn't do very well. It's mother's purchased and, surprisingly, only true friend. Mrs Havel leaves around five. No maids or butlers, Mr Gratelli. Not what you've seen in the movies. Only one here, for the most part, is mother.'

'Probably could spend days in here without running into each other.'

'True,' he said making it sound like a confession. 'What can I say? Ask mom.'

'A mother's love . . .'

'How is Julia doing? Have you heard?' Maldeaux asked.

'She's back home, healing, I think.'

'I'm glad she made it through,' Maldeaux said. 'I understand she's somewhere in Ohio.'

'Iowa.'

Maldeaux smiled. 'I'm not very good when it comes to all those states out in the middle of the country. A lot of vowels.'

'You've not seen her or talked to her since the attack.'

'I stopped by the hospital. She was unconscious. I didn't go back.'

'Why?'

'I thought better of it. One dinner does not create the kind of intimacy that would entitle me to share that kind of pain. I'm sure she has family and close friends. I'd think that she'd want to be with them, rather than a one-night suitor. I know I would.'

'Have you given up on your eggs?'

'Just postponed them for a few minutes. Do you have any idea at all who might have done this to her?'

'No.'

'Is it possible that once she is past the shock, she might be able to identify her attacker?'

'I don't know.'

'We're here such a brief time. Alive, I mean. You're not guaranteed any time. And the very best you can expect is seventy to eighty years. Then most people go through it like cows. Not doing anything. Most people live lives of – what was it, some poet said – "people living lives of quiet desperation?" I'd say most people live lives of endless routine. The time they have their coffee, the way they get to work, the Sunday afternoon football game.

'This murderer. I could probably understand why someone might do something like this,' Maldeaux continued. 'But again and again? Why? It's horrible, grotesque, but it's fascinating. What is he trying to do? Is he trying to get it right? Will he keep doing it until it's just the way he wants it? Or is it some electric impulse in his brain jetting in from the primitive animal unconscious to impose its will, again and again, merely a dumb but dangerous animal. The blind will of a shark?'

'I have no idea,' Gratelli said. 'You're attaching this to the serial killer. What makes you think that?'

'Oh, I've talked with David. What kind of person is this, do you think?'

'We've got a profile from the FBI. Who knows how close it is?'

Maldeaux shrugged, sighed. 'I was reading the other day about black holes. In space. They've just discovered that there are such things as drifting black holes, wandering around the universe. The only way they know they exist is that there is a residue of light still on their hungry mouths.'

'Your point?' Gratelli asked.

'We don't know so many things. We want things to make sense so we create rules and force them to fit. What if this . . . this attacker doesn't fit? What if he suddenly lurches in another direction or never does it again, or does something completely different?'

'I have no idea,' Gratelli said. 'That doesn't take me anywhere, Mr Maldeaux.'

'Probably an ordinary fellow,' Maldeaux said, 'standing next to you at the counter in a department store or,' Maldeaux smiled, 'sitting across from you at breakfast.'

'You're not an ordinary fellow,' Gratelli said.

'No.' Maldeaux said it almost solemnly. 'I participate in life. I don't mean the social club or political kind of participation. I mean participation in life. Feeling a part of it as deeply as possible. I want to take life in through every sense as deeply and as often as possible. That's why I like to cook, Inspector. See, smell, touch, taste. And if you bite into the peppers, we will hear a little crunch. Sure you don't want to stay?'

'No, thank you. But I'm sure it's time I left you alone.'

'Actually, Inspector, you have no idea how much time I spend alone.'

'I see pictures,' Gratelli said. 'Pictures of you here and there, always with people. You are alone then, too, you're saying.'

'Yes, precisely what I'm saying.'

'Did you feel as if you were with someone when you were with Julia Bateman?'

'Right again,' Maldeaux said. 'Oh look, there's Mother now. She was out here all the time.'

Gratelli looked at the woman coming from the far end of the back lawn, a handful of weeds in her gloved hand.

THIRTEEN

Mickey McClellan was at his desk, still waiting for the people at the Cassidy Group, an advertising agency near Jackson Square, to track 'the' Cassidy down. Sammie Cassidy had proved elusive. The office was empty, quiet. He hated this more than anything other than the hours near nightfall; chained to the desk, ear numb from hours on the phone, attempting to track down the fraudulent insurance claims, cases in which Bateman's statement or testimony might have truly pissed off the claimant. He was also trying to discover the whereabouts of one Darvy McWilliams.

According to Paul Chang, Julia testified against him at a parole hearing for Darvy's bizarre behavior at Julia Bateman's laundromat some years before. A long, long shot. He had dismissed the idea when Paul Chang presented it. But there was little else to go on.

All this boring phone work and for what? If Bateman was just one of the chicks who got it from the same guy, this insurance claim stuff didn't mean a damn thing.

He put the phone in the cradle. He took a deep breath. One of the inspectors was standing on a chair, tacking a Giant's poster high up on the wall. Next to it was a professionally printed sign. It read:

Old age and treachery will overcome youth and skill.

Great cop motto for a department filled with the over-forty crowd.

The phone book may have been the hard way, but there was no Darvy McWilliams. McClellan was down to the sixth McWilliams.

'Looking for Darvy,' he said to the woman who answered. There was a long silence. 'Darvy McWilliams,' McClellan said, trying to get a response.

'I heard you. Who are you?'

'A friend of a friend.'

'Mr Whoever You Are, you ain't never gonna talk to Darvy, you hear what I'm sayin'? The boy is dead.'

'Darvy A. McWilliams, I got here,' McClellan said, though he was pretty sure there weren't that many Darvys in the world.

'Mmmn,' she said. It was the sound of disgust.

'This is the police, ma'am.'

'Then you oughta know. He was dead in his cell. You hear what I'm sayin'?'

'I hear,' he said softly. 'I hear.'

He put the phone back again, gently. He believed the voice, but he'd check it out anyway. Death was a damn good alibi.

He wasn't having much luck with the rest of the list either. No answers. Disconnected. He'd already come to Samuel Baskins. This was another of Paul Chang's suggestions. McClellan had to admit that it had been stubbornness that kept him from questioning this guy earlier – though the likelihood of some guy living in the Tenderloin going all the way up to Russian River – a guy who was too injured to work or pretending to be – seemed pretty far fetched. If the guy was bilking his company, wouldn't it be better just to play along? His phone line was busy, which indicated he just might be home.

McClellan ran into Gratelli on first floor between the metal detectors and the elevators.

'How'd it go?'

'Wanted to fix me breakfast,' Gratelli said.

'Ooh la la,' McClellan said. 'What else?'

'He's looking for a wife.'

'Sounds like he's lookin' for a husband.'

'He's pretty relaxed. Pretty casual. Doesn't sound like a guy with a tortured libido. Where are you going?'

'Samuel Baskins.'

Gratelli smiled.

'Do us a favor,' McClellan said, handing Gratelli a crumpled scrap of paper. 'Here, why don't you take our little woman tycoon? I'd probably just piss her off. She's got some sort of snooty PR agency down on Jackson Square. She's only gonna be there until six. We better get her now. She's one fucking busy broad.' McClellan turned to go, changed his mind, turned back to Gratelli who was trying to figure out the handwriting on McClellan's note.

'We're down to the dregs, Gratelli,' McClellan said. 'If these don't lead somewhere, I don't know where in the hell to go next.'

Sammie Cassidy met Gratelli in the waiting room and guided him through a maze of workstations to what appeared to be a media room. A huge wall of electronic gear – monitors, CD players, videotape machines, reel to reel tape recorders. He sat on the leather sofa and Sammie sat opposite him on some extremely modern chair, her black suit-coat and slacks blending with the leather on the chair. She looked more tough than snooty – a bit harsh, maybe even hard, in her cropped black hair. But her smile seemed genuine.

'What can I do to help?' she asked.

'Tell me what you know about her, about her friends, her life,' Gratelli said.

'I wouldn't know where to begin.'

'You're friends?'

'Yes. Mostly work-out buddies,' Sammie said. 'We met at the gym, hit it off, so we decided to schedule our time at the gym together when we could. After that we'd go somewhere, sometimes. You know, coffee, a juice bar, sometimes for a drink or something to eat.'

'No other times. Like maybe double dates?'

Sammie's face burst into laughter. 'Double date.' She laughed some more.

'I'm sorry. I'm out of touch with this sort of thing. You might even be married for all I know.'

She seemed to sober immediately. 'No, I'm not married, Inspector. But we didn't double date or really even see each other socially.' She looked at him, as if weighing her words carefully, then obviously decided not to say more than, 'No, just workout buddies.'

'No?'

'No.'

'Why not?'

'Just didn't. I mean. One has friends . . . for different things. This was just the way we knew each other. She was busy. I am very busy.' Her look suggested that was more than just an answer to Gratelli's question. It was a hint for him to hurry up and move on.

'You guys work out a lot together?'

'I go every day. She went three times a week.'

'You must be very fit,' Gratelli said.

'I try to be.'

She was getting very agitated. Gratelli changed his tack. 'You ever notice anyone hanging around the gym or maybe outside? Anyone you might think is suspicious especially now that you know what happened?'

She softened again. 'I've thought about that,' she said. 'I can't bring anybody to mind.'

'She ever talk about anyone or anything that was troubling her.'

'Not recently.'

'How about going back a bit?'

'No. There was some guy in a laundromat she had to testify against. She was a little worried. The guy she used to work for was trouble, I understand.'

'Trouble?'

'Hitting on her. Pressuring her. Sexual harassment. But that was a long time ago, now.'

'What about David Seidman?'

'What about him?'

'Your impression of him.'

'I don't have one. She said he was a nice guy. I don't think she was in love with him. Inspector, listen. I'd love to be able to help. We weren't confidantes. We didn't double date and we didn't talk about our sex lives. We worked out, talked about diet, sometimes about our careers, women trying to make it. We weren't giggling schoolgirls talking about crushes. Fortunately, our conversations weren't that trivial.'

A young man was outside the glass doors of the office trying

to get Sammie Cassidy's attention. She waved him off. 'I have
to go,' she said to Gratelli. She stood.

'One more thing?' Gratelli asked, rising to face her.

'Sure.'

'Where were you on that night.'

'What? The night she . . . ?'

'Yes.'

'For heaven's sake,' she shook her head. 'What on earth . . . ?'

'I'm asking everyone.'

'I worked here until ten.' She closed her eyes. 'I had a late
bite at Beetlenut's. Went home.'

'Alone?'

She was silent for a moment, brown eyes glaring. 'Yes. Alone.'

'That's me. Now, how about you?' the man behind the door
asked.

McClellan was out of breath. He'd climbed three floors of
the tenement-styled apartment house to be confronted by a
terrier of a man who wore some sort of back and neck brace.

'McClellan, Mr Baskins. I'm with the police.'

'What's your business, officer?' Baskins was as prissy as he
was curt.

'Seems like I've got a Mother Theresa complex today and
I'm visiting the sick, crippled and the dying.'

Baskins looked puzzled for a moment, then shrugged. 'I give,
officer. This is what I need, another surreal day. One that makes
no sense at all. There has been a succession of these, lately.
And you are quite effective.'

'What?' McClellan asked.

'Never mind. Just tell me why are you here. I don't have an
automobile. I don't play my music loud. I don't have any pets.
I'm in bed by nine. What could I have possibly done?'

'Do you know a guy named Ezra Blackburn?' McClellan
asked, head shaking 'no' in disbelief at one more nut case.

'Never heard of him.'

'You two guys would really hit it off.'

Baskins sighed deeply, folded his arms and stared at McClellan
as if daring him to continue in this absurd conversation.

'How about a Julia Bateman? You know a Julia Bateman?'

'No. Am I supposed to know these people?'

'Bateman was a gal who parked out front here waiting to get

a good look at you, thinking maybe she might catch you jumping rope, bench pressing five hundred pounds or carrying a refrigerator back from K-Mart.'

'I have absolutely no idea what you are talking about.'

'Well I think that's probably the case, Mr Baskins. Been nice talkin' with you.'

Out on the streets, McClellan saw a guy he used to arrest regularly when he was in burglary.

'Hey, Barnaby. How they hangin'?'

'Low as they go, Governor.' Barnaby looked up. 'Oh, sorry didn't recognize you. You been eatin' well.'

'How about you? You rich yet?'

'You know me, man. Rich one day, homeless the next.'

'You gotta home now?'

'Just got out. Lookin' for one. You got something for me?'

'Nah. Take care Barnaby. Get a job.'

On the way back to his car, McClellan passed a few massage parlors. Vietnamese, most of them now. He pushed the button by the door. He heard the buzz. He walked to a small wooden counter surrounded by struggling tropical plants. 'Cho Cho here?'

The woman nodded.

In the little room, McClellan tried to forget about everything. Just a few minutes of escape, he prayed. A moment or two when nothing mattered. Rest. He felt the healing hands. He hoped he wouldn't feel guilty afterward. Be quiet, he told himself. Retreat.

FOURTEEN

From the air, Iowa's farmland looked like a quilt on an unmade bed. The pattern was not composed of the neat, flat squares and rectangles of Kansas, Illinois or Indiana farms. The land in Iowa rolls. Circular and oval patches are not uncommon – showing a tendency toward independence if not creativity, showing a willingness to work with nature not impose itself upon it.

The ride from the airport in Cedar Rapids to a farmhouse just outside Julia's hometown of Iowa City was full of slow rises and gentle falls. The blacktop curved sometimes over and sometimes around the smooth swells of earth.

It was mostly quiet with Royal Bateman behind the wheel, alert for the slow-moving, horse-drawn Amish carriages. Julia huddled inside a blanket, alone in the back seat. She took reluctant comfort from the land just now beginning to show rows of green sprouts in the rich dirt. The only sounds were the wind whistling in the window gap her father always maintained to keep the air fresh, the steady drone of the engine and the occasional rattle of her wheelchair.

She had ridden in the back seat of a Ford, several of them over the years, looking at the back of the same head many times, so many times. This Ford was fairly new, but blue and large like the others. The familiar head was covered with silver not black hair and there were deep, rut-like wrinkles cross-hatched on the back of his neck.

'Harriet's a nurse,' Royal said finally.

'I know, Dad,' Julia said, catching herself before saying 'Daddy.'

'Stay there a few weeks, you'll be ready to come home with me. I can't take care of you as well as she can. I have to work. This is the busy time.'

'I know.'

'Of course you know. I'm just worried you'll think I'm deserting you or something. Harriet can be a pain sometimes.'

'I'll be fine. I like her. I like her place if I remember it right.' Already her language seemed to simplify itself. Simple sentences conveying simple messages.

'She's happy to have you. She's looking forward to your coming, you know,' Royal continued.

'Me too.' It was still a little painful to talk. To take a breath.

'She'll never say it, of course.'

It seemed odd to Julia that her father, so anxious in San Francisco and even on the plane to Des Moines, now seemed so relaxed, so in charge.

There's a smell about old houses, especially farmhouses, that suggests a memory of all the freezes and thaws, of all the wet and dry spells. Harriet's home, perched on a hill that sloped down to a white gravel road, had that scent about it. Julia took a deep breath, drank it in. She could feel herself relax.

Funny, how sometimes smells were more powerful than sight to illuminate memories lying in wait all these years in darkness. She always knew when her father had his hair cut. There was a lotion he used, and a powder – the unpronounceable, the very foreign and in her youth, the very exotic Pinaud. The scent lingered at least for the day.

Her mother's kitchen had a distinctive scent – apricots in the morning, especially before the afternoon when harsher, meatier smells took over. Her mother would boil dried apricots to spread on her toast. Lilac recalled her grandmother. These scents came back to her vividly.

Harriet's farmhouse smelled of cold and emptiness. Disuse. It was a house that had less and less about it as time went on. In fact, land no longer connected Harriet's house with its farm history. The adjacent space had been parceled off to the Amish families as Harriet needed the money. Her late husband's medical bills pretty much wiped out the savings. It didn't make much difference, though. Harriet had no special need to spend. With the exception of food, there wasn't anything in the house that wasn't at least thirty years old.

For Julia, it was painful to see the farm dwindle.

The Amish had been farming it for years. Harriet's deed now showed little more than forty feet behind the house and the long slope that ran down to the road in front. But she had a view worth a fortune. She knew it. The picture from her living room window was rolling Iowa land at its most beautiful. Above it, there was a lot of sky.

In cities like San Francisco, it is easier to forget about the sky.

Harriet too seemed to be dwindling. She had always been smaller than her brother Royal, but she seemed to be losing her physical presence more quickly. Their coloring, too, was different. But their common origins could not be questioned. Squareness of face and the deep-set wrinkles tied them together immediately. It was clear they came from the same stock. That's how Royal would have phrased it.

She spoke even less than her brother. Those who did not know her well thought her a sour, bitter woman. Those who

knew her knew better. While she was, as the Batemans and
many Iowans were, conservative with most of their resources,
especially money – and had no tolerance of waste – they were
generous with their time and energy. Knowing just how untel-
ling Harriet's face could be meant the slightest variance would
reveal a lot.

It appeared to Julia that Harriet was thrilled with the idea
that she nurture Julia back to health. And, like Royal, Harriet
would see that this time Julia would remain on Iowa soil.

Harriet had cleared out the first floor parlor for the bedroom
so that Julia wouldn't have to maneuver the steps.

'I aired it out for two days,' Harriet said, 'so it shouldn't be
too stuffy in there.'

'Thank you Aunt Harriet.'

'Too early for much out of the garden,' Harriet said busying
herself with unnecessary pillow fluffing. 'But we'll get your
strength back.'

The tomatoes that came from the Ball Jar were sweet. The
creamed corn was heaven. The secret was a dash of sugar,
though Julia wasn't supposed to know. She wouldn't be able
to chew the steak she saw sizzling on the broiler. Having guessed
as much, Julia was served ground beef. Julia hadn't the heart
to tell her she'd sworn off red meat altogether and had given
serious thought to becoming a vegetarian.

Royal and his sister ate quietly. Julia remembered it was all
right not to speak. Such silences were taken as rude among
most of her city friends; but here long, quiet periods were signs
of comfort. Perhaps some of the quiet came about because
neither Royal nor his sister would want to remind her of the
ordeal. They were being respectful.

But in Iowa words like 'plain' and 'quiet' and 'simple' were
qualities, virtues even. That Grant Wood came from Iowa was
not lost on Julia. It amused her and comforted her. She had to
hide her smile because of the question it would pose and from
the pain it would cause her to stretch her mouth muscles any
further than it took to slip in a bite of skinless stewed
tomatoes.

Royal left at sundown.

It was warm enough to leave the windows open and Julia
luxuriated in the soft cool breeze that passed through the screens.

In the morning, she looked out of the window. She could see the laundry hanging out to dry to the side of the farmhouse across the road. Not much in the way of color. Black and white, mostly, waving in the breeze like cartoon ghosts. A large chestnut-colored horse stood ready in front of a black carriage, unattended. The sky was blue. The sun was out. White puffs of clouds moved so slowly they seemed to have been hung there, so much laundry on the clotheslines. The picture could have been from an illustrated children's book, showing America in the 1800s.

She slipped on the blue terry cloth robe that hung on the hook behind the door, and rolled out toward the sounds in the kitchen and the smell of oatmeal.

'You used to like it with raisins,' Harriet said.

'I still do.'

'Good, because that's the way I made it.'

The brown sugar was on the table and so was a pitcher of cream. Real cream, no doubt. Harriet had never succumbed to margarine or two percent milk or sweetener – at least not by the time Julia packed up and headed West. Apparently, Harriet remained among the unconverted.

The bread was homemade. There was just one place setting on the oak table in the kitchen. A bowl of oatmeal, pitcher of milk and a clump of pale butter on the bread plate. There was a tall glass of orange juice beside it.

'I had mine a few hours ago,' Harriet said.

'What time is it?'

'Approaching six,' she said. 'I thought it might be good if you slept in after the trip.'

'Thank you for letting me sleep.' Julia was happy the light sarcasm would go unnoticed. It was still hours earlier in California. She'd adjust.

Harriet disappeared. It was quiet. Very quiet. Julia remembered that Harriet had no radio, no television. Her only contact with the world was the Sunday edition of the *Des Moines Register*.

Oddly, the sweet smell of the butter as she brought toasted bread to her lips was repugnant. Was she so unused to fresh food she would have to learn to like it over again? Maybe it was sour. She smelled it again to see if she could detect it being spoiled. 'Off' the farmers might say. A wave of nausea spread through her body.

Later, Harriet said that Royal would be back for supper. 'Another good thing about having you here is that I'm more inclined to see your father. He's in need of regular cooking. If it were left up to him, he'd starve to death.'

In the afternoon, Julia wrapped a cotton blanket around herself and sat on the porch staring out at the farm across the road and the outbuildings visible to the west. Nothing seemed threatening.

No sign of street crazies yelling obscenities. No electronic madness. No noise except for the wind in the trees and the occasional slam of the wood-framed screen door. It was not likely that people in the nearby farms and towns had heard very often of AIDS or the humiliation of big city poverty or days when the air was too brown to breathe, let alone jog. Here, only the infrequent sight of an automobile stirring up the dust from the white gravel broke the fairy tale spell.

None of this dispelled the pain in her body when she moved, but it was a relief from it.

In Harriet's hands and on Iowa soil, Julia could feel the healing begin.

It wasn't until the third day that she realized the room she slept in was the room Harriet's husband had died in. She recalled the last months of Everett's death, of Everett getting thinner and thinner, moving from the rocker to the bed, a handkerchief to his mouth, withering away. Perhaps this was the official room of transition, Julia thought. Her returning, Everett's passing.

When the family visited Everett, they would go in briefly. Say hello, be social until Harriet suggested the kids go outside. Julia and her cousins would have to recite some event of the week – what they learned in school or Sunday school.

Everett would nod. Toward the end, he would merely stare. Julia remembered it was like the light going out inside the old man. Little by little the light dimmed. Then it was gone.

'Oh God,' she said under her breath. Her grandmother died in this room. And her mother spent time here before she made her last trip to the hospital. A return home was not just a return to a place, but to a history. She hadn't prepared herself for the memories. Not all of them were pleasant.

On the night of Julia's fourth day, the dreams started. Vivid and sensual, they began with an immense sense of all is right with the world. Julia would be in a small boat floating on a quiet lake. Then the sky would darken. Finally she would not be able to see. Something would nibble at her. And inevitably she would either be dismembered or devoured.

There were variations. In all of them she was alone. She was confident that this pleasant and overwhelming sense of well being was eternal. Then, of course, something or someone – in the darkness – would begin to tear at her body.

Harriet was the kind of person who did things for people but didn't like to be done for. Except for the dreams, Julia's first two weeks back were nearly bliss – a complete vacation. She did nothing for herself to speak of, wasn't allowed to help. Some days she sat on the back porch, a place used later in the season to shuck corn, snap the green beans and shell peas, preparing the harvest for canning; where onions, turnips and carrots as well as white and sweet potatoes were dusted off and busheled for the cellar.

By the third week Julia was on her feet assisted by a cane. She moved slowly and haltingly. But she moved.

Royal came for dinner every evening and complained about gaining weight from Harriet's cooking.

'A man's not supposed to be a bag of bones,' Harriet said.

'It'll cost me a fortune to have my buttons moved,' he said, enjoying the audience for their small and loving squabbles.

When asked if she had any calls, Royal told Julia that a fellow named Paul had called several times and so had a 'David,' and that both had been told Julia would call them when she was well enough.

'I'm well enough, Dad,' Julia said.

'It's too soon to even be thinking about that place,' Royal said. He said it with the tone that implied this was the final word on the subject. He went about eating quietly.

Julia watched how the temples above the ear pulsed as he ate.

Dinner was generally quiet, unlike it had been when her mother had been alive. Harriet, much more than her brother, lived by the motto the Batemans passed along to their children, 'think your share and say nothing.'

By dinner's end, Royal announced that in another week Julia would be ready to move into town.

The week that followed Julia readied herself mentally to

return to the big, square white brick home on Church Street in Iowa City – the home she lived in from age eight to the day she was married. No doubt to her old room. Two years ago, when her mother died and her father tried to convince her to move back home, the idea of living in that house was the furthest thing from her mind.

Today, it wasn't. It didn't seem exactly right that a thirty-six-year-old woman would move back in with her father, but considering the alternative, it didn't seem all that wrong either.

Rain fell on the Sunday Royal moved her to Iowa City. Her room was very nearly the same as it had been while she lived there. A sewing machine had been moved in and had settled in the corner that once held Julia's record player. The Moody Blues poster had been taken down. The accents had been taken, but the sense of the room was still the same. Julia moved toward the closet. Her clothing had been removed. Hanging on the long transverse pole were items of greater value – a wedding dress and a tuxedo in a coffin of thick clear plastic. There were other pieces of clothing – a fur wrap and a long, dark fur coat.

It was late in the afternoon when she went back up, telling her father she needed to nap. As painful as it was, she investigated the boxes that were in the deep, slant-ceilinged recess of the closet. She wasn't sure what she was looking for, but was obsessed with the search anyway.

Several of her dolls – none of which she'd ever played with – were in a box within a box. All in perfect condition. Some would fetch some serious dollars from those who collect such things. Stacks of birthday cards. High school yearbooks. Her diary, still locked. Key missing. She picked it with a sewing needle she found in a box by the sewing machine.

Most of the entries were short and terse, not the romantic ramblings she expected of her teen-aged self. The longest passages were about her desire to emulate Jacques Cousteau. Despite being thousands of miles from any ocean and about as landlocked as you could be, Julia remembered her fascination with deep sea diving and how her father encouraged her to do something more practical. Nursing would be nice, he suggested. Her mother had been asked to agree and she did.

There was mention of Donnie Patton ever more frequently. His eyes. His voice. The long talks. About the future. About dreams without stunting compromises with reality. Then suddenly Donnie Patton appeared no more. She had put him and the event by the Cedar River back and out of her mind. Nothing else appeared either. The remaining half of the diary was blank.

That evening, at dinner, Royal let it slip that she had received more calls. From Paul, mostly. But there were a few from David Seidman and one from a fellow with a strange name he couldn't recall. Royal had told them Julia was not yet ready to talk, to be reminded of what happened.

'I was here. How did I miss the calls?'

'I had them transferred to the store – automatically. The phone company calls it something . . .'

'Call forwarding.'

'I didn't want you thinking about it all,' Royal said, not apologetically, nor even sympathetically. His voice had the hard, cold ring of authority. Absolute authority.

Not since leaving home had Julia ever permitted such control over her life. Now, she was quiet. Inert, really. She wondered why she hadn't thought much about Paul and David. Especially Paul, who had been such a close and understanding friend. She would call them. Later.

'You best let these things go,' Royal said as if he knew what she was thinking. 'You're here now, where you belong.'

At first, staying in her old room was comforting. The house, which hadn't changed, gave her a sense of security even when Royal left for work as he did invariably at six forty-five every morning of the week except Sundays.

Julia prepared dinner and more than once Royal remarked she was as good a cook as her mother. She was sure he didn't mean it, but was pleased that she could be helpful. A few times she mentioned she ought to get a job.

Usually, he wasn't encouraging. However the last time, over Sunday afternoon dinner at Aunt Harriet's, it was apparent he had given it some thought.

'In a little while, Julia,' Royal said. 'If you like. Maybe you could work for me. Maybe help us modernize the business a bit. Get us a computer or something. You know about those things, I imagine.'

Julia hadn't been to the nursery since she got back. But it was another familiar place, another place to reconnect her to the past rather than the future. She could almost smell the Spruce and Hemlock, the flowering crab apple trees, the lilacs.

'I meant something kind of temporary,' Julia said, 'while I try to figure out my future. I still have a business there.' Strange how 'there' was a distance now measured in time as well as miles. As the familiarity of home invaded her senses, San Francisco seemed to recede. It wasn't as real. On one hand she understood that it provided insulation from the horror. On the other, it frightened her. A strange fear. It was as if she were losing who she was.

Royal's face went hard. He looked at Harriet. Her solemn face didn't betray a thought or feeling.

'Paul called last week.' She could sense her father tensing as she spoke. 'We're just talking right now. He's kept everything up. He's very good.'

Harriet got up and put on the coffee.

'You don't take oak trees or maples and put them in the desert, Julia. And you don't take palm trees and plant them in Ottumwa.' She had heard this before. Royal believed that people, like plants, did their best in the geography of their origin. 'That city is no place for you. I should think that would be quite obvious by now.'

The remainder of the evening was quiet. Royal didn't finish his plate and resisted the blackberry pie. Harriet packed the pie, along with some other items from her garden, into the cardboard box Julia put into the backseat of the Ford Victoria.

'Why don't you come into town for dinner one night this week,' Julia asked Harriet.

'I'm not much for coming into the city, anymore,' Harriet said. 'Iowa City is a little too busy for me. I get into Kalona once a week. That's enough for me.'

'Cheese,' Julia remembered. Kolona was small by any standards. The clearest memory Julia had of the Amish town was of the black horse-drawn wagons backed up to the old brick building where they made cheese. She remembered the smell of horses and milk.

FIFTEEN

The neighborhoods around the Bateman's Church Street home in Iowa City suggest the pleasant perils of the 1950s families – the Cleavers, the Nelsons – missing cookies, lessons about telling small lies and other minor misunderstandings. Nice, modest, well-kept homes, kept but not manicured lawns, splashes of garden color. Quiet. Safe.

Within walking distance of her home was Hickory Hill Park. There was a cemetery near. Despite having lived there all of her childhood, she could never remember its name. Just as she was about to look up and see the name above the gate and memorize it, the large statue visible ahead always stole her gaze and her thoughts.

For the most part, it was a relatively normal little cemetery – concrete stones embedded in little mounds of green lawn. Around them were narrow avenues that would curve and, eventually, lead visitors back to the tall iron-gated entrance. Fresh cut flowers and patriotic flags were plentiful despite the fact that it wasn't the Fourth of July or Memorial Day.

Julia found the walk through the cemetery both appealing and profoundly sad. Towering over one black-topped avenue was the Black Angel. Her head down. Her dark, weathered bronze wings folded over her like a large, heavy cape.

The Black Angel frightened her when she was a child. She would have nightmares that heaven was far less desirable than people made it out to be. Now, looking at the face, the posture, the cape-like wings, Julia didn't feel fear at all.

The expression on the angel's face wasn't what she had remembered. She wasn't sure if she had ever seen the angel's face before. The angel's eyes showed not so much sadness as compassion. The angel's wings spoke of protection. The face of the angel showed determination.

Julia sat on the ground beneath it and began to cry. She knew she wasn't done yet. It wasn't over.

The next few days she was drawn back again to the Black

Angel, wanted to hide under the shroud-like wings. She looked forward to the walks and to her stay with the angel.

Less appealing were the errands that took her from the solitude of the house. The pharmacy and the food co-op were more civilization than she cared to encounter. Some people in town still knew her. She could see the concerned look on their faces when they noticed her. Though her face and body were nearly healed and her walk almost normal, many had to have known her story – or part of it. Human nature being what it is, Julia imagined that what part of the story they didn't know, they invented.

Those she knew, who insisted upon engagement, she would engage briefly. She would be polite with them; but she would excuse herself quickly with one alibi or another. The horror came when she came face to face with Wayne in the Co-Op. He had rounded the corner by the wine. They had come face to face. There was no way out – for either of them.

'Julia? For heaven's sake,' Wayne said. 'I heard you were here. How are you?'

'Fine.'

'Good. You look fine,' he said.

Funny, she thought, how after all these years, she could still detect when he was being insincere. But something had changed.

'How have you been?' she asked, looking around, hoping to see something or someone to rescue her. She could be insincere too. Insincerity was important in awkward moments like these.

'Fine.' He nodded. There was a kindness in his face she didn't remember.

'You staying?'

'I . . . am visiting . . . visiting my father.'

'How is he?' Wayne asked.

'The same. He doesn't change.'

'No,' Wayne laughed awkwardly. 'No I'm sure he hasn't. Well, I've seen him, of course. From a distance. I've never gotten up the courage since . . . since the divorce.'

Oddly, Wayne, who once dominated her life physically and emotionally, seemed powerless. The look on his face she thought was kindness now seemed more like uneasiness. He seemed as troubled and embarrassed running into her as she was meeting him.

'Yes. I'm kind of in a hurry, Wayne. I'm glad you're fine. You're looking great. Happy even.' She looked around for a passing life raft.

'Thanks to Jesus Christ,' he said. 'I know, I know. Sounds crazy. I won't bore you with it. Just wanted to let you know that I'm not that person anymore. I've asked for forgiveness from God.'

'That's good, Wayne.'

'I should have asked you too.' He looked nervous. 'For forgiveness, I mean.'

'Long time ago,' she said. 'Got to go.'

'Something to think about,' Wayne said. 'The Lord, I mean.'

'Yes,' she said, nearly running back into one of the aisles.

When she found the mayonnaise, she headed toward checkout. Wayne and a woman about his age and two little blond boys were gathering the bags. They seemed happy in the world they created.

Julia felt like an impostor. She was only pretending to live here. Only pretending she was one of them.

Iowa City was a wonderful place; but she couldn't shake the notion that she had come back to ghosts, that she hadn't come here to live at all, but to die quietly, passively, defeated.

She knew at that moment, she would return to San Francisco. It was only a matter of telling her father. She had to go back in order not to be defeated by the evil that sent her away. She had to go back because that was her home.

SIXTEEN

It was a routine call for Gratelli and McClellan. There was no reason to believe that it was related to the others. Just a call. A suspicious death. The grandchild of the owners of an old Edwardian in the Haight found the body. Gratelli and McClellan had the luck of the draw. They were back on other cases now that the trail grew cold on the tattoo artist killings and Julia Bateman was back in the Midwest. The task force was still in place, but only nominally. The media had refocused, without the periodic infusion of fresh kills.

McClellan stood above the remains. Not much there. He stood, staring. Almost transfixed on what was little more than a skeleton. The skin of the face was stretched over the bones like thin, worn leather over wood. But all flesh beneath it was gone. The physical matter of this former being was being slowly absorbed.

Gratelli knelt down. There were leathery patches of flesh on the rest of the body. Enough to identify it as a female. A nude female. And there were marks, indistinguishable now, where a rose might have been etched.

'She's one of them,' Gratelli said.

'Earth comes. Takes you away,' McClellan said. 'Not a bad thing.'

Gratelli looked back at the house. A young boy, maybe two, stood in the doorway, above the steps. Eyes open wide, thumb in his mouth. Face blank. He was the one who found her, Gratelli was pretty sure.

At the foot of the concrete steps stood an old rocking horse.

A lot of time had passed since Earl Falwell had seen the outside. He was entitled to a speedy trial, his lawyer argued and now there was some chance that the guy who pressed charges was losing interest in being a witness for the prosecution.

'Time was money,' the guy said. His work was completed in San Francisco and he had something important going on in Boston. Meanwhile, without bond, Earl had done some time for it, hadn't he, the guy said to the prosecutor over the phone.

Meanwhile, Earl had shared the cell with a succession of goons, crackpots, and losers. He was about to get the most recent – a guy called 'Cobra' the guard said as the ferret-like human angled into the room.

'Shit,' Earl said, disgustedly.

'Who was you expectin'?' Cobra asked. 'One of the Spice Girls?'

It wasn't until later when Cobra took off his shirt, baring his scrawny, bony chest that Earl noticed the tattoo. How had he missed it? The guy's whole right arm was a snake. The head and eyes were on the back of the hand.

'Why the fuck you do that?' Earl said.

''Cause it fascinates. That's how them snakes get their kill, you know.' The guy got up off his bunk, came over to Earl.

Cobra raised his arm. 'Snake moves like this and some little beady-eyed rodent gets hypnotized.' Cobra kept moving his hand.

Earl had to hand it to him, the work was real good. Maybe it wouldn't be all that good in a better light. Maybe it was the way Cobra could turn his arm and flex his muscles. The way his fist looked like a snakehead. Whatever it was, it sure did look like a snake. It was fascinating. He could be watching a real snake move. Made him feel weird. It was almost like doing acid or something.

Then Earl felt something smash against his temple, something hard, solid. He felt himself going down. Earl thought he might have been out for a second because he saw the little guy sitting on the edge of the mattress, grinning.

'If it'd been a snake, it'd a bit cha,' Cobra said with a toothless laugh.

Not for a moment did Earl think about clocking the guy. Cobra was crazy. Strength had nothing to do with it. Earl could kill the guy, but anything short of that would be worse for Earl. He was already wondering how he'd get to sleep with this guy in the same cell.

'That's good,' Earl said, getting up on his feet. 'Real good.' He wobbled for a moment. Dizzy. You had to know the difference between wild and crazy. Wild meant you could take a guy on and take your chances. Crazy meant some old fart like Cobra would cut your nuts off while you slept. Earl would either have to kill him or make friends. 'That's damned good,' Earl said wondering if Cobra knew Earl was sucking up.

Cobra didn't say anything.

Earl didn't sleep well that night. A thousand things were on his mind, though it would be difficult to say what they were – except that one of them was crazy Cobra. The one thing, the one surprising thing that wasn't on his mind was girls, the lonely young women. Not much. He thought more about survival. The thought that maybe he wouldn't do it anymore had crossed his mind.

If he dreamed that night, he didn't remember. But for some reason his mother and father were on his mind. Didn't know why. Maybe it was how Cobra's smash just kind of came out of the blue. His dad would do that sometimes. A fist would just come crashing down seemingly out of nowhere and many times for no reason Earl could guess. He and his older sister would sometimes get it that way – out of the blue.

Earl could remember when he was five, how his old man jerked his thirteen-year-old sister out of the shower, her screaming and getting whacked, falling back into the tub and against the tile, naked and wet and unconscious. Blood swirling in the water. The look on his sister's face. Earl thought she was dead. She had a strange, dreamy look.

Earl's father stormed out and Earl stayed there staring at his sister, his naked sister with those small breasts and the small patch of hair between her legs. He had seen his sister naked before, but he turned his eyes away then. Now he couldn't take his eyes off her. He couldn't stop looking. She wasn't looking back.

He stared at his naked sister, staring at that almost blissful look on his sister's unconscious face, the odd angle of the long, graceful neck. His sister was beautiful. She had escaped, he thought. It was OK. She was beautiful and OK and free. He stared, eyes riveted on the delicate, swan-like curve of his sister's neck until his mother came in. She was calm. She was always calm. Mean sometimes, but calm. She pushed Earl away from the doorway and went in. Somehow she managed to revive her.

'How many times have I told you not to provoke him when he's like this,' his mother told his sister who was still too shaken to understand a word. Earl walked back by the bathroom again. His sister was shivering, wrapped in the towel. Earl was still thinking about earlier, about the look on his sister's face. Again he left, but crept back one more time. His mother was drying his sister's naked body. Earl had drifted off into some sort of reverie when the force of his father striking him lifted his feet off the floor and flung him against the wall in the hallway.

'Fucking little pervert,' his father said.

But that look, the look on his sister's face. She was always agitated, confused, frightened – in pain. Always that look. But there, in the tub, she was calm for the first time. She was beautiful. Only time she was.

From then on, Earl stayed away from his family as much as he could. He stayed in the basement a lot. The other thing he did often was to go into the clothes closet, climb way in back. He'd stack things in front of him so that he would be all sealed off. He took comfort in the closeness of it, the darkness. In the summer it was cooler. In the winter it was warmer.

Inside, all curled into himself, he was safe. His father wouldn't be able to cuff him on some strange whim, some anger no one understood. He wouldn't hear his mother's complaints, her saying how stupid he was. Safe from classmates who used to call him 'termite' because he was so small and because he chewed up his pencils, and then later called him 'fruit' and 'fag boy,' because he was small and thin and too early pimply.

No, there in the closet, reality proceeded in muffled tones, sounds blanketed by wool coats and cotton dresses.

Earl would pretend he was an animal. A squirrel or rabbit mostly. And sometimes he would take some bread inside with him. White bread. He'd roll it up in little balls and eat it and think about being an animal and sometimes he'd sleep. A squirrel or rabbit; something small and helpless and frightened, snugly and warmly hidden from the world.

Earl had no friends. In the second grade, he made friends with chubby Michael Sandinski, a sloppy, ugly kid with a whiny and ugly disposition who also had no friends. Sandinski lived a few blocks away and had a bedroom full of toys.

They had decided upon the little green miniature soldiers that had been Sandinski's dad's when he was a kid. Somehow, a realistically molded wild cat – a leopard or lion or something – made of white rubber was thrown in with the set. It was beautiful, Earl thought. Raring, proud, leaping, handsome, fast, powerful. More powerful than the stupid green soldier. Sandinski had no interest in the wild animal, had tossed it aside. It didn't belong with the other plastic pieces scattered out on the floor. Earl chose it. That didn't bother Sandinski. As they divvied up the soldiers, Sandinski picked one who stood eternally in a boxing stance, right arm giving the air an upper cut, to be Sandinski. Earl wanted to be the horse. The leopard was beautiful. Proud. Strong. Independent. Free. He wanted to be the leopard.

Sandinski said Earl couldn't. It was a rule. A guy had to be a guy, not an animal. A guy could not be a leopard. But once Earl saw the leopard he didn't want to be anybody or anything else. They argued. Earl punched him. A couple of times. Blood came out of the kid's nose. Earl took his wild animal and ran.

*   *   *

All the cops in homicide, except Gratelli, lived beyond the city limits of San Francisco, some as far as two hours away. McClellan lived in Petaluma. Like the others, he didn't want his kids growing up in the city. Mickey didn't want to accidentally run into some psycho he'd put away for a few years while he was dining with his family at the local Denny's or picking out bananas at Safeway. Distance was a good thing.

For McClellan, distance was also a great way to deal with problems at home. Travel cut four hours out of his family life. Good for him these days. But not good for Beth. She had threatened to leave before, usually in anger and the end of an argument she seemed to be the only one having. Frustrated, enraged, she had actually taken the kids to her sisters just outside Sonoma on two occasions. But this time was different. Mickey McClellan knew it. He knew it was coming, but when? Her decision to divorce him came not after he came in a few sheets too many to the wind. It came cold, quietly, at the breakfast table.

The sun was coming into the cheerful yellow kitchen. The light played in her still blonde hair. Her hair was a little shorter and her frame a little heavier than when they married. But she was still attractive. Her face, despite the fact she wore only a modest amount of makeup, was still younger than her birth certificate stated.

Beth's voice held no anger, no sadness. Not even a trace of disappointment. McClellan knew it was coming now. He had sensed it, but didn't even begin to understand how to keep it from happening. He wasn't sure why he wanted to hold on, but he did.

'Why?' he asked.

'You really don't need me to explain it.'

'I've provided.'

'You've provided, yes. And well.'

'We have a nice house,' he said. 'I worked a lot of extra hours to get this, to set up Sarah and Kyle for college.'

'Yes. We have two nice kids out of it. Made it worthwhile. In the end, Mickey, I believe we'll both be short on regrets. That is true for me. I hope it will be true for you. We have that, our kids.'

'Then why?' he asked, though he really didn't need to ask. It was more a delaying tactic until he could come up with some argument, some reason that would make sense to her. Make sense to him.

'What we don't have is a marriage. We have nothing in common. We don't sleep together and when we're awake we don't particularly enjoy each other's company.'

'I don't sleep around,' he said.

'You can if you want.'

'I don't slap you around,' he said, instantly regretting his statement.

'Am I supposed to be grateful for that, Mickey?'

'No, of course not,' he said. 'Tell me what to do. Tell me how I can make it better.'

'I did that five years ago. Mickey, there's nothing here anymore. It's a good time for us to go our separate ways. The kids are off making their own lives now. It's about time I did.'

'What about me?'

'I don't know. You're over twenty-one. I have no more children to raise. You're not my responsibility. You have your work. You have your friends on the force.'

'I don't,' he said. 'I don't have any friends.'

'What about Vincent?'

'Vincent's all right. We work together. He goes home, has his life. The rest of them, the others they don't even fuckin' like me.' He winced when he realized he'd used the word. 'I'm sorry. I don't know what makes me say that.'

'It doesn't matter. I'm used to it. From your lips, it's like saying "apple" or "refrigerator" or something. Look, it's over. For the last fifteen years, I haven't been included in your life and you haven't been interested in mine. I don't even know who you are.' Sadness did creep into her voice for a moment. 'And I'm not sure you do either.'

Beth got up, went to the sink.

'Is it somebody else?' he asked quietly to her back.

'You might not understand this,' she said not turning. 'There is someone else but had there not been we would still be having this conversation.'

Her back tensed. She was still afraid of his rage even though he had never taken it out on her. She had witnessed it. It could be devastating.

He surprised her by not getting angry. 'Have you seen an attorney yet?'

'Yes. The papers are being drawn up.' She turned around to look at him.

He seemed calm. Deflated.

'You can have everything, you know?' McClellan said, matter-of-factly.

'You have the right to remain silent . . .'

'I mean it Beth.'

'I do too. Someone needs to advise you of your rights. I don't want everything. We can work it out.'

'When?'

'Soon,' she said. 'I can move . . .'

'No, I couldn't stay here. This is definitely your house, the kids' house.' He looked around. He nodded, smiled. 'Definitely your house.'

'Too big for me,' she said. 'We can sell it.'

They looked at each other for a moment. They seemed to understand. More than that, they seemed to agree.

'I'm sorry,' she said.

'Me too,' McClellan said.

'I know what's happened to these young girls is pretty hard to take.'

He felt very calm, almost relieved.

'The world's a pretty sad place sometimes,' he said, tapping the hard edge of a manila folder on the top of the table. 'We'll forget about them in a while.' It's happening already, he thought.

He looked at Beth who had turned back to the sink.

This wasn't how it was supposed to be. His dress blues were still new when he married Beth. He thought the future was pretty clear, pretty well planned out. McClellan fully expected to work his way up the ranks, retire while he was still relatively young, maybe have some sort of second career while on pension, have a cabin by the lake where he'd have a small boat and where he and his children and eventually their children would spend leisurely days together.

He looked forward to being a grandfather. He'd do better. He'd have the time. Life was just too screwy right now.

He'd done well by some standards. Homicide was one of those assignments nearly everyone wanted. Pretty much top of the heap. Overtime was plentiful. A couple of years, he'd earned as much as eighty-five thousand dollars. A lot of hours, yes.

Base pay was fifty-six thousand. But that's how the house in Petaluma came about. That's how college happened for the kids.

Somewhere along the way, though, something went wildly wrong. He'd changed. He knew that. He knew why, too. He never really knew the world was as sick as it was. There were people out there willing to sell or even kill their kids because they didn't have anything better to do that day.

Spend five years in Sex Crimes like he had and it'd be damn hard to hold on to the notion that people were basically good. There were people out there who could only get their sexual gratification from humiliation or violence or chopping up their loved one into little pieces. Look at those poor, dead, brutalized young women. Look at Julia Bateman, literally beaten within an inch of her life and then branded. She'd live with that. Maybe she wasn't dead. But . . .

In those early days he never really understood how squalid lives could be. He did now. Only cops, firemen and ambulance attendants knew how it was. They walked into the bedrooms, the bathrooms, the attics and the cellars of strangers. They saw humanity wallowing in filth – rancid food, urine, blood and human feces. Bruised and battered babies. Animals didn't live that way unless humans had something to do with it. They didn't do that to each other. At first he could separate that world from his own and from the larger world where crimes and perversions were smaller. It got harder.

Would he get to see his grandchildren? He'd be a fucking strange old man by then, he thought.

'I'll find a place,' he said to Beth's back. He waited for a response. Maybe, 'you don't have to hurry.' None came. He got up to leave.

'Mickey?'

'Yeah?'

'I appreciate your . . . uh . . . understanding.'

'No problem.'

He opened the folder – began to examine the list of men who went to prison about the time the murders stopped.

SEVENTEEN

The room surprised Earl Falwell. For one thing, it was really small. For another, there were no mirrors. This wasn't like the interrogation rooms in the movies or on TV. Just a little five-by-six room with acoustical ceiling tile, the kind used to absorb sounds, as wall covering. The whole place made him feel a little crazy, all closed in.

'My name's McClellan,' said the heavier cop, the one who looked a little bloated. 'That's Gratelli.' Gratelli had deep bags under his eyes. Gratelli was pretty ugly, Falwell thought. A face you couldn't read. Sad, dog-like eyes, thin lips. Hair in his ears.

The two cops sat across the narrow table, close enough to reach across and grab Falwell by the throat if they wanted to. But they didn't seem excited enough to do that. They seemed kind of slow. Kind of boring. Not at all what he imagined. This was Homicide?

Falwell reminded himself to be quiet. Polite. Short answers.

'So, Earl,' the bloated cop said. 'You ever been up on Potrero Hill.'

'No.'

'How 'bout that hill above Haight Street.'

'Nope,' Earl said. He knew what this was about now. He thought he'd been home free. The guy he beat up finally dropped charges – after Earl spent ugly time in jail waiting – probably because the beating victim didn't want to come back from Baltimore or Boston or some place like that. And he was just about home free. Just a couple of more questions they said before they set him free. And here he was. In Homicide. Talking about the hill above Haight Street. Earl Falwell's right foot started keeping time a beat no one including Earl could hear.

'Nope?' McClellan said. 'You live near the Haight, don't you?'

'You know where I live.'

'Yeah and you never been up the hill over there?'

'Nope.'

'Twin Peaks? Sutro Tower? You know what I'm talking about?'

'Yeah, but I never been up there.'

'You jog much?'

'Nope,' Earl Falwell said. He wondered if he should get his attorney. Not if he just kept saying 'nope.' Thing was if he asked for an attorney he'd be admitting he thought this was something serious. He thought he'd better ask.

'Looks like you work out some,' McClellan continued.

'I don't jog. What's this all about?'

'Don't you know?'

'I don't know anything.'

'You work out at a gym, maybe.'

'Yeah.'

'I notice a lot of gay guys work out.'

'I ain't queer.'

'You like girls, then.'

'Yeah, what kind of question is that?'

'I don't know, just a question of whether or not you like girls.' McClellan looked at Gratelli. Gratelli had nothing to say. He looked bored, so bored, Earl thought the guy might die from it. 'So, you going with somebody?'

'I been in jail.'

'Sure. I know. But your girlfriend came to visit you, didn't she?'

'I ain't seein' no one right now.'

'How long's it been?' McClellan asked.

'How long's what been?'

'Since you've been with a girl.'

'I have girl friends.'

'How long's it been?'

'I don't know.'

'C'mon, a good looking guy like you, cool guy like you gotta get a little. You gotta a chick that'll help you out, you know?'

McClellan acted like they were just two guys talking about chicks.

'You're talking weird,' Earl said. 'Why are you so interested in my love life?'

'Gratelli here kind of pegged you as being gay, didn't you Gratelli?'

Gratelli didn't acknowledge the question.

'I'm not queer,' Earl said, trying again to remind himself they were playing games with his head. Better not to play along.

They couldn't know what Cobra had made him do. And that didn't make him queer anyway. Don't bite on this one, don't get pissed, he reminded himself.

'We've got a couple of dates and times here, Earl. Thought maybe you tell us what you were doing during those times.'

There were twelve dates and times and Earl didn't have an alibi for any of them. Though he couldn't remember exactly what the dates were, they seemed to correspond to the incidents.

'Who could remember things like that? I don't keep a diary or nothing. What's supposed to have happened on those dates, anyways?' Earl asked.

'We have some girls got themselves killed,' McClellan said.

'You think I did 'em.'

'Did you?'

'No. Why would I do that?'

'You're alone an awful lot.'

'I am,' Earl said. 'I like to be alone.'

'No friends?' McClellan asked.

'No. Like I said, I like to be alone.'

'You said you had girlfriends. Maybe you could give me the names of some of those girlfriends. We could talk to them. Maybe they could bail you out on a couple of those dates.'

'Am I arrested?'

'Nah, nah, nah,' McClellan said. 'Just questions.'

'Maybe I should get an attorney.'

'Not now,' McClellan said. 'Maybe later. Just between you and me and the fence post over there,' he said gesturing to Gratelli, 'what are you into?'

'What do you mean?'

'Sex.'

'I don't get it.'

'C'mon Earl. A guy, alone a lot. Healthy. Into anything kinky?'

'I don't know what the fuck you're talking about.'

'Now, Earl don't say "fuck". Gratelli, over there, is a sensitive guy. Goes to church. Right Gratelli? He don't like people saying "fuck" and things like that. You fucking understand?'

'Fucking A,' Earl said.

McClellan laughed.

Earl laughed, relieved.

Gratelli didn't.

'The kid's got a sense of humor. I like him,' he said to
Gratelli, then back to Falwell. 'I like you. Listen, what I like
from a woman is respect, you know. I like it when a woman
shows me she respects me, willing to do what I ask. Sub-servant.
You know what I mean?'

'Subservient,' Gratelli said.

'We don't know the difference, do we Earl? But we know
what it means, don't we Earl?'

'No,' Earl said.

'It's kind of like you want total control, Earl. So the girl
don't give you any problems, any resistance, any back talk.'
McClellan bent down so that he and Earl were nose to nose.
'Otherwise you can't get your tallywacker up.' McClellan
smiled, backed away and turned toward his partner. 'Vince, why
don't you take a walk.'

Gratelli got up, left the room, closing the door behind him.

McClellan leaned over the table.

'C'mon, Earl. Tell me. We won't get heavy here, but what
kind of girl do you like. Young, old, full chested or maybe the
slender, model type?'

'Hey, I like girls. That's it.'

'That's it?'

'I don't talk about my sex life, man.'

'I was gettin' a little bored. I thought we could talk about
women. But hell, maybe Vince was right.'

'I ain't . . . look, don't matter. I don't care what you think.
I don't give a shit whether you think I'm a fag or not. I ain't
talking about my sex life with you and if you think you got me
on something, why don't you just let me call my lawyer. I'm
supposed to be out of here.'

'You got a lawyer, Earl?'

'I'll find one. It's the law, right?'

'I just don't understand why you're so shy when it comes to
sex. Says here in this little folder,' McClellan said, tapping a
file folder, 'says you got caught looking in a window late one
night in Daly City. Peeping, Earl, peeping at some sixteen-year-
old girl.'

'I was looking for my dog.'

'Cops say they come upon you and you got your pecker out.'

'I had to take a piss.'

'So what was it? Were you taking a piss or walking your dog. Or maybe you were petting your monkey.'

'My what?'

'Monkey.'

'I don't have a monkey.' Earl looked confused.

McClellan shook his head. 'Half the world's got a monkey, Earl.' Still nothing from Earl. The detective gave up. 'So where's your dog now?'

'Like I said, he ran away. Never seen him again.' Earl grinned. He felt like he won one.

'Neighbor said you were standing up on some bricks, looking in that window at that young girl in the bathroom. Funny place to be taking a leak.'

'I was put on probation. I stayed clean. That's over with.'

'Don't you still like naked young girls, Earl? I mean you kind of like looking at them, but you don't much want them looking back.'

Earl Falwell was starting to feel small, like he was shrinking right there in the seat.

'Thing is, Earl,' McClellan continued, 'we have a few young girls who got strangled to death. And we thought you might know something about it.'

'I don't.'

McClellan kicked the door and in a couple of seconds, Gratelli, came in, sat down.

'Earl says he doesn't know anything about these girls getting killed.'

'You believe him?' Gratelli said matter-of-factly.

'I don't know. He doesn't give me much reason to believe him. I mean it's all kind of a sex thing, you know, Vince, and Earl here gets all uptight about sex.'

'That's the way it is with these guys,' Gratelli said.

Earl's heart began pounding. He wondered if the cops could hear it. Maybe he should just let it all out. Get it over with. They're still playing their cop games, acting out, being cute.

'You charging me, or what?' Earl asked, trying to keep his tone from being angry or frightened or too cocky.

'You're kinda rushing through this, Earl. You gotta be somewhere?'

'I been inside for months. I'm kinda in a hurry, yeah.'

'OK, get outta here,' McClellan said. 'Oh, Earl?'

'What?'

'What kind of car do you own?'

'Chevy.'

'Chevy, huh. Report says you have a Camaro.'

'A Camaro is a Chevy,' Earl said. 'Where you been?'

Once the kid left, McClellan put his head down on the table.

'Hey, you OK?' Gratelli asked.

'Sure,' McClellan raised his head. 'What the hell you think?'

'You can have the car tonight.'

'Don't need it. Live real close now.'

Gratelli didn't say anything.

'End of the line,' McClellan mumbled.

'What do you mean?' Gratelli asked.

'No place to go, nothing to do. The world's all fucked up.' He stood up. 'Look, why don't we get some electronics on that boy's Camaro. We still got the car impounded, I think. Take him awhile to fill out the paperwork.'

'You think he's worth the trouble?'

'No, I don't. His IQ is about room temperature. He's not the kind of guy I'd picture doing it. Other than brains he could be a fit. Except he don't own a van. And he doesn't stutter.' McClellan shrugged. 'That's what the experts say, isn't it. He's supposed to stutter.'

'Antisocial behavior they said. They got that right,' Gratelli said. 'We also know he's a peeper.'

'Young girls,' McClellan countered.

'Almost all of them were young.'

'Not Bateman.'

'He made a mistake. Maybe that's why he got violent. We know he can get violent.'

'I can't see him doin' the Bateman chick at all. Didn't leave nothin'. You know?'

'But she's got the mark. He's in jail, the crimes stop,' Gratelli said.

'Why do we bother?' McClellan asked.

'The mark puts them together somehow,' Gratelli said, ignoring McClellan's rhetorical futility. 'I want to know.'

EIGHTEEN

David Seidman sat on the bench in a long row of benches by the lockers. He was fully dressed. The only thing that needed attention was his salt and pepper hair which curled into little ringlets when it was wet. He looked up to see his competitor just now coming from the shower room. Thaddeus Maldeaux was as cocky and exhibitionistic as ever. He came strolling toward the locker with his towel around his neck rather than around his waist.

'Didn't you used to have hair on your chest?' Seidman asked.

Maldeaux laughed, rubbed Seidman's chest fur. 'Sure did. A little vanity is good for the soul. The word we use these days is "buffed".'

'So who are you trying to be, some Calvin Klein model?' Seidman said bitterly. He felt embarrassed. He wasn't sure if it was for Maldeaux or for himself. Probably himself. Maldeaux looked younger. He wasn't. People thought Maldeaux had more money. He didn't. He looked more fit. He wasn't. He just looked younger and more fit. God gave him better bones and enough confidence to walk around a locker room without his clothes, like he was out for an evening stroll on Mount Olympus.

'You hear from Julia?' Maldeaux asked, finishing the process of drying his tanned body.

'Julia?'

'Yes. Right. Julia. Is she OK?'

'I called shortly after she left for Iowa. Couple of times. Her father said she couldn't speak, then later wouldn't speak. I finally got through to her and . . . hell, I don't know . . . didn't seem like the same person. Kind of dead.' Seidman winced. 'An unfortunate phrase.'

'A thing like that, David. It's utter destruction. Any word on who did it?'

'No. They're still trying to make a connection to those rose carving strangulation cases. But it doesn't make sense.'

'Really?'

'I thought I told you about those.'

'Well yes, but you didn't mention it in connection with Julia.'

'We haven't talked much since then.'

'No, we haven't.' There was a moment of silence. 'Spectacular game, David.'

'You won,' David said.

'Yes. But you played really well.'

David was quiet. 'C'mon,' Maldeaux said. 'You have to get a life. This unrequited love with Julia was dragging you down anyway. You two were just, what do they say, farting in the wind.'

'Colorful. You have a way with words.'

'True though, right?'

David nodded. 'I guess. I still miss her.'

'You two never even slept together, did you?'

'Teddy, stop it. It's none of your business.'

'You're right. Wasn't very gentlemanly. But, don't be so uptight. Sometimes, you're such a prude. Let it out. If you don't, some day you're going to pop your cork big time and it won't be pretty.'

Seidman looked away.

'C'mon, live,' Maldeaux said, poking him with some force on the shoulder.

'This is living isn't it? I should be thankful. Not many assistant D.A.s can get an afternoon in Hillsborough for a little tennis.'

'You've worked hard. You deserve it.' Maldeaux slipped on his shirt. 'No leads on this rose guy?'

'No, I've followed it. I'm following it. I talked with the lieutenant in Homicide. It's all cooling off. The cops looked through the records, found some dude named Falwell, of all names. Not a "Jerry" though. An "Earl". Kid had a minor sex crime on his record. He was popped for battery and, while he was off the streets, the murders stopped. It's interesting, but you can't hang a whole lot on it. A lot of people came and went in that time when you count California's prison population. And the guys on the case don't think he's bright enough to have covered his tracks so well. He owns a Camaro and that fits with the description of a car at one of the crime scenes. It's all real vague, way too circumstantial.'

'Sounds plausible. How much do you need?'

'Who knows?'

'You should. Aren't you the prosecutor?'

'I doubt if I'll be on this one. Too close. The lieutenant says the guy could be good for it, but the cops say it's not ready. If it's him, the murders will start again. The cops will be looking out for him this time. On the other hand, Gratelli's partner says a guy with the intellect of a Falwell wouldn't be able to get away without leaving something. Pubes or something. The murderer is too savvy. Too clean. They dusted the car, vacuumed. Nothing. Aside from the IQ factor, the Quantico profile doesn't paint him out of the picture or in the picture for that matter.'

'What do they say?'

'White male, not sure about age. Lonely. The usual. Can't help himself. Maybe he wants to, maybe he doesn't. Probably in awe of women, worships them. Doesn't want to want to do the dirty thing. Not like you at all.' Seidman laughed. The sound was hollow and he cut it short.

'Can't you just run a photo of this guy by Julia? You suppose she could identify him?'

'They did. Faxed it out to the Iowa City Police. No I.D. She might not have seen him. A ski mask. If he ever took it off, she doesn't remember. Maybe something will come to her.'

'You think she might eventually remember him?'

'Possible. With time. Maybe with some help,' Seidman said, looking into Teddy's eyes. 'Since you're so interested, it's not uncommon for there to be some amnesia – even in accidental cases. Victims can't remember anything immediately, then after a time they often remember everything except that which actually preceded the trauma.'

'Really, never?' Maldeaux asked.

'Sometimes never. Sometimes they get some of it back.'

'So, maybe, right?'

'An outside chance.'

'At any rate, she's in Iowa, right?'

'For now.'

'She's coming back?'

'Don't know. She's not cut off everything here,' Seidman said. Was there hope in his voice? Dread?

'All right, enough gloom. When are we gonna get you some women?'

'Just pick one out of the herd, right Thaddeus?'

'Don't start using that high moral tone, OK? Women are equal to men. Superior in most cases. But let's not forget sex is part of the human condition, not just the male condition. Men and women want it. So, David, it's all right to have sex with women. Some of them even enjoy it.' Maldeaux grinned. 'And if you should ever have sex with a woman, remember you don't have to marry them.'

'I have sex with women.'

'News to me.'

'Oh c'mon, I just don't talk about these things.'

'Not even to me?' Maldeaux asked, slipping on a pair of boxer shorts. 'You pay for it, right?' When Seidman didn't say anything, Maldeaux said: 'That's it. Bingo! Mr Holier than Thou puts the cash on the nightstand.'

'Not so loud.'

'Assistant Prosecutor. Going to run for mayor some day.'

'Hey, that's enough. You know now. You never heard me say prostitution should be illegal. So shut the fuck up.'

Maldeaux sat down next to his friend. 'Talk to me, David. I'm concerned, really.'

'No, let's just move on to another subject.'

'C'mon, David. You're acting like you did when you were a senior in high school and refused to take your turn with Cindy what's her name.'

'It's all very clean, very quiet and very safe and very pleasant. Not at all like what's going through your jaded little mind. So shut up.'

'Were you doing this when you were seeing Julia?'

'Yes. It was a separate thing.'

'I bet. Quirky, kinky stuff with the girls you can't bring to charity events.' Maldeaux laughed.

'Enough. You know . . .' Seidman was flustered. 'I'm a guy . . .'

'So it appears.'

'I have needs. Julia and I are . . . were working on romance. It wasn't there at the time. In the meantime, I can't play monk. I don't feel the need to be celibate. But what I do is my business. Unlike you, I don't want my private life public knowledge.'

'You ever read Genet?'

'Not my cup of tea.'

'*The Balcony*, remember. The judges needed to do penance for all the punishment they'd dished out. They'd go to prostitutes and humiliate themselves in front of them, kiss their feet, beg for the rod?'

'I didn't read it.' David's face was in full blush.

'Here, you, Mr Prosecutor, punish the guilty and those who can't afford to be innocent,' Thaddeus said, putting on his shirt. 'You try to be fair, I know. But you win most of the time. Still some criminals go free, some innocents are punished. You must be punished. The riding crop, or whip?' Maldeaux's laugh continued.

'I don't want this kind of talk.'

'I'm just having a little fun with you. Learn how to laugh, David. It makes life much more bearable. Enjoy life. Live.'

'You're such an ass.'

'Aren't you at all curious about what makes us tick? Look at that preacher. What was his name? Swaggart. Preaching hellfire and damnation during the day and then has some woman in black lingerie whip him. Gets his butt in a sling, more or less, with some dominatrix. You know what a dominatrix is, don't you?'

'Will you get off it?' Seidman said. He stood. 'You don't see what I see every day in court. You, in your fairy tale life know nothing about what really goes on out there. Just because you've seen the Ganges, Teddy, doesn't mean you suddenly know what it's like to be an Indian.'

Maldeaux smiled. 'I don't think you quite get it.'

'Get what?'

'What I do, how I live. I do live, David. That's where we're really different.'

'I'll see you around, Teddy.'

NINETEEN

'How about dinner?' Gratelli asked McClellan. 'We can go shopping first. I know this little boutique on Maiden Lane.'

'All right, all right. I make a friendly gesture. I just thought we'd grab a bite. On me.'

'Now I know there's something wacky on this fucking planet.'

'Well?'

'Sorry Gratelli, me and Jack Daniels got a date this evening.'

'I know it's not Friday, but I'm in the mood for stew at Joe's. And I hate eating alone in that place,' Gratelli said.

'Let's stop by our boy's abode first,' McClellan said, waiving a warrant, 'while he's still filling out papers.'

'Eerie, huh?' McClellan said. 'How can you live without windows? Fucking bat.'

'Vampire maybe,' Gratelli said, going through the drawers of the bureau.

'No teeth marks, but definitely a neck fixation.'

'Kid's got a lot of underwear, but all of it appears to be his.'

'The place is fucking strange,' McClellan said, looking at all the half-burned candles. 'No books, no letters, no dirty magazines. Nothing. Just candles. Fucking candles everywhere.'

'Candles in the john,' Gratelli said from inside. 'Body oil of some kind. Oh, here are some magazines. Some muscle magazines.'

'Naked guys?'

'Half naked guys. Not porno. Muscle shit.'

'Sheets, lots of sheets, sheets and towels,' McClellan said, opening a door and examining the shelves. 'The kid's clean enough. His mother would be proud of him.'

'No pictures, you notice that?'

'No nothing. Oil, lots of oil, and candles and sheets, towels and some magazines.' McClellan looked under the bed, lifted the mattress. 'These guys are supposed to keep something.'

'Not a trophy in sight. No locks of hair, no panties, no newspaper clippings.'

'Like I said, this guy's not bright enough to be as smart as he is.'

Gratelli laughed. 'OK, Yogi.'

The restaurant was in the Tenderloin, on the corner of Limbo and Hell. There was a crowd, but it was really too early for dinner. The dinner crowd at Original Joe's didn't get there until eight.

McClellan, slipping across the leather seat of a booth, recognized a few judges. There were some District Attorneys and lawyer types and some cop types as well, but there were no friendly waves of recognition. No one thought a whole lot of Mickey McClellan.

Even so, the crowd was more to his liking. He wasn't uncomfortable. Here, no one sampled the latest release from Napa. No one was asking for some strange beer from a microbrewery in Oregon. This was the hard stuff the guys were sipping on. Vodka. Scotch. Gin. Later, it'd be rack of lamb or stew like your momma made.

'Hey!' the waiter said. 'Don't tell me it's Friday.'

'It isn't,' McClellan said. 'Gratelli's feeling sentimental.'

'Jack Daniels?' the waiter asked McClellan.

'Right. Double.'

'How about a martini?' Gratelli asked.

'You want that huh? A martini?' the waiter grinned.

'A sudden wave of nostalgia along with the sentiment,' Gratelli said. 'You still know how to make one.'

'Sure, why not?' the waiter said. 'It's all the rage. Everybody wants a Martini now. A Martini and a cigar. Regular Dean Martins. So you want a Martini? Absoloooootly. Whatever you guys say.'

'That's Gratelli, Mr Trendy,' McClellan said. 'Don't you think?'

'Whatever,' the waiter said.

'That's what I like about this place, Vincent,' McClellan said when the waiter was out of earshot.

'What?'

'The waiter is a heterosexual. Where do you see that? Everybody in here is a fucking heterosexual. That's the way it's supposed to be. All is right with the world.'

'What do you care? You think you're some movie star, guys are gonna fall all over you if they see you?'

'Oh shit, I don't. I don't. I don't care. OK. Just an observation. I don't care about fucking anything.'

'Where did you move?' Gratelli asked.

'Found a little place around the Panhandle. Not too expensive.' He was calming down again.

'Good,' Gratelli said. 'I get a place to open up in my building, we'll talk.'

'Rent's too high.'

'I just said we'll talk. That's all. You got something against talking?' McClellan shrugged. Gratelli continued. 'So you got plans?'

'Plans? Plans for what?'

'You're out of the house. Your life is changing. I was just wondering.'

'Is that what this is? A little therapy for a deranged cop?'

'You have to do something. You can't just go home from work, drink the night away and come to work and that's it?'

'Sounds like a plan to me.'

'It doesn't to me,' Gratelli said.

'You're not living my life the last time I looked.' There was a moment of silence as the waiter brought back the drinks. When he was gone, McClellan leaned over the table. 'So your life is so fucking exciting?' McClellan asked, taking a gulp of the drink the waiter put in front of him.

'I don't say it has to be exciting,' Gratelli said.

'I don't like opera.'

'Doesn't have to be opera. You could take up woodworking or a . . .'

'Strangle some kid, go to prison, learn a trade. How's that?'

'Leave work at work.'

'You know a fucking leopard goes off, kills one of those little gazelles. And you say that's terrible. But you know that's nature. And you bite the fucking bullet on that kind of shit. Gotta eat. But this isn't nature anymore. It's something else.' McClellan's face reddened as his voice rose. 'I don't know what it is. It's not survival of the fittest. It's survival of the sickest. What the hell did those little girls do to wind up naked and dead and rotting in the fucking sun? This isn't nature's balancing act. It's fucking sick.'

He realized that everyone was looking at him. He let out a deep sigh, shook his head, fiddled with the menu.

'One of them is found by a dog, a fucking dog. Another is discovered by some little kid in a backyard, the corpse being swallowed up by nature. Doesn't that get to you?' McClellan asked in an intense whisper.

'I don't dwell on it.'

'You can do that. Just go off to the opera. Leave work at work, right?'

'It's always been that way,' Gratelli said.

'You always been around? You've been observing the human condition since the day Christ was born?'

The two were quiet for a while. Halfway through the stew, McClellan asked Gratelli what else he did when he wasn't working.

'I play my records,' Gratelli said. 'I read. On Saturday I catch a game or maybe a movie. Once a week I take the train to Colma.'

'You visit the dead people? That's all there is in Colma.'

'I don't know about that, but I go to the cemetery, yes. On a sunny day, I sit in Washington Park. Sometimes there are weddings at St Peters and Paul. Or maybe I watch the people. The sad people, the happy people. The dogs. The point is there is life there. Life goes on. It's good. Sunday I go to Church.'

'Church? You believe in God, Gratelli?'

'I wouldn't know how not to.'

'You figure out the great mystery?'

'I'm a little man, Mickey. I try to solve the little day to day mysteries.'

'Well Vincent, I'm happy we had this talk so we could discover just how much we have in common.'

'We're both trying to stop this guy, aren't we?'

'Forget about work,' McClellan said. 'Isn't that what you keep sayin'? Eat, drink and be merry, right?'

'Right.'

'And tomorrow?'

Earl's lawyer had arranged things. Most things. Not the car. Earl had to wait until he got some money before he could wheel his Camaro out of hock. But the rent had been paid. Nearly anyway. He was only a month behind and he couldn't be evicted on that. The money came out of his vacation pay at the store when he was terminated. The mail had been taken in by the landlord. Other than the stuff that went to 'occupant,' there wasn't much of anything. But the lawyer didn't want people to know the place was unoccupied.

There wasn't enough money to keep the phone and to pay for the electricity, but, according to the lawyer, Earl should be happy he salvaged the living quarters.

The bodily injury charges had been dropped; and even though he was glad to be in his dark little one-room cave, he was on edge, a scary, dangerous edge.

The dead phone reminded Earl how long it had been since he had talked with his grandmother. She would be worried. He might have to call her collect. He didn't want to do that. It would make her worry more. But she had probably tried to call. She'd be worried anyway. Hell, he was worried.

That last conversation with the two cops in that little room was too close. He was pretty sure they were just checking it out. If they had something, really had something, they'd have said more. His past arrest record was no big thing. The Camaro I.D. was the worst part of it.

But if they had a license plate, or even a color, they wouldn't have let him off so easy. And the homo thing, that was just to get him all screwed up, make him crazy, so he'd give something away. He didn't give away anything, he was sure. He ran the conversation back over his brain as best he could. No. No slips.

He looked around the room. He couldn't tell if anyone had been there messin' around other than his lawyer. Maybe the lawyer had been a little nosy. Probably. The cops maybe. But there was nothing to see. He didn't keep anything. Just the photos. For a moment, he was seized with panic.

Nothing about the killing, he thought, then relaxed. Embarrassing yeah, but not anything they could use against him. Earl went to the refrigerator, pulled out the meat tray, undid the tape holding the envelope underneath.

Didn't look tampered with. He'd check anyway. All three Polaroids were there. He'd taken fifty or so, but saved only the three. He cut the others into little pieces and threw them in the neighbor's trash.

If the cops took a peek at these, they would think he was all fucked up, taking naked pictures of himself. Fuck, he thought, they think he's all fucked up anyway. They were right, weren't they? But taking pictures of yourself all shaved and naked wasn't illegal. Just weird.

The photos looked good. Sharp definition to the muscles. He'd have to work like hell to get that back. Even a few months without the right equipment and off the 'roids and you're screwed. He went to the bathroom, lit the candles, catching glimpses of himself in the full-length mirror on one wall. He undressed. Somehow, it didn't excite him. Maybe he should go ahead and shave his body. Maybe that would help. He was tired. That seemed like a lot of effort. Later.

Maybe he should dump the photos. He put the photos, one on top of the other, and grabbed the scissors. He would cut them up in little pieces and scatter the cuttings in trash cans around the city so no one could put them back together again. Even that required more effort or interest than he could muster.

Later, he thought. He put them back where he found them, using new tape.

In bed he felt empty. He ought to be glad he didn't have the desire. He didn't feel driven. Not to do that, anyway. He was edgy though. Unsettled. Not his body. There was nothing left to drive it. But his mind. He couldn't make sense of what was going on there. Edgy, angry, impatient. But he had no idea how to calm it. The way he felt, though, he almost wished he had the desire. Somehow, not knowing what he wanted, he was starting to feel worse. Now there was no reason to move, to open his eyes.

It was like something filled his chest, a pressure kind of; a kind of pressure that started to feel like it was going to explode, like it was all out of his control. But what? What could he do about it. It was anger, he was pretty sure. But at what? At who? He knew life was unfair. That couldn't be it. It wasn't just unfair to him. It was just the way of things.

He was free from the family. No one was calling him names any more. He was out of jail. What was it? What was this thing that was so ready to explode?

It was rare when Gratelli couldn't sleep. All he could think about was McClellan, and those thoughts were disturbing. If one were sensitive, any conversation with his partner could be disturbing; but what made Gratelli uneasy was that his partner had been getting quieter. He wasn't bothering so much with keeping up the tough guy act. He seemed to be taking the deaths of the girls personally. Anger had turned to futility. The 'end of the line' remark wasn't vintage McClellan.

McClellan had grown increasingly quiet during dinner, refused to respond to guaranteed hot buttons and was nearly morose by the time dinner was over.

A lot of things were coming down on the guy. All at once. The marriage, the embarrassment of having the investigation taken away – most of it anyway, and the case itself. Nothing to do really. Julia's survival was supposed to have moved the whole thing along. But she wasn't much help. Now things were at a standstill. Gratelli knew that the only hope for finding the killer, besides an unexpected confession, would have to come from another victim. A new victim. Would there be one? Was he wishing for one?

The Panhandle was a drive across town from North Beach, but not a long one. Even in the rain – the heavy drizzle – at this time of night Gratelli could be there in ten minutes. There was a space out front – the same space that had been there when he dropped McClellan off at his new digs.

There were four apartments in the building. Three had names, none of which were McClellan's. One was unmarked. That was apartment A, just as you came in. Gratelli knocked. No sound. No answer. There weren't many places near there where a guy could go for a drink. Maybe down into the Haight, but the bars down there weren't likely McClellan hangouts.

He knocked again. He put his ear to the door.

Gratelli wondered if he'd done the right thing. Maybe Mickey had called one of the various 'escort' or 'massage' services. Maybe the pot-bellied Irishman had tanked up on a bottle of Jack Daniels and was out. Then again, the reason Gratelli drove all the way across town was to find out. And Gratelli wasn't acting on curiosity. He had a bad feeling. McClellan's normally abnormal behavior was more abnormal than usual.

'Mickey! You in there?'

No answer.

The lock wouldn't be much of a challenge. One more time. McClellan may be inside, half drunk, and think that the guy busting in was some stranger. Like any cop, McClellan had to be considered armed. And if he was drunk – a likely condition given the hour – also dangerous. Gratelli was content enough with life. He didn't want to die just yet.

'This is Vincent, Mickey. I'm coming in.'

This time, Gratelli heard a sound.

'Shit.'

He heard a thud on the floor, the scraping of furniture and then the knob turned. But the door didn't open. 'Shit.' There were some clicks and the door opened to reveal a half-steady, bleary-eyed McClellan. He still had on his suit jacket, but was without pants and shoes. His dress shirt was open. The tails hung down over the boxer shorts.

'What the fuck is this?' McClellan asked.

'Welcome wagon,' Gratelli said. 'I've been asked to officially welcome you to the neighborhood.' Gratelli looked over the slouching McClellan to see the Irish cop's gun on the table beside the bed. 'You got company?'

'You. Don't I see too fucking much of you during the day, you gotta haunt my nights as well.'

'Yeah, well . . .' Gratelli stammered. He'd forgotten what excuse he'd thought up on the way over, the one he'd use when called upon to explain his presence.

'Yeah, well what?'

'I wanted to talk about that kid, what's his name? Falwell?'

'Earl,' McClellan said.

'Yeah, Earl Falwell. You gotta minute?'

'No, no, no,' McClellan said. 'You never wanted to talk about a case . . .'

'I'm spooked. I'm afraid we didn't search his place all that well.'

McClellan ran his hand through his hair. 'There was nothing in his room except a few fucking muscle mags, Gratelli. Zero. Zilch. I don't even think he reads those magazines, just looks at the pictures. The kid's got to be the dimmest bulb on his family tree. He hasn't got the smarts to snap these little girls' necks and not leave at least one fucking clue. We talked about it. OK? Goodbye. Sweet dreams.'

Gratelli was relieved McClellan bought the story about coming over to discuss Earl Falwell.

'I couldn't sleep,' Gratelli said.

'So you thought I shouldn't sleep either. Nice of you.' McClellan turned to go back toward his bed, sitting down on the edge. Gratelli followed. There were two pint bottles of Jack Daniels. One was empty. The other was nearly so. The pistol bothered him. So near the bed could merely mean that McClellan was too tired, too lazy to take off the holster and simply wanted the weight of the piece off him. Or it could have been so close because McClellan was thinking about doing something with it.

'That's it, huh? You come over to talk about a case even though in fifteen years you never did this?'

'Seemed to bother you too,' Gratelli said.

'Not any more. Nothing fucking bothers me.'

'Why don't you put your pants on?' Gratelli said, getting up and grabbing the pants that had been carelessly tossed on the floor. As he handed them to McClellan, the wallet fell out.

'Why?' McClellan said. 'We going somewhere?'

'No.'

'The President going to pay us a visit?' McClellan tossed the pants on the other side of the bed. 'I spilled something on them.'

'Then take off your coat and tie, for Christ sakes,' Gratelli said.

McClellan smiled big. 'What's this to you.'

'You look silly,' Gratelli said.

McClellan laughed. 'I am silly. Fucking silly.'

'Your kid?' Gratelli said, picking up a small, faded color portrait of a young blonde teenage girl. An old photo.

'No, I bought it in a museum. Who the hell would it be?' McClellan said, his big grin getting smaller. 'Look, what is this?'

'Nothing,' Gratelli said. 'Just seemed like you needed somebody to talk to.'

'About what?'

'I don't know. Things.'

'I can go to confession.'

'Good for you,' Gratelli said. 'I don't want you doing anything stupid.'

'That's the way I do everything,' McClellan said.

'You want to talk about it?'

'It?' McClellan shook his head. 'It? It what? What it?'

'Your life. Your marriage. Something's going on.'

'I haven't paid attention to my wife in fifteen years. She decides to leave me and I'm all fucked up about it. Figure. I got two kids, moved out of the house long time ago. I'm not even sure I said goodbye or good luck. I feel deserted, sad. Figure that! I ignore my entire family forever, and I feel deserted because I'm not close to any one of them. I don't know them. I got nothing. I got no life.'

'Wait a . . .'

'No you wait. It gets better. I make good money. There's people in India begging. I got more than enough to eat. There's hundreds of thousands of people starving in Africa. I'm healthy. There are people sick all over the world. Name it. Cancer. AIDS, diseases they ain't even got names for. I'm fucking sorry for myself. Why? What right . . . ?'

'No, you're angry because you can't do anything about it.'

'I can't do anything about anything. We got this killer. Seems like we got killers all over the place.'

'Do what you can.'

McClellan stood up, went to the window. 'It's a dump, Gratelli. A fuckin' dump.'

'You all right?'

'You thinking of leaving now? I had a perfectly good drunk going on and you come in here, get me sobered up. For what? There's this world and then there's nothing. Do you know how fucking frightening that is?'

'I thought you were Catholic.'

'Thanks a hell of a lot. That helps. Something worse than nothing. You find it.' He turned. He was grinning. 'Gratelli, you're a real pisser. What in the hell are you doing here?'

'You want to grab a bite to eat?' Gratelli asked.

'What are you doing here. You don't even like me.'

Gratelli winced.

'What do you mean?'

'What do I mean? That's a laugh.'

'I know you are trying to do your job.'

'You don't like me.'

'There's a lot about you I don't like,' Gratelli said. 'That's true. But I'm here aren't I? Doesn't that count for something? Maybe I don't want to go steady with you Mickey, but since I'm here, do you want to go out for a bite to eat?'

McClellan came back to the bed, shaking his head. He seemed amused.

'No. What I'd like to do is get on with my drunk. Short of that . . . forced to accept your Boy Scout efforts to help an old lady across the street whether she wants to go or not, I'd like to sober up, shower, change my clothes. I could use a pack of cigarettes. I'll put some coffee on,' he said. 'I wonder if you wouldn't mind going out and getting me a pack of Camels?'

Gratelli thought his partner looked relaxed for the first time. Oddly, he seemed suddenly sober. Suddenly lucid.

TWENTY

Earl Falwell woke up for the third time that night. For a few moments after each, he thought he was still in the cell with Cobra. The little asshole had got to him. More ways than one. Each time Falwell woke, not sure he was out of the dream, he sighed in relief, letting his head drift back into the pillow. He'd glance at the tiny but constantly burning night light for reassurance and close his eyes.

But this last time he couldn't get back to sleep. Earl was troubled by the idea that the cops connected him to the girls' deaths. Those thoughts put other thoughts in his head, starting with the girls. The killings. The time after the killings. Earl searched his mind for better pictures. Clearer pictures.

He had the same problem in prison. He could not bring them into his mind clearly. The faces were no longer distinctly separate. He felt empty. There was nothing to feed his fantasy. He wasn't ready to go out; but he was ready to settle his mind – to reconstruct, to excite himself, to satisfy himself, to sleep. To make all of these confusing thoughts go away. To stop all of this from eating him alive.

There was nothing he could do tonight. He hadn't been able to pick up his Camaro. Tomorrow was the earliest. If he could get the bucks.

He would try harder. He lit the candles, put on the CD. He slipped off his underwear and slid into bed, uncovered, trying hard to clear his mind. He didn't like the feel of his body. It was softer. Too soft.

Earl Falwell could tell. He couldn't get it, couldn't get the thing going that would bring him rest. Must be because it's his first day out. The cop questions. Got him all jumbled up inside his head. Got him thinking about things he didn't want to think about. He got to thinking about his sister and about what his dad did to her. And what he did to him. About jail. About Cobra. Earl didn't want to think about this shit. If he couldn't get it off his mind lying there, he'd have to get out.

He slid over the edge of the bed, dressed. It would be cold outside. He couldn't remember a warm, San Francisco night. And there had been precious few dry ones.

Even so, he wasn't prepared for the hard rain.

It was still dark in San Francisco. Five a.m. Earl Falwell had not yet slept. He dressed in the near dark, faced the dark outside when he opened the front door. He walked north on Stanyan, past Haight and the entrance to Golden Gate Park, to Page Street, then headed east. It was cold. The rain angled at him. Pellets stung his face. It felt good. He walked through the darkened street.

Most of the homes and buildings were dark; but there were lights on here and there. Earl wondered what was going on in all those rooms. He attempted to imagine all the rooms in the city, in the country, in the world and how many different things were going on. People eating, sleeping, pissing, bathing, working, watching TV, fucking, killing. He wondered if anyone was being killed now. He was sorry he did not have his car.

He cut over to Oak Street, then headed east again. He saw someone on the grassy strip known as the Panhandle, which, if you looked on a map, was a kind of rude finger of Golden Gate Park sticking back into the city between Oak and Fell. Earl moved toward the figure. It was hooded and hunched against the rain, but facing Earl as he approached.

At first Earl thought it was a girl. The figure was slight.

'What's up?' Earl asked.

'Not much. How about you?'

'Bored. Just walking.' The face was young, male. So was the voice.

'Yeah, me too. Bored.'

'And lonely?' Earl asked.

'Who isn't?'

Earl wasn't sure how the guy meant it. 'So, enjoy the night, huh?' Earl moved past him.

'Wait,' the guy said. 'You have to be somewhere?'

'No,' Earl said, turning back around.

'Why don't you come to my place?'

'Why?' Earl said.

'We'll figure out something,' the guy said.

'I'm not into drugs.'

'We don't have to do drugs.'

'What are you into?' Earl asked.

'What do you like?' The guy lit a cigarette.

Earl noticed the guy had that sad, pained look around the eyes. Eyes that looked older than the rest of his soft face.

Rain was coming down. The guy's face was wet. Almost looked like he'd been crying. The guy looked agitated, frightened, confused.

Earl felt an odd stirring in his brain. He didn't feel as he had before – with his sister and the others. Not exactly. Whatever way he had felt before, there was anger in it now.

*   *   *

Gratelli found the same parking spot he'd had earlier – a minor miracle despite the short time he was gone – and pulled the Taurus into the small space. The light was still on in McClellan's apartment. In the dim street lamps across the street he saw two figures, talking to each other in the rain. Noticed one of them lighting up.

'Smoking'll kill you fella,' Gratelli said aloud but to himself. Conversations this time of night, Gratelli thought there was no doubt a more dangerous deal being struck – drugs more likely. Sometimes after dark this wasn't the best of neighborhoods. A little crack, a little meth, a little heroin. And who knows what goes down.

Gratelli tried to shrug off the wetness once inside the building's entry hall. He went to McClellan's door. It was unlocked. He went inside. It was still. Too still. McClellan was not in the main room.

'Mickey?'

There was no answer. No one in the kitchen. The door to the bathroom was ajar. There was light behind it. He looked at the bedside table. The pistol was missing. Gratelli knew what he'd find. There was really no need to open the door. He did. He had to.

Earl followed the young man into the rear entrance to the apartment building. Only a little light filtered down the dingy stairway from the landing above. Earl put his hand on the fellow's shoulder before the first step.

'Here,' Earl said. 'I don't want to go up.'

'What?'

'I said I don't want to go up.'

'Just for a few minutes,' the guy said. 'You don't have to do anything.'

'Take off your coat.'

The young man turned, took off his coat. Before he showed a nervous anticipation. Now he showed a nervous caution.

'It's warmer up there,' the young man said. 'We can relax.'

'I don't wanna relax.'

'Something to drink maybe?'

'No,' Earl said, taking the guy's coat and throwing it on the steps. 'Drop your pants.'

'Hey, I want to do it with you, but not like this.'

'C'mon.'

'Hey, maybe this isn't a good idea.'

'Turn around,' Earl said, grabbing shoulders and forcing the guy to face the other way. Then Earl put his arm around the guy's neck, holding him firm. 'Drop the pants.'

'I don't mind getting a little kinky,' the guy said. 'But this isn't . . .'

'Shut up,' Earl said, increasing the pressure on the stranger's neck. He heard the rustle of the pants fall. He felt powerful, really powerful. 'I'm getting tired of getting fucked,' Earl said. 'About time somebody else did.' He didn't know whether he said this out loud or just thought it.

'Use a condom,' came the strained voice. 'Please use a condom.'

Earl felt the boy's warm body against his own, pushed in, felt the warmness engulf his flesh. It was as if it was this that caused his trembling to stop. Now he had the power. This time for real.

Gratelli went out to the car, made the call. Then he went back inside. There was a note. It read: 'Fuckin' awful thing to do to you, I know. Remember, nothing you could have done. Nothing anybody could have done. I was past all that.'

Gratelli wadded up the paper torn from McClellan's notebook and stuffed the wad in his pocket. He sat down on the edge of the bed. Mickey had tried to minimize the mess. The tile in the bathroom was far easier to clean than mattress and carpeting. A deadly dose of something might have been easier; but Gratelli didn't know of too many cop suicides done with pills. That just wasn't the way. You ate your gun. That was the way.

Stupid. All of it was stupid.

Gratelli tried to figure out what he felt. He was stunned. Perhaps he was in shock. He looked around the room. Pretty anonymous. 'End of the line,' McClellan had said. If Gratelli had been a bit sharper, he would have seen this coming. His visit, the friendly, not-too-personal chatter fell way short. McClellan had needed professional help.

Gratelli would have to tell Beth. He didn't know her that well. McClellan had been right. They didn't have dinner together. They didn't visit each other. They weren't close. Only accidental glimpses into each other's lives.

Still, it was up to him to break the news. No one else was
any closer. McClellan had alienated most of his peers and virtu-
ally all of those in charge. If he hadn't made Homicide before
making so many enemies, somebody would have found a way
to get him off the force. Nobody knew McClellan very well,
Gratelli thought. Including McClellan.

Gratelli went outside to wait for the cops to arrive, noticed
one of the figures from before crossing the grassy divide back
the other way. Whatever was going down had gone down,
Gratelli thought.

Two cop cars pulled up. Lights flashed, but there were no
sirens. In the back of one was the lieutenant.

'Who'd a guessed? Jesus!' he said, covering up his neck with
the collar of his long coat. 'You OK, Vince?'

Earl knew something had changed while he was in jail. No
question. He couldn't have explained it even if he'd had someone
to explain it to. Maybe he grew up.

Lying in bed, he had no urge to light the candles, to feel his
own body, to listen to music. There was a dullness in his mind,
but he wasn't confused anymore. The baby monster grew up to
be a real one. Eat or get eaten. At first he never figured Cobra
to be that smart, but Cobra had it right. Cobra hadn't tried to
help him. He just took what he wanted. But Earl learned something. There was nobody to help. Just get tough. Don't take any
shit. Get what you need. Take what you want if you figure you
can get by with it. Be a little smarter than Cobra. Don't get
caught.

What happened in that back stairway was done by someone
he was becoming. Someone who wasn't lonely anymore,
wasn't sad anymore, who wouldn't worry about the rightness
or wrongness of what he had done. He still couldn't sleep.
He didn't care. Earl Falwell had found a new power, not over
unsuspecting women; but over whoever he wanted to have
power over. Earl Falwell wasn't frightened anymore. He was
in charge. Like Cobra. Like his father and stepfather. Prison,
however brief it was, was a turning point. Things would be
different from now on.

TWENTY-ONE

Helluva time for Bradley to call, Paul Chang thought. He had thirty-five minutes to get to the airport to pick up Julia, and Bradley, very unlike him, wanted to talk. And Bradley, also very unlike him, didn't come to the point.

Something about opportunity. Change.

'What! Bradley tell me what. Or wait until you get back and we'll have dinner and drinks and we'll talk until dawn.'

'I'm not coming back,' he said. 'I'm staying here. In Florida. I've got an invitation to spend some time in New York.'

A brick drops inside Paul's stomach. Heart flatlines. He hadn't thought about that possibility.

'Oh,' he managed.

'You've got a life, right?' Bradley said. 'Julia's coming back . . .'

'Yes . . . yes . . . um yes, as a matter of fact, she's nearly here.'

'I mean, it was you and Julia, anyway, wasn't it?'

'Well yes,' Paul said, puzzled. 'She's my friend.'

'And you've got her back after all.'

'I guess you could say that.'

'I guess I did say that. Listen, Paul, this is kind of really abrupt, you know?'

'Go on.'

'I've met someone.'

'Oh.'

'His name is Chen. He's a model. From Vietnam. Chinese actually from the Cholon district. It's very exciting.'

'I see,' Paul said. 'That's not a surprise, you know.'

'I know. And I'm being an ass. Maybe that will make it easier.'

'It'd be strange if it were a Moscowitz or O'Brien or even Rodriguez. I'm sorry, don't worry about it. Enjoy . . . have a good. . . what the fuck . . . have a good whatever. I mean it, don't worry about it.'

'I hate to do this by phone.'

'Well, I'll box up your stuff and you can let me know when . . .'

'Just my leathers,' Bradley said.

'All right.' Paul tried hard to keep emotion out of his voice. Not too cool, though. Friendly.

'You're really being nice about this.'

Paul looked at his watch. He felt a little hypocritical.

'I am disappointed,' Paul said, knowing he was about to launch into something. 'The really sad part of this isn't our going our separate ways. The sad part is that we're going to continue to go the same way. You've found another almond-eyed, dark-haired, smooth-bodied exotic creature. And me? I will no doubt begin my search for another pretty blond. I won't even care if he can read or write.'

'Ouch,' Bradley said.

'Ouch, ouch. One for each of us. I'm serious. The mind won't matter. The heart won't matter. I know better. Don't you?'

'Me?' Bradley said. 'What do I know. I'm just a pretty face. Just a blond. I better go too.'

'Chen awaits?'

'Could be. Yes.'

'I wish I could say "goodbye" in Chinese, at least.'

'What can you say in Chinese?' Bradley asked.

'Kung Pao Chicken. How's that?'

'Bye.'

'Not good enough,' Paul said, then clicked off the phone.

Julia Bateman sensed the differences immediately. The people and the pace. At the San Francisco airport, the generally slow-paced vanilla world of an insulated Midwest was replaced by the largely fuel-injected swirl of humanity here at the shaky edge of the continent.

Paul was never on time. Sometimes early, sometimes late, but either he was shorted a sense of time and got lost in it or it was a characteristic of his passive-aggressive personality. Or both. She loved him dearly. She was pretty sure he was the one she most longed to see. But there was still a question about Thaddeus. She couldn't get him off her mind.

When Paul finally arrived, the moment of awkwardness she feared didn't materialize.

'When we get back I'll make myself scarce so you can acclimatize,' Paul said.

'Not for long,' she said. 'I want to jump in. Tonight I want to go to that Thai restaurant across from Hamburger Mary's and have Thai beer and something hot and spicy.' Her excitement broke. 'Oh God, I bet you have plans. I always do that. I'm sorry.'

'I don't have plans.'

'Tonight's not a Bradley night?'

'Bradley who?' Paul said.

'What?'

'He found another Asian youth . . . one from the old country. Or some old country. Vietnam.'

'I'm sorry.'

'So tonight is yours. We'll have a feast. But remember I'm allergic to coconut.'

'How about peanut sauce?'

'No. Love it. And peanut butter.'

Gratelli sat at his desk. Opposite and butting against his own was McClellan's desk, pretty much as it had been left. Any minute, it seemed, Mickey would plop his plump amorphous body down in the chair. The sudden whoosh of the cushion would be accompanied by random obscenities. Gratelli tried to concentrate on the folders – the ones that pertained to Bateman. While another stack, much larger and pertaining to the others rested on the upper left corner of the battered Formica.

The folders yielded little. There were no real suspects in the slaying of the girls. There were some remote possibilities with Bateman; but those didn't make a great deal of sense with the others. Earl Falwell looked good for both Bateman and the others. But unless he was giving a Dustin Hoffman job of acting, it wasn't likely that Earl could have avoided some sort of DNA trail. No blood. No hair. No semen. No fabric samples.

In the case of Bateman, most leads were dead ends. A couple of guys she testified against had concrete alibis. The guy from the laundromat had an unimpeachable alibi. Death. No alibi for Baskins, who may have resented her spying on him, if he knew. But the sexual aspect didn't fit and he didn't appear to be strong enough – even without a neck brace – to be that dominant. Then again, a flashlight to the head of the victim goes a long way in the domination department.

According to McClellan's notes and the conversation they

had after the interview, it was possible Ezra Blackburn could have done it; but how would he have known about the engraving? As a former insurance investigator, maybe Blackburn had some official connections somewhere. Any one of a number of cops who were first on the scene and could have taken a close enough look to describe the rose tattoo. The medical examiner's office, maybe.

The silly charge that McClellan himself could have been involved should have been resolved quickly by getting the measurements of the skylight the intruder dropped through. McClellan's girth would have been a pretty tight fit. This wouldn't have been a McClellan choice for an entrance. He wasn't exactly in shape for Olympic gymnastics.

Apparently some members of the task force implied that a cop would be smart enough to set up something like that. Pick the lock on the front door. Break the skylight to suggest that was the point of entry and avert suspicion. It still didn't fit.

Who did that leave? Someone Julia Bateman knew? Seidman? He could easily have known about the engraving. They had a relationship, of sorts. He'd be smart enough to know how to destroy the evidence. He could have a real kinky side. A lot of people did.

Who else? Not Paul Chang. Surely.

Why? For what purpose? To take over the business? Murders have been done for less. Even so it didn't work. On the other hand, judging by the photos Chang took, the books he owned and the clippings he saved, Paul wasn't one hundred percent out of the running. Chang seemed like such a likable, whole-some guy. Maybe he was just an artist attempting to document our violent times. Sweet guy, right. On the other hand, Jeffrey Dahmer convinced a Milwaukee cop that a naked, fleeing, bleeding Cambodian youth was actually the other half of a mere, slight domestic quarrel. Ted Bundy was a genuine charmer. The Menendez kids didn't look mean enough to blow their parents to smithereens. Not every mad dog looked and acted like Charlie Manson.

Gratelli picked up the phone. Called Paul Chang. He didn't know what he would say. Maybe he would talk to him about the symbolism of engraving a flower on the inside of victims' thighs. Maybe he'd have Paul Chang keep track of Earl Falwell. Mix it up.

As Gratelli prepared to leave a message after Chang's recorded message advised of his inaccessibility, Gratelli flipped through the photos. He had pretty much avoided them before, especially the photographs of the killer's etchings which were carved high on the victims' inner thighs. It had seemed to him, even with all his years in the police force, to be a prurient thing for him to do, an invasion of privacy oddly more repulsive by the fact that all of them were dead. Except for Julia.

'I want to talk to you about the Bateman case,' Gratelli said after an impertinent beep on Chang's recorder. 'If you're willing, I need you to help. Call me if you're interested.'

All the marks looked alike and were in the same place, including Bateman's. However, there was one small difference. Julia's mark showed two small thorns on the stem of the rose. The others didn't.

What did that mean? At first it seemed that this was evidence that the two weren't connected at all. But, a moment later, it occurred to Gratelli that the added thorns might very well have meant a change in the killer's attitude. Or, merely that with Julia, the victim had, for the first time, fought back. Was it an editorial comment?

'Jesus!' he said. The other cops looked at him.

'Why don't we go somewhere.' It was David Seidman's voice on the telephone. 'Somewhere way away.'

'I just got back,' Julia said. She looked around her tiny room. So small compared to her home in Iowa.

'I've had a lot of time to think, Julia.'

'So have I.'

'I want to show you another side of me,' he said. 'Before we head out in different directions. Let's do something spontaneous. Let's go to the airport and take the very next plane out of here.'

'I don't want to travel, David. Really.'

'We won't tell anyone. No one. Not even Paul.'

'Paul would worry himself sick.'

'This isn't about Paul. It's about us.' The 'us' resonated. 'We're supposed to be together,' Seidman said. 'I know we are.'

'Not now.'

'I know what you've been through. I can protect you.'

'David . . .'

'There's nothing more to say,' he said. 'Why do you do this to me?'

'I don't want to do anything to you,' Julia said. What she had sensed before was now overt. Recognizable. 'I don't mean to. There's nothing I can say either. I'm just very tired from the trip.'

'I thought you'd want to see me.'

'Not now.'

There was dead silence on the other end.

'David?' She asked in the quiet.

She heard the disconnect.

The distinct aroma of coconut, peanut and sesame blended with other spices as Paul and Julia toasted each other. She had a brown bottle of Singha beer. Paul had the Thai iced tea.

'I missed you,' she said. 'I hate to say this, but you are the only person I missed. If I thought for one minute I could get you to Iowa City, I might not have come back.'

'I don't think so,' Paul said.

'Why?'

'We can talk about that later. But not before I tell you how much I missed you. If only you were a guy.'

'I think I'll find a way to take that as a compliment.'

Neither of them had spoken of the attack. Not at the airport or on the ride home. Not on the long walk from her Hayes Street apartment to the restaurant on Folsom. He didn't want to spoil her mood; but the longer he waited the more difficult it would be. Eventually the subject would become taboo. That wouldn't be good, either.

'You remember Inspector Gratelli?' She looked puzzled. 'Dark, hairy, sad-looking guy with big hands,' he said to jog her memory. There was an awkward moment. 'We don't have to . . .'

'I remember. Vaguely. I don't remember much of it. Not much before, nothing during and not much after until Iowa. But yes, I can picture him.'

'He's sort of still on the case.' He waited for some sign of approval, an OK to go on. He didn't get it. Paul continued anyway. 'I'm helping. Just thought you ought to know.'

'Help him do what.'

'Find out.'

'Find out what?' She recognized she was being coy. 'I'm sorry.

Please don't. No need. Look, Paul. I'm going to need you as a friend, not as a vigilante. I don't want you obsessed with this. You'll draw me into it. I don't want in. And . . . anyway . . . we have our own work, don't we?'

'You don't care.'

'I do care, Paul. I want to kill him. I could do grotesque things to him. I want to inflict pain . . . torture him. But I'm not going to chase my tail. If the police had anything, they would have called me. I can't keep looking back. I don't want you living back there either.'

She held out her bottle of Thai beer for a toast. 'To the future,' she said.

TWENTY-TWO

The call came at one a.m. Earl had been asleep, but not for long and not deeply. It had to be a wrong number or the guy from the other night, Earl thought as he swung his legs over the edge of the bed. What few people he knew wouldn't call him at all probably, except Grandma O. No one, including her, would call at midnight unless it was seriously bad news. He could find the phone in the darkness. This wouldn't be good, he thought.

'Hello,' he said hesitantly.

'Earl?'

Earl was pretty sure it was the guy, but not one hundred percent sure. It could be a doctor or someone.

'Who is this?'

'Now, Earl you have to listen for awhile. I'm not trying to hurt you. I'm not going to turn you in. I just want to tell you what I know and warn you.'

'Warn me?' Earl said reflexively.

'I'll get to that Earl. Will you listen to me?'

'Don't talk too long,' Earl said. He knew that didn't make much sense, but he was unsure of what he should do.

'I won't Earl. I'm on your side. Listen. Don't hang up. I know about the girls. The ones you strangled. You didn't really want to do it, did you?'

'Fuck,' Earl said. This was pretty lame. Social worker language. He'd heard it before. Here he was afraid of this wimp. 'Get on with it fuckhead.' Earl felt tough again.

'Come on, Earl. You didn't want to at first, did you?'

'I ain't sayin' I did nothing. You keep talking and I'll hang up when I get bored with this shit. OK?'

'OK, Earl.' Now the voice got harder. 'So you are a tough guy now. What are you going to do about the witness?'

'What witness?' Earl asked. He'd said it before he thought.

'The witness. The one on the hill. Sutro, you know? You, your Camaro and that girl? The naked girl?'

'So why haven't the cops arrested me if they got somebody so sure I done it?'

'Because she was scared. Now she isn't. You're not off the hook, you know that. The cops have talked to you, right?'

'Who says you're not a cop?'

'I wouldn't be giving you a chance to eliminate the only thing in this world that can convict you. When she's gone, you're home free.'

'So, who is she?'

'I'll tell you when it's time.'

'Don't jerk me around. Why do we have to wait?'

'Because I want it done right, when the time is right, when we're sure no one is watching you. I'll let you go now.'

'Who's watching me?'

'I don't know if anybody is, Earl. You are a suspect. We both know you are. We just have to make sure the time is right.'

'I didn't say I did anything, you know?'

'Right Earl. I know.'

'Listen . . .'

'What?' the voice asked, sympathetically.

'I don't know.'

'You want to talk for awhile?'

'No. No I don't.'

'I understand these things. I really do.'

'Bullshit,' Earl said, but not with much authority.

'You feel OK?'

'I fuckin' feel fine,' Earl said belligerently. He hung up the phone. What made him angry was that the guy didn't really want to know if he was all right. He was just digging in, trying to control him. The caller, in all his anonymity and his knowledge had the power. Earl slipped on a pair of jeans and a pair of Nikes, not bothering to lace them up. Why is it somebody else always had the power?

He went to the door.

Gratelli looked at the clock – 1:10 a.m. He wondered why he was awake. Then he remembered the dream. It was Mickey. The dream was a replay. Gratelli walked into the bathroom, and there was Mickey crawling out of the tub. The side of his head had been blown off. His white shirt was soaked scarlet. He cursed in much the same manner as he had when his bowl of noodles were cold or the traffic was snarled.

'Fuck, can't I do anything right?'

'Damn,' Gratelli said. Was there more to it? If there was, Gratelli didn't want to know. It was clear to Gratelli that he'd been bothered by McClellan's death more than he cared to admit. He'd been slacking, too. Coasting. All he really had to do these days, besides a few court appearances on previous busts, was Bateman. And he wasn't sure where to go with what little he knew.

He rarely let things get to him. Something was getting to him now. It was some damned combination of Bateman and McClellan.

Once he got a new partner, Gratelli thought, the cases would begin to flow. He'd be back in the swing. Things would return to normal.

Paul had eventually given up on the tea and had three – or was it four – Singhas. A positive belief in the future – as required by their initial toast – needed a little reinforcement. It wasn't clear that either was convinced.

He'd walked Julia back to her place, arriving there by ten, going immediately to this address on Stanyan. He had a photo of Earl Falwell, the person who lived there. The likeness showed pockmarks and dull eyes on an otherwise average Caucasian face. This was probably the ugliest picture of the kid ever taken. There was no such thing as a looker on a mug shot – unless you use your imagination.

The stake out on Falwell held little promise, Gratelli told him. It was true the killings had stopped while Earl Falwell was incarcerated. But it was also true Earl Falwell had been out long enough to renew his efforts if he were the one. Maybe the killer had long since moved to some other part of the country or the world and continued his nasty ritual where the connections wouldn't be made. Maybe the killer was dead. Killed himself. Not an improbable end to this kind of thing.

Bateman's may have been a separate crime in any event. Certainly, the occurrence in that cabin that night was different from the others, perhaps different enough to change the killer, to alter the patterns, to force him to stop or move on or completely change his procedure. Hell maybe the killer was dead.

Julia Bateman had gone to bed. Then, too restless to sleep, she got back up, put on a robe and paced. The dinner had gone well. A few beers and the restaurant took on a golden glow. The exotic smells, the mix of people, the music and chatter – all made her feel alive again. But a little anxious. By the time they were ready to leave, a light, drizzly fog moved in and they walked back.

Maybe she shouldn't have had the coffee. Maybe it was the time change. Jet lag. Whatever it was, she was on edge. She had put on some music. Every CD she tried irritated her. Too fast. Too slow. Too romantic. Too cold. She picked up a thick Margaret Atwood paperback; but it proved too complex for a mind that seemed to flit around like a butterfly. She shut out light. Maybe she could sleep now.

The steam radiators had caught up with the chill. Now she felt hot. The room seemed stuffy. No air conditioning. She went to the windows, pulled the lever down and pushed out, her body leaning out over the fire escape. She caught the cold breath of a summer night in the city. She caught movement across narrow Ivy Street – an indistinct figure in the window. It took a moment to realize what he was doing there. What had been discomfort now had a dark, eerie edge. She recognized the symptoms of panic creeping into her mind. She took a deep breath. She shut the window, pulled the shade down.

She picked up the phone and dialed Paul.

'Thanks for calling,' came the response. 'I am not available at the moment. If you'll leave your name and number and a brief message, I'll return the call as quickly as I can.'

'Paul,' she said in the loudest whisper. Then, realizing it was a little foolish, she spoke in a nearly normal voice. 'Paul, pick it up. Please.'

She repeated herself, waited. Nothing. She thought about going down the hall. She had a key. No. She was over-reacting. She thought about calling the police. No, no. She wasn't ready for an all-nighter and the questions.

It wasn't the killer. He wasn't in the window for her. Was he? Then who? He was in the window before she got there. He couldn't have known she was going to open the window. Had he even noticed?

Julia went to the kitchen, found a bottle of white rum and discovered the half-empty bottle of tonic water in the fridge. It was several months old. It had to be flat. She'd try to settle her nerves. First day back and it felt like the day had gone on for weeks.

Julia went to the window again, peeked from the side of the shade. He was still there. She didn't want to be alone. She didn't want to go out into the night. The alcohol hit her stomach like peroxide on an open cut. Had she made a mistake by coming back?

Iowa wasn't the answer. But was coming here a solution? She didn't know. She didn't have answers. She wasn't sure she understood the questions. And all of that frightened her almost as much as the peeping Tom.

Earl went out his door, crept from the rear of the three-story Victorian, down the narrow walkway between the houses, toward Stanyan. He didn't venture far enough to be seen in the hazy glow of the street lamps. No life on the street that he could see. He scanned the row of parked cars. The drizzle had coated most of the windows so it was difficult to tell if there was an occupant in any of them. He watched for some sign of movement.

He was familiar with most of the cars – a couple of them he had thought about hot wiring and just taking off. Maybe for San Antonio or Atlanta. Some place totally new. Away from the cops and the phone calls.

There was a tan Toyota he hadn't recalled seeing before. And there was a VW bug. The windows were fogged. Either someone had just parked it or someone was in it.

Just as he focused in on what would be the driver's window, a hand swiped across it. It startled Earl. His body lurched involuntarily. Someone was watching. Could be a couple making out or talking after a date, Earl thought. Could be someone was watching him. Could be the guy who was calling him now. A guy with a cell phone.

Anyone who had staked out Earl's place would know any movement would have to be on Stanyan. No way to watch from the rear. And it would be difficult for anyone leaving from the back to go anywhere but the front to leave. No alleys. No paths in the back.

The late night drizzle coated Earl's flesh. His fear turned to anger. Then, like some sort of electrical charge, he became confident. If someone were stalking him, he'd turn the tables. It was as if his brain was lit. He had a feeling similar to the one he had with his young victims. Heartbeat increased, brain cleared, sharp. The excitement was also sexual as it had become for that guy in the Panhandle. This was even better. Earl Falwell had reached some sort of new level.

This was exciting. Danger. A contest. Putting his own life on the line. The scared killer who preyed on weak, unsuspecting young girls was history.

Paul's cat investigated the newly cleaned window, crawling on Paul's lap, moving up on his shoulder. Paul swiped at the window again. He thought he saw something move near the house he was watching. It was taller than the ferns that seemed to wall the space between the buildings.

'I did a really stupid thing,' Paul said to his cat. He wished the mark he'd made on the window would fog up quickly. He blew on the space that had been cleared.

'Christ, Chat, what do I do, someone's coming over here,' Paul said, knowing full well the cat would do nothing to protect him. 'Why couldn't you be a Rottweiler or something? Look at that?'

Earl's body caught the soft light of the street lamp. He had a body that would have served Calvin Klein well. A body that bore firm muscles, narrowing down to a flat chiseled belly. As it crossed the street and came closer, the commercially porno-graphic image bore the face of Earl Falwell, more handsome, more frightening than his picture.

Rather than race away and blow any cover he might have, Paul decided to stay and talk his way out of it. Checking on his girlfriend, that was it. Wondering why she wasn't home. Admit to a little jealousy. He rolled the window down.

'Hi,' Earl said.

'Hello, what's up?' Paul said.

'That's what I was gonna ask,' Earl said.

'Just waiting here,' Paul said, hoping the nervousness he felt wasn't apparent in his voice.

'For what?'

'It's kinda personal.'

'Yeah,' Earl nodded. 'I think maybe it is kinda personal because somebody tells me on the phone that somebody is minding my business. Like scoping me out, you know?'

'Well rest easy . . .' Paul said, pausing. He'd almost said 'Earl.' He continued. 'Rest easy, guy. I'm waiting for my girl to come home. I think she's seeing someone else. Just playing private eye, you know?'

'Funny, I get a call saying I might be watched and I come out here and sure enough someone's parked out here.'

'I don't know anything about that,' Paul said. He wondered who'd be calling Earl. 'Why do you think they'd say that?'

'I don't know. What's her name? Your girl?'

'Trish,' Paul said. He wasn't sure where he got the name. He never felt more white.

'She lives around here, you say?'

'Yeah.' He wanted to change the subject before he got trapped. 'You're going to catch cold.' Paul nodded toward Earl's drizzle coated torso.

'You could too. Why don't you come over to my place.'

'What?' Paul was confused by the friendly attitude.

'Couple of lonely guys, huh?'

Was it that obvious? Paul asked himself. 'Just thought you were getting pretty wet out there. And cold. I'm fine. I really want to know who comes back with Trish. If it's a girlfriend, hell, who cares? But if she's seeing some other guy . . .'

'Yeah?' Falwell said, challenging Paul's statement. 'I like your sweatshirt.'

Paul Chang looked down. The shirt read: 'Boys will do boys.' Christ, Chang thought. His stomach pitched. He was so used to being gay, he gave no thought to what he put on for the evening.

'My place is just over there,' Falwell said. He reached in,

put his hand on Paul's shoulder. 'We can talk about your girl.'
Falwell smiled.

'Uhhh . . .' God, Paul thought. Was he actually thinking about
doing it? About going with Earl? He'd played rough before.
He'd taken some chances. The guy was coming on to him. 'No,
I don't think so. Not tonight.'

'What have you got to lose?'

Paul tried to disconnect his brain from his penis. It was
difficult because there was a legitimate intellectual process going
on. Well, one legitimate, one quasi-legitimate. One was the
intimacy of strangers which was both an emotional need and
an artistic pursuit. The other was his task to learn more about
Earl Falwell. How better to find out about him than spend some
time with him in his own environs. Paul had already blown his
cover.

'Don't think so,' Paul said, not quite losing the battle with
his brain. Earl was bigger, tougher. What would happen to . . .

From Paul's belt came the electronic beeps.

'What's that?' Earl asked.

'My beeper,' Paul said, pulling it out. Looking at the number.
It was Julia's. 'Listen, I've got to go.'

'You can use my phone,' Earl said, his fingers tightening on
Paul's shoulder.

Paul turned the ignition key. The engine engaged. 'I gotta
go. It's an emergency.'

'Just a few minutes,' Earl said. His fingers clamped around
the back of Paul's neck, the other on the steering wheel.

'Gotta go,' Paul said, turning the wheel and accelerating,
wrenching himself and the car free, spinning Earl's body down
on the wet pavement. As Paul drove from Stanyan to Haight
and up Haight Street, Paul wondered who it was telling Earl
Falwell he was being watched. Nobody knew about it except
for Inspector Gratelli – and the inspector didn't seem likely to
broadcast it.

'I wonder if I would have died tonight,' Paul said to his
cat. Whatever Earl did tonight or seemed likely to do, it didn't
necessarily connect him to the dead girls or to Julia Bateman.

TWENTY-THREE

The phone was ringing when Earl got back inside.

'What?' he answered.

'Where were you?'

'Talking to the guy you sent over,' Earl said.

'Someone I sent over?' the voice replied.

'Fuck, you did. Don't deny it.'

'Earl, I didn't.'

'Chinese guy. A fag.'

'Earl, listen. Don't go crazy on me. I'm on your side. You do what you do because you have to. I understand it. It's what you need. Like air or water. The world's a tough place. You've got to survive. I know that. Everybody does what they have to do. I could go on for hours about all the stuff that people do to each other – all legal. Killers. Make things that get people addicted and kill them. And society thinks you're bad. It's what you get by with. That's all that counts.' There was a pause, then the caller continued: 'You didn't have it easy did you?' Another long pause. 'Who cared about you?' Nothing. 'Tell me.' There was more silence. 'Earl?'

'What?'

'Who cared about you?'

'I don't know what the fuck you're talking about.'

'Who gives a shit about how you feel? Who understands how lonely you are? Who in the hell ever talked to you like you were a human being? Like you were a decent guy? Who ever held you, loved you, wanted to protect you? Who calmed you after your nightmares? Who cares about whether you live or die? That's what I'm talking about.'

Earl thought about Grandma O. She was separate. He never talked about her to anyone. If he did, it would spoil it.

'No one, I guess,' Earl said.

'See, that's the point. The only one who cares about you is you. You have to protect yourself.'

'Yeah? From who? You?'

'No, Earl. I'm trying to help, remember? From this woman

who saw you on the hill, above Haight, remember? She can identify you. She can identify your car.'

'I'm tired,' Earl said.

'Go to bed, Earl. Get some sleep. I'll let you rest, OK?'

'OK. Thanks.'

'You're welcome, Earl. We'll talk later.'

'I just don't know,' she said to Paul after explaining what had happened. 'Since I've been back, everything seems dark, more desperate. A nightmare. For a moment I thought that this guy up there in the window was him. Why not? It could have been. It's like I'm waiting for the moment when he returns or when some other monster comes out of the dark.'

'I know.'

'I panicked. But I'm afraid I'm going to go from one panic to another. I'm scared. I'm scared of being scared.'

'Don't apologize, Jules.'

'I'm sorry,' she said. 'I normally take these things in stride. Now I feel sorry for the poor pervert across the alley. Just lonely and screwed up.'

For a moment she looked as lost and forlorn as she had in the hospital. As she did then, Julia Bateman stared down at her hands.

'Don't leave me here alone,' Paul said to her, remembering how she'd been at the hospital – staring at her hands and lost. 'You just got here. I need you.'

'It's all just too strange, Paul.'

'That it is, dear girl,' he said putting on an Irish brogue. 'But Father O'Chang is here for ya, lass.'

'That's good to know. What part of your life did I screw up by beeping you?'

'Neither of us will ever know.'

He wasn't about to tell her.

'You want me to stay the night?' he asked.

'No. But go lock the window, will you. I really don't want to see him.'

'You could come stay with me. I've got one of those things people take along on camping trips . . .'

'Those things with the zippers?'

'Those very things.'

'I don't know what you call them.'

'I can't think of it either,' Paul said. 'But I've been trying to find an excuse to sleep in it. What's his name left it.'

'What's his name left the whatchamacallit?'

'Right.'

'Bradley,' she said.

'Yeah, him.'

'You miss him?'

'I don't know. I kept thinking life was going to be like the Brady Bunch.'

'How was that supposed to happen?' Julia asked.

'I don't know, exactly. We could get some puppies and name them Greg and Peter and Bob and . . .'

'And Marsha and . . .' she said.

'I forget the girls,' he said.

'Go home.' She took a deep breath. 'I can handle it. Some milk and cookies and Hawaiian music and I'll drift off to Paradise.'

'Bye toots,' Paul said, kissing her on the forehead. 'I'm a phone call away and I won't be going out anymore tonight. I'll just pack up some of Bradley's depressing artwork and his strange diaries.'

Morning streamed in through the side window. Only the general, dispersed light nagged Julia from sleep. It was quiet. Strangely normal. For a few moments she had forgotten the months in Iowa, the trip back and the tiny attacks of panic gaining a hold for the final, sorry disturbance across the alley.

A car door slammed down on Ivy Street. She slipped out of bed, went to the little white tiled mosaic bathroom. She checked out the fact of her existence by looking at the mirror.

Yes, it was one Julia Bateman, not too much the worse for last night. Actually not too much worse for the last year or so. The body the attacker left her – broken and bruised – was almost back to normal. The broken nose showed only the slightest bump now. She smiled to show herself her teeth. The new dental work was good. Though they weren't all real, she might have a slightly better smile. She had aged faster than the calendar. A kind of five years for one toll, she now felt better about exchanging for the gift of life.

Actually, in some ways, with the jogging and exercise in Iowa City, she was probably in better shape than before. She was certainly trimmer.

'Get on with it,' she said to her image, applying that to both the day and the rest of her life. Funny, after all these months, the scent of the spilled perfume still lingered.

The phone rang. It was Inspector Gratelli.

Apparently she wouldn't be getting on with it without dragging a bit of the past along behind her.

'I'm sorry to be bringing this up again,' Gratelli said, settling on the small chair opposite the one by the desk where she sat. He had quite a day ahead of him. This interview, then a quick drive up to Petaluma for the viewing. McClellan's widow had asked him to come. Had asked him to speak at the funeral later the same day. He would rather have faced a firing squad. But he agreed. 'It's important.'

'That's all right,' she said, thinking perhaps she had been a little too curt.

'Are you OK now?'

'Yes, I am. I'm pretty sure.'

'You've just gotten back, I know. Are you sure you want to talk about this now?'

'It's fine, really.' It wasn't fine. She just wanted to get on with it. With all that had gone on yesterday and last night and a rough sleep, Julia was on edge. On top of that she had fed her jangled nerves three cups of coffee in the half-hour between the inspector's call and his arrival.

'Have you thought about this at all?' Gratelli asked.

'Yes . . . but I'm not really sure what you mean.' She stood. 'Can I get you some coffee?'

'Sure,' Gratelli said. 'But what you need is a shot of bourbon.'

She laughed. 'I know. I know.' She sat back down. 'You want to know if I can remember anything more than I did when we last met.'

'Right.'

'No. I don't remember anything. Nothing solid anyway. Coffee?'

'Sure.'

'Cream? Sugar?'

'I'm not particular Miss Bateman.'

'I have both.'

'I'm sorry,' Gratelli said. 'I take my coffee black. What I meant was I wasn't particular about your memories being solid or not.'

'It's vague.'

'What?'

'It's crazy,' she said.

'Good.'

'Butter.'

'Butter?'

'Butter. The smell of it. Makes me nauseous. I don't know why. Well, I'm not sure I know why, except that I associate it with what went on that night.'

'I don't mean to be indelicate,' Gratelli said. 'Did he use it in some way? On his body perhaps?'

'I don't know. I don't think so. I just don't remember feeling it. I remember smelling it.'

'Was it like coconut butter?'

'I don't think so. No.'

'I remember smelling butter and . . . leather.' She felt nauseous, just recalling the scent.

Gratelli squirmed in his narrow seat. He seemed like a Frankenstein trying to sit in a child's chair.

'Leather,' he said as if trying to lodge it in his memory. 'Was he wearing leather, you think?'

'I don't know. I remember seeing a dark form, something covering the face, but only for a split second. The light was shining at me, directly. Then it swirled. And he hit me with it, I guess.'

'I've read the reports over and over. Nothing. I would think . . . though I can't be sure . . . that there would have been some mention of butter or an oily presence on you. There wasn't.'

'Did you find anything other than blood?'

'No. Nothing. Unreasonably so. Your blood, your hair . . .' He shook his head in disgust. 'Enough of that. Did you have a sense of size, height or weight?'

'What I said. I remember. Average. It was. Average.'

'Fat, muscle? What?'

'I don't know. Solid, I suppose.'

'The butter,' Gratelli said, his face showing a switch in his thoughts. 'Could it have been on his breath?'

'Yes, perhaps. Maybe. I don't know.'

'Cologne?'

'Yes,' she shrugged, then smiled. 'Perhaps, maybe. Then

again, it could have been my body reacting to the shock. With the medicine I took, sometimes food tasted metallic. Maybe I was smelling myself.'

The phone rang.

'Bateman Investigations,' she said, beginning the one-sided conversation Gratelli easily overheard. 'Oh hi.' (Pause) Thanks, but I'm afraid I can't. (Pause) I'm going out of town. (Pause) I know I just got into town. It's not Iowa City. Going to check on the cabin. (Pause) I know. I know. (Pause) I appreciate that. Thank you.' She put the phone back down on the desk. She looked at Gratelli whose interest was now obvious. 'I know. But I need to do this.'

The phone call over, she took their cups to the little kitch-enette and refilled.

'Are you done with the cabin?' she asked Gratelli when she returned.

'What do you mean?' Gratelli was also curious about the phone call. Who was she telling about a trip to the cabin? Whoever it was must have been angry because the caller had not given Julia a chance to say 'goodbye,' or Julia was angry because she didn't say 'goodbye.'

'Can it be disturbed? Evidence or something?' she asked. 'Paul said he went up there after – I guess it's been awhile – and it was still roped off, taped off, I think he said.'

'Should be OK now.' Gratelli looked puzzled. 'Are you going up there?'

'Yes,' she nodded but seemed to be thinking of something else. Then she focused again on Gratelli's presence. 'Just some things to wrap up. Papers, cleaning. Get it ready to sell. Despite what you may think, I don't want to live there.'

'You could have someone else do it.'

'I don't want it haunting me.'

'I could go up with you,' Gratelli said.

'No, that's all right.' She knew she was being stubborn. But it wouldn't help if she couldn't face life on her own terms, without her father, without Paul even and certainly without the police.

'We could talk on the way,' Gratelli said.

The two of them talked for another forty-five minutes. Gratelli picked up nothing else that was helpful, not even permission to go up to the River with her.

* * *

Earl's day at the dock wasn't going well. He'd gotten in late and suffered a barrage of remarks from his supervisor. When he buried himself in his work, his fellow dockhands thought he was trying to show them up.

'You're moving too fast Falwell,' said a pot-bellied redhead.

Earl said nothing, but slowed down some. He was trying to get some thoughts out of his head. For a while, after getting out, Earl was able to work hard, come home tired and forget. Forget the girls, forget the guy on the telephone and the fucking woman who could I.D. him and his Camaro, forget Cobra, forget that kid he killed on the back steps of the apartment building. But last night stirred things up again. Not just the phone call. There was the Chinese guy spying on him and Earl spying on the Chinese guy. The possibilities. What would have happened? What did Earl want to happen?

The pattern Earl had before getting locked up and screwed over was part of then, not of now. What was now? He didn't fucking know.

'What's it gonna take to slow you down, fuck up?' asked the redhead, his face in Earl's.

A couple of others came toward the two of them.

'I don't want any trouble,' Falwell said. 'I just want to do my work and when it's time to go home, go home. So leave me alone.'

'You keep working at that pace, you might have an accident,' the redhead said.

'You are an accident, you fat ass. Beat it.'

This wasn't the first time they'd been rude to him. But it was the first time he'd been rude to one of them.

The redhead was in his face. Earl couldn't understand what the guy was saying after the first few obscenities. What the redhead was doing was sweating and spitting. His mouth became an ugly gaping hole and his tongue just a wiggling piece of red flesh. The guy's breath smelled like garbage. It was like the gaping garbage mouth was going to eat him.

Earl punched him. Seemed like he punched him before he even thought about punching him. The guy's face spurted blood. The face didn't go away and Earl punched it again. He didn't know how many times he punched the face. Suddenly he was being pulled backward by tentacles curling around his body, tightly around his arms and his neck and his waist, tugging at him, pulling him away.

It didn't matter what the weather was in San Francisco. More than likely, a few miles north or south, the sun would be shining and all those who believed California was the land of golden light generally had their preconceptions reinforced.

The light came in with some force, through the blues, yellows and reds of the stained glass window. It was a small church. McClellan's body was not there. His family was. Beth and her two college-aged kids, a blond boy and a blonde girl – the ones whose photos were in McClellan's wallet that night – sat in the front pew.

There were others in attendance. Aside from the dozen members of Homicide and the lieutenant, there were maybe a dozen more. Gratelli guessed them to be family.

It was Gratelli's time to speak. He hadn't wanted to, but Beth had indicated if he didn't, no one would. And it was important, she said, that someone say something.

'Despite the raunchy, hateful words he had for the general population and every single adult member in it, he held out hope for the young, the very young. He was able to see the last glimmer of innocence in the eyes of children. That was enough to keep him going. He thought perhaps this one or that one would make it. Maybe this one or that one wouldn't be corrupted by greed or stupidity or fear. For all his pessimism, he still held out hope that the world would be what it was supposed to be. He ran out of hope.

'Mickey McClellan is dead. He wasn't as tough as you thought he was, as he tried to be. The world didn't turn out right and he lost all hope that it ever would.

'I wish I could tell you otherwise.'

Gratelli sat down. The minister stood, went to the front of the congregation.

Gratelli heard only the first few words before he tuned out. 'We must all have hope, Inspector . . .'

TWENTY-FOUR

The building wasn't remarkable. Big, brick and slightly down from the peak of Nob Hill. It had been a men's club. Still was for the most part, though now you could see women scattered about at the tables. If you looked more closely, the older men still sat together, accepting the inevitable women members but not in the depths of their old-family, old-moneyed hearts.

The interior was quality but had never been trendy. Because both Thaddeus Maldeaux and David Seidman were far from first generation members, they seemed oblivious to the power around them and uninterested in the menu open before them.

'We didn't do anything, David.'

'She fell for you,' Seidman said.

'No. Not really.'

'You have that way about you, Teddy.'

'What way.'

'Getting what you want.'

'I don't want Julia.'

A young black man in a white jacket filled their water glasses.

'I'm a smart guy,' Seidman said. 'Reasonably bright, I mean.'

'More than reasonably. Look at you. Look at your record in court. Look at your political standing. You're going to be mayor, I'm sure. Then maybe governor or senator. If we can get you out of those little tanning booths, the sky's the limit. Maybe president.'

Seidman wasn't smiling.

'If you're going to get cancer, you might as well get it right on the beach. As you know San Franciscans aren't too keen on guys with tans.'

There was another long, dark, brooding silence.

'I'm not seeing her, David,' Maldeaux said sternly. 'Get that through your little obsessed brain.'

'I know. I'm over it. Day by day it's easier. I'm not even angry with you. But you pointed out to me . . . oh nothing. It's so strange, you and me. It's like you skip through life. Wherever you go, the rain falls on the other side of the street. Somehow, somehow I'm always struggling to keep up.'

Both went silent as the waiter came, took their order.

'Police have any leads on this strangler?' Maldeaux said after the gentleman left and in a tone that indicated he wanted to change the subject.

'He's not a strangler,' Seidman said. 'He breaks their necks.'

'The paper says . . .'

'Homicide doesn't want to correct the general impression. We've gotten a dozen confessions. Only the killer knows how it was really done.'

'Oh. No leads, though?'

David sighed. He seemed uninterested. 'No more deaths.'

'You were saying something about a Jerry Falwell?'

'No, no. Not Jerry. Earl, I think.' Seidman shook his head, trying to dispel something from his brain. 'Doubt it. Boy just came through again. Just like last time, he got in a fight, pounded some guy's face until it looked like raw meat. Homicide still gets an alert – as do we – when he comes through the system.'

'Nothing to tie him with . . .'

'Probably no connection. Listen, I'm sorry for all that whining.'

'I'm a friend, right? That's what it's about.'

'Of course. When I get hold of something, it's hard to let go.'

'I know,' Maldeaux said. 'You don't like to lose. That's why you do, my all too serious friend.'

The salad came.

'We'll talk about something a little lighter, what do you say?' Seidman said.

'The fellow across the way won't be bothering you,' Paul Chang told Julia Bateman.

'What? What do you mean?' There was a stack of old invoices, checks and checking account statements in front of her.

'I talked to him,' Paul said, thumbing through an old copy of *Newsweek* magazine.

'You did? Why? I mean, what a strange thing to do.'

'Is it?'

'No,' she said. 'I guess not.'

'He's terrified you'll report him. He's had a brush or two with the police.'

'Then he should stop, shouldn't he?'

'He knows it. He's tried to stop. He's seen five therapists.' Paul flicked through a few pages, saw the story on the killings. He checked the date. The magazine was three months old. 'He can't help it. Actually, he didn't know you were home.'

'He keeps track of that?' Julia asked sharply.

'Said he's careful not to stand by the window when someone can see him.'

'I thought that was the point.'

'Not for you to see him. He knew you'd been gone. Didn't know you were back.'

'Why does he do it in the window then? He wants someone to see him?'

'Yes. Apparently Mrs Clark in the apartment right below you not only likes our friend to do it, she does it for our friend. Mutual.'

Julia couldn't help but laugh. 'God, why don't they just do it together?'

'Spoil everything. Take all the fun out of it. It's just how life works sometimes. I sort of understand it.'

'You would,' she said. 'You find that all pretty interesting, don't you?'

'Yes. The world is willing to talk about everything in their lives. Really, think about it. Go into detail. But not sex. That's why the twists and perversions. It's the taboo that forces people to hide their little private fetishes, where they have a chance to fester. No one wants to talk about it.'

'I'm putting the cabin on the market.'

'Good.'

'I figure it'll take a few days to get it ready, get it listed. All that stuff.'

'You can have somebody do that, you know?'

'Not all of it. I have stuff there.'

'We'll go up some afternoon,' Paul said.

'I'm going up this weekend.'

'I'll go with you.'

'No. Stay here. What have we got that's active? Anything?'

'We can still bill for Baskins. I completed the stake out – with a little help from some friends. Apparently his injuries are for real. We've got an appointment with Mr Harvey on another injury case. And three autos we're to locate. I've been working on them. Listen, let me come up with you. It's exciting up at the River this time of year.' He grinned. 'And I'm a free man.'

'Free or not. I want to go up. I want to face it. I need to.'

'You can stay at a hotel or a bed and breakfast up there.'

'No, I need to stay there,' Julia said.

'One moment you're Zazu Pitts and the next you're Sylvester Stallone. What happens if Sylvester becomes Zazu in the middle of the night and you're up there all by your lonesome?'

'I don't know much about these things,' Gratelli told the clerk at the men's fragrance counter at Macy's.

'What's there to know?' said a blond youth cheerfully. 'Find one you like.'

'You have Old Spice?' Gratelli asked the clerk, whose answer was a 'you know better than that' glance. 'I didn't think so. Listen, I'm trying to find a cologne or after shave that smells like butter.'

'Butter?' the clerk asked.

'Yeah, butter.'

The clerk looked as if he'd been offered a dish of onion ice cream.

'No.'

'Subtle kind of thing,' Gratelli said.

'The butter, you mean?'

'Yeah.'

'Is it that you want something that smells like butter?'

'Yeah, I'm trying to get a date with Mrs Butterworth.'

'OK,' the clerk said. 'You've smelled it yourself, this scent?'

'No. Someone described a smell, a scent whatever you call it. And it was something like butter.'

'And it's a cologne.'

'I don't know,' Gratelli said.

'Could be suntan oil, maybe?'

'Maybe. How much you know about this stuff?' Gratelli said, waving his arm over the dozens of bottles on the counter top.

'I know the brands, but I'm not a perfumer.'

'Oh? I hadn't thought of that.'

'You're pretty serious, aren't you?'

'Yes.'

'Let me make a call for you.'

Gratelli hadn't spent much time thinking about Earl Falwell. Neither had the nearly defunct task force. But the system was still in place. They had been notified of Earl's assault arrest and had forwarded a copy in an envelope to 'Inspectors McClellan and Gratelli.'

Gratelli, noting how much impact McClellan's death had upon others, wasn't all that interested in Falwell; but he thought that maybe it was worth checking some things. Search the apartment again, for example. Maybe because of the suddenness of his arrest and the length of time since he had been a suspect – not to mention the halt in the killings – the apartment might reveal something it hadn't earlier. Gratelli had no problem getting a new warrant to search Earl Falwell's apartment. And he coaxed Barnaby Richardson from Narcotics to help him search. Richardson could find a flea in the desert.

Very little, if anything, had changed in Earl Falwell's apartment in the back of a Victorian home on Stanyan. Gratelli stood there for a moment, having his Xerox copy of the view he had earlier. The other cop was already into the search.

Physically Barnaby Richardson was an unlikely officer of the law. The small physique, elfin face and mental agility, however, made him an excellent undercover agent and his ability to ferret out hiding places had no match.

'A cave dweller, hmm?' Richardson said, shortly after entering the dark interior. The narcotics cop went immediately to the shelf holding the CDs. 'A trophy hunt, is it?' he asked, referring to the usual practice of a serial killer which was to keep something that belonged to the victim.

'Whatever,' Gratelli said. 'It's been a long time since the last kill – that we know of. We found no trophies the first time we searched. Maybe you'll have more luck.'

Richardson didn't seem to be too interested in which CDs Earl collected. Richardson was more interested in what was inside. Wearing latex gloves, he went through each one, putting each one back, very carefully. When he was done he made sure they were all neatly aligned.

'You notice anything, Gratelli?'

'The place is dark. Not much here to reveal what kind of person he is – other than he's nocturnal.'

'He's neat,' Richardson said. 'Very neat. Here's a kid you say isn't too bright, leaves no clues at the scene.'

'Maybe it's neatness, not brightness.'

'Sure. Also means he's careful.'

Gratelli covered the more traditional hiding places, checking out walls and floors in the closet, up and underneath the drawers in the bureau, heating ducts, under the carpet. He checked the bathroom tiles. Using Richardson as a model, Gratelli was careful to put each item back where it had been found.

'Well, what have we here?' Richardson said from the kitchen. He emerged with photographs.

Gratelli's countenance brightened. 'Photos?'

Richardson's face held less promise. 'Interesting, but not what you'd hope. Even so . . .'

Gratelli looked. Polaroids, not of the victims, but of Earl Falwell himself. Oiled and naked. 'Not a hair on his body,' Gratelli said, flipping through the photos showing Earl in various poses.

'I don't know if that's being neat or just kinky,' Richardson said.

'This puts a whole new light on things,' Gratelli said, more to himself than to Richardson.

'That would explain no pubic hair left at the scene,' Richardson volunteered. 'But that's about all.'

'A freshly bathed body, free of body hair, a little oil to keep the body tissue from scaling, a hood over his head . . .' Gratelli's voice trailed off into thought. What traces would the killer leave behind?

'You see a hood?' Barnaby asked.

The kid not only had a fairly substantial vacuum cleaner for his small, one room apartment, but an abnormally large number of specialized cleaning products for kitchen and bath – items that Gratelli and McClellan had overlooked or at least gave no importance to during the first search.

The bag of the vacuum cleaner had been emptied recently.

Gratelli and Richardson spent hours in the small apartment, but found nothing other than the Polaroids that were incriminating – and those weren't anything on which to base an arrest. It wasn't illegal to take a picture of yourself or to shave your body.

However, it did give Gratelli reason to heighten his interest in Falwell. He would interrogate him again tomorrow.

On the drive back to the Hall of Justice, the image of Falwell's oiled flesh danced back to Julia Bateman's comments about smelling butter and leather.

He had foolishly not paid attention to the various lotions in Falwell's bathroom and linen closet. He had seen Johnson's Baby Oil. There was tanning lotion. Was there butter in the refrigerator? Where would there be a smell of leather?

For a moment, Gratelli's mind flashed back to the leather chaps in Paul Chang's apartment. He dismissed it.

Perhaps after the interrogation tomorrow, he would go back to Earl's apartment and check out these little details himself.

TWENTY-FIVE

'How did he get out?' Gratelli spoke into the telephone. 'Oh, who bailed him?' There was a pause. 'Find out.' Gratelli wanted to talk with Earl Falwell, wanted to take one more shot. McClellan had done the interview before. He was better than Gratelli at interrogation. But maybe a different approach would mean a few different answers.

He had spent the morning testifying on an unrelated case. It was one McClellan was supposed to handle. McClellan had done the report and most of the work. Gratelli's testimony was thin, bordering on flaky. He was embarrassed and angry.

He was still thinking about Falwell. He hadn't gotten out after his first arrest. No one wanted the kid, as Gratelli remembered it. Falwell was stuck in jail for months because he didn't have the bail and, apparently, anyone willing to post it. What changed in Falwell's life? Who cared enough about him to bail him out? And bail him out so quickly. Who knew he was in?

Gratelli stood. Falwell's small, dark apartment wasn't designed for visitors. In fact there wasn't much in the way of creature comforts even for the resident creature. If you wanted off your feet, there was the bed. There were two visitors. One was a uniformed policeman, Gratelli commandeered. He wasn't about to spend a few hours alone with some guy who had a history of beating people to an inch of their lives with his bare fists.

'You remember me, right?' Gratelli asked. He held two envelopes in his hand. One large brown one. One smaller white one.

'Yeah.' Falwell said. His head was aimed down at the floor, but his eyes were on the inspector. 'You were with the fat guy at the station.'

'Earl, you could be in a lot of trouble.'

'How's that?'

'Killing people.'

'I didn't kill nobody. Beat up one guy on the highway and beat up this bastard at work. They're still walking around.'

'How'd you get out?'

'Whaddya mean?'

'Bail. Who got you out?'

'Magic, man.' Earl looked up, grinned.

'You gonna be difficult?'

'Don't wanna be. Don't know.'

'Don't know who posted bail?'

'Nope.'

'Friends. One of your friends maybe? Your boss? A relative?'

Earl kept shaking his head. 'No relatives, no friends. My boss fired my ass. Don't imagine he came through. Call him. Ask him.'

'I'm asking you.'

'I don't know.'

'Nobody you can think of? No one pops into your mind?'

'Why do you keep asking me the same question?'

'Because you're not telling me the truth.' Gratelli spoke flatly, without intonation. 'You have a good guess, don't you?' There was a long silence. 'OK,' Gratelli continued. 'I have some photos I want you to look at.'

Earl shrugged.

'Come over here,' Gratelli said, spreading the contents of the larger envelope on the bed. He fanned out the photos of eight victims. Their faces. The bodies. Close-ups of the engravings.

Falwell came over, stared for a moment, looked away.

'What do you think?' Gratelli asked.

Earl said nothing.

'C'mon, Earl. Answer me. What do you think?'

'What are you showing me that for?' Earl blushed. Deeply.

'I want you to see them. Familiar faces?'

'No.'

'You the artist?'

'No.'

Gratelli picked up one photo. 'What is it carved on this girl's thigh?'

'How do I know?'

'You don't know?'

'No.' Falwell wasn't looking at it.

'Guess,' Gratelli continued, still holding the photo up to the boy's face. 'Turn around, look at it. I said look at it.'

Falwell turned slowly. 'A flower.'

'What kind of flower, Earl?'

'I don't know.'

'What does it look like?'

'I said I don't know.'

'A common flower, isn't it?' Gratelli said. 'Tell me what it is.'

'I don't know.' Anger was building. 'I guess it could be a fuckin' tulip, couldn't it?'

'A tulip?' Gratelli was stunned. Could be a tulip. Christ, Gratelli thought. He looked at each one of the pictures. Where had he gotten the idea it was a rose? 'I have some other photos to show you, Earl. I don't want you to get upset.'

'I don't get upset,' Earl said, still excited. He was breathing heavy.

'Yeah, and I have a date with Rita Hayworth.'

'Who?'

'Never mind.' Gratelli pulled color copies of the Polaroids. 'Got another celebrity for you to look at.'

'What?' Earl grabbed the sheets of paper from the inspector. 'Where in the hell . . . you were here . . .'

Gratelli looked at the uniform cop, hoping he was staying alert. He was.

Earl was still sputtering.

'Calm down. I don't give a shit what you do. It isn't a crime. Just some questions.'

It appeared that Earl was doing all he could to keep from exploding in anger or tears.

'Sorry, Earl,' Gratelli said. 'We'll give 'em back.'

'You stole . . .'

'This is the warrant,' Gratelli said, pulling folded papers from his pocket. 'A few more hours on it, Earl. You want to see it?'

Earl shook his head. 'What difference would it make? A guy like me doesn't have any rights.'

'I do have a question though. Why do you shave your body?'

Earl no longer had the pink color of embarrassment, but the paleness of anger. He wasn't answering.

'I'm gonna go look in your bathroom,' Gratelli said. 'Stay here with the nice officer and cool down. Be thinking of an answer.'

It took awhile for the whir of thoughts to slow enough for his brain to think anything remotely rational. Earl brought himself back from the verge of cracking – of lashing out like he did at that guy in the Honda and that guy at the dock. It was close. He had caught himself just in time.

Now he felt defeated. Wounded. Near dead. What else could someone know about him that would bring him so much shame? He couldn't talk to them. They wouldn't understand. He didn't expect to be let off, but they wouldn't understand. They would never see how beautiful those girls were after he had brought them peace. They would never believe him. Hell, he didn't believe himself in the light of day. Which was right? Night or day? Which one was he, the killer when it was dark? Or the asshole sissy-ass during the day? No, if he was one thing, he was a monster. A fucking monster. Life was shit. He was worthless. What was the point of going on? What difference did it make for him to be on the inside or outside? It was all the same. Inside, it was easier, wasn't it? Didn't have to decide things. Didn't have to worry if someone was going to catch you, put you away. You were already away and only death could catch you and it didn't matter because death could catch you anywhere.

It wasn't so fuckin' bad in jail. First few weeks or so would be hell. After that he'd adapt. It would be the same, only easier. He wouldn't have to pay rent, fix food. Easier.

Maybe he should just tell them. Get it over with. That was what was intended for him, wasn't it? He wasn't smart enough to do anything good anyway. Couldn't be a success. Yeah, he was smarter than people thought. But he'd never amount to anything and nobody fuckin' cared.

Except Grandma O. She cared. She believed him. Loved him. Understood him. Yeah, Earl thought, he'd give in, give it all up after she was gone. He couldn't just go off to prison or death without seeing her first anyway. He'd have to tough it out. Christ, the effort was almost too much.

He looked at the uniformed cop. Didn't say a word. Neither did the cop. Just stood there and stared, probably laughing his ass off thinking about those pictures of Earl without any pubes, posing naked like that, oiled up and excited. Cop is thinking Earl is a retard, a perv.

'I'm a pervert,' Earl said to the cop. 'So?'

Cop didn't blink.

It was a game, Earl thought. Otherwise they'd arrest him. Now they're harassing him. Trying to get him to break. Damned if he didn't almost just let it all out. The tulip thing.

He'd have to hold on. He'd have to pretend real hard that he didn't care. Even so, he felt small. Real small.

Gratelli checked the bathroom for anything that would yield a fragrance – something buttery or leathery. He sniffed at the baby oil for fragrances, replaced its cap. There was a bottle of Hawaiian Tropic tanning oil. There was a plastic container of Vaseline Intensive Care Lotion. Gratelli had the same size and brand of lotion in his bathroom. The difference was that a bit of lotion had congealed at the spout of his own bottle. Falwell's half-empty container was spotlessly clean.

'What are you doing?' Earl asked Gratelli when he came back in the room and checked the floor of the closet.

'I'm taking these with me,' he said, carrying bottles of oils and a bar of soap.

'How am I supposed to get clean?'

'Confess,' Gratelli said, checking the floor of the closet.

'Now what are you doing?'

'Just browsing,' came the reply.

Gratelli noticed one pair of leather sandals. Open, just one broad strap over the ankle and another over the toe. Falwell was wearing an identical pair at the moment.

Was it possible that the combination of leather and butter came from some mix of oil and the sandals? Was Julia picking up on a scent that was an accidental combination?

Gratelli looked at the bottom of the sandals. Flat. Smooth.

Didn't make that much difference. Nowhere did the attacker leave footprints.

'I'm taking the sandals too. Keep the ones you've got.' Gratelli noticed that Earl looked worried. 'You have something to tell me, Earl?' Gratelli said while he was still down on his knees, face in the closet. There was no answer. Gratelli stood, went to Falwell, who seemed to have himself under control. Maybe Gratelli should have pushed when the kid was upset. McClellan would have.

'Earl. We're closing in on the killer.'

'Good,' Earl said. 'Find the bastard. Then you'll leave me the hell alone.'

'You sure, Earl?'

'String him up by the balls.'

Now it was Gratelli who was confused. Earl had said it like he meant it.

'You want that, huh?'

'You better believe it. I want him dead and buried. Probably more than you.'

Gratelli gathered up the photos from the bed, again noticing how the scar tissue engravings looked more like rosebuds than tulips. But the fact remained, none had thorns except for the artwork left on Julia Bateman.

Tulips? Roses? Maybe it made no difference at all.

TWENTY-SIX

'Can't you stay out of trouble?' asked the now familiar voice on the telephone.

'How did you know?'

'Know what?'

'The cops were here.'

'They were there? Just now?'

'Yes. You knew that. You knew just when to call,' Earl's voice was full of accusation.

'The truth is I wanted to hear the words "thank you" from your very own lips.'

Earl recognized the sarcasm in the voice. It was how a lot of people talked to him – amusing themselves at his expense.

'You got me out?'

'Yes. You don't believe me, but I've been looking out after you. I'm the only friend you have.' Earl thought of Grandma O. Didn't say anything. 'Now, there's something I need you to do and it will help both of us,' the voice continued.

'What?'

'The witness.'

'You want me to . . .'

'That's right. The way you did the others.'

'I don't . . .'

'Listen Earl, you said yourself the cops were there. They're closing in. We don't have much time. I can't keep calling. The next step is for them to bug your phone. Then if the witness makes a positive I.D. of you and your car . . . Earl . . . that's the end. That's the end of you. You can't help me. I can't help you.'

'I don't know . . .'

'Earl? She's a pretty woman. Alone. In a cabin, out in the woods at night. Earl, what are you waiting for?'

'I don't do that.' There was silence on the other end. 'I don't do that,' Earl repeated.

'I know,' the voice said. 'I'm sorry. You'd have rather not have killed them, I know. That was the only way.'

'Yes.'

'Earl?'

'What?'

'This is the only way. They will put you away. There will be a horrible trial and you will be humiliated. And people will make fun of you. You'll be sitting right there in the middle of it all. The people who don't hate you will laugh at you. No one understands you. I do. But who else? You can do it.'

'When?'

'Tonight. It has to be. Earl, are you with me?'

The caller's logic and Earl's distrust argued for dominance in Earl's brain. He still felt the humiliation of the Polaroids. What a freak they must think he is. Nobody'd understand.

'Earl. Are you with me?'

No answer.

'Take a deep breath,' the caller said. 'Please. Take a deep breath and relax. You're in control. You know what you're doing. Look how long you've fooled them. The best in the business.

San Francisco's finest. Hell, the FBI. Psychiatrists. Criminologists. You've done it. You know what to do. There's just this one little slip. The witness. And you can take care of her. They don't know you know about her.'

'It's a trick,' Earl said finally. 'Everything. Getting me out on bail. Cops showing up, leaving. You calling. It's a trick. Like I said before I don't even know what you're talking about.'

Highway One. Beyond Mill Valley, and then up the winding road. Julia Bateman's cobalt blue Miata caught flashes of sun and flashed them back in her eyes. The ocean on her left crashed against the rocks, but she could not hear the surf above the wind and the drone of the engine. However, the smell of the salt water was ominously familiar. Point Reyes. Tamales Point. Past Bodega Bay. Inland toward Monte Rio.

Escaping the sea. Rolling hills. Then the pines and the eucalyptus. New scents and intensified memories.

She would not turn back.

Perhaps she was foolish. But it was the only way she could face life with some modicum of control.

She made the cabin before dusk. Even so, it was dark and stale inside. The windows were closed. The heavy draperies she rarely ever closed were pulled tightly, even over the broad window beside the front door. The skylight had been boarded up. That was all that had been done since that night. But aside from the staleness of the air, the place was relatively clean and neat.

She checked the refrigerator and cabinets. She would have to get in some things. Julia was eager to leave while the breeze swept through the place. She would go into Gurneville to pick up some coffee, some fruit and yogurt.

While she was there, she added a bottle of dry sherry to the list.

It was dark by the time she got back. She was nervous again. She found the .32 in the desk drawer. Julia carried it with her as she checked the rooms, the closets, under the bed. Nothing had been disturbed.

She laughed. She sat still, bidding her mind to be still. She took a deep breath. The quiet she first sensed wasn't quiet at all. Night sounds. Bugs. Crickets mostly. The more she listened, the more it seemed they were turning up the volume.

She closed the sliding door to the back balcony, locked it. Pitch black now. She looked out of the floor length window beside the front door. Pitch black outside.

She poured a half glass of sherry.

All she really had to do was get through the night.

'Hello,' Earl said into the phone. He was out of breath from doing sit-ups. He knew who it was. He wouldn't admit it to the caller, but he welcomed the call.

'Earl?'

'Who else?'

'Earl, this is the only chance you've got. It's now or never.' There was silence. Earl didn't know what he should do. He wasn't going to hang up. Not right away. 'I can tell you how to get there. I can tell you how to get in. I can tell you where she'll be.' Another long pause. 'Earl?'

'What?'

'Do you hear me?'

'Yeah,' Earl said. He looked down at his body. Appraising it.

'Listen, let me tell you. If you hang up, I'll not call you again. And you can fry. You'll be a piece of bacon in a skillet.'

That wasn't the way they killed people in California, Earl thought, but he understood.

'Tell me.'

'Tell you what, Earl?'

'How to get there.'

'You going to do it?'

'I don't know. I gotta think some more. But if you don't tell me before I hang up, then I can't, can I?'

Gratelli had called the police up north, asked them to patrol in the winding roads around Julia's cabin.

Gratelli was sure Julia Bateman was not in any danger from the likes of Earl Falwell. Though not disqualified as the murderer in the other cases, Gratelli was not convinced he was the one to assault Julia, to beat her until she hung on the precipice of death.

Gratelli had his reasons for believing this. One of them was that the person who attacked Julia had engraved a rose on the inside of her thigh. A rose with a thorn on the stem. The serial killer, quite possibly Earl Falwell, had carved out a tulip. Something everyone had overlooked. In the beginning, someone called it a 'rose.' And it became a 'rose,' until Earl corrected them. Now, suddenly, the 'rose' had a thorn? Had Earl added the detail on his own? Not likely.

Who else had access to the intimate details of the victims who might also have a personal motive? Seidman surely did. A jilted lover.

The call Julia Bateman received while Gratelli was there was from David Seidman. She had blown him off again. If it was to happen it could very well be tonight. Then again, if by some long shot Earl Falwell was the one who attacked Julia Bateman, how would he get back to the scene? His car was still impounded. He knew he was being watched. He had no way of knowing she was returning to the cabin.

Gratelli sat back in the large, overstuffed chair in his apartment, the one situated between the speakers of his stereo. He had already dropped the needle into the first groove of the LP. He wasn't sure if he was patient enough this evening to wait for the voice of Placido Domingo to transport him to another plane of existence.

It was almost as if someone switched on a light inside Earl Falwell's head. He was awake. Seriously awake. His body seemed to pulse with electricity. His mind was clear. He knew what he was going to do. It was a little different than before. They all had been, since prison. Since Cobra. A cycle had been broken. Another had begun. He had no idea what path he was on, but even that was somehow exciting.

It wasn't the sad longing that would lead him to the young street girls. It wasn't the cold, bitter and immature desire for physical satisfaction that drove him to rape and kill the young man. What he discovered was his own world. The world of the others had always confused him. Their lives. Their needs. Their rules. They were right. He was stupid. Now it didn't matter.

He would not be caught again. Not in the daily traps set by ordinary people. Not in prison. He would have none of it. He would kill the woman. And once he found him, Earl Falwell would kill the caller.

*   *   *

An irritating ringing intruded upon Domingo's aria.
'Yes?' Gratelli said.
'Seidman is walking his dog.' It was Paul Chang.
'His dog?'
'A little white terrier of some sort. Doesn't seem to be in a hurry. Got his slippers on.'
'I appreciate you doing this for me,' Gratelli said.
'Sure, but it's really for Jules.'
'I know, call me if things change.'

TWENTY-SEVEN

S leep came reluctantly and without commitment. Julia's mind hovered around consciousness in a stark, gray place. The dream was more like a vision because she understood the shadowy hallways and the opaque windows were not real. Neither were the shapes of transparent draperies that danced in an invisible wind.

Julia was cold. She crept back into consciousness long enough to pull the comforter from her feet up, over her body, and over her shoulders. Slipping back into the vision, Julia felt the heavy down comforter. It folded over her like the wings of the dark angel.

Earl Falwell pegged the burgundy Oldsmobile parked down the street, off Stanyan. He knew GM products backward and forward. He knew he could get in and get it started.

Paul Chang called Gratelli, reported that David Seidman had gone to bed. Alone. Or possibly with his terrier. He would hang out a while longer.

The black asphalt drive still held a touch of the day's heat. Earl could feel it through the soles of his bare feet. His clothes were stacked neatly beside him as he crouched naked a few feet from the glass window.

The night sky held only half a moon. Even so, there were shafts of light spiking through the holes in the scented pine. In the streaks of gold light Earl could see a clear, slight shimmering of the California fog and feel its fine mist on his flesh. There was a sense of the universe pulsing. And gradually Earl felt himself become part of it.

At least for the moment, Earl had shrugged off any sense of himself, that which had a history or a future. This self that was the culmination of all that preceded the moment. Inside, beyond the glass, was not a witness, but prey. Even that wasn't a thought now, but the beginning of the act.

Suddenly the universe went quiet, empty. All of his muscle and bone and flesh were part of a single, sustained movement. Earl's body lunged at and through the glass, but not before a moment of recognition. Seeing himself, however faintly in the reflection of the moonlight against the sheet of glass – powerful, naked, crashing into himself.

Julia heard the crash. It seemed to be at a distance. Yet she knew it wasn't. It was near. Someone had come for her. She could not move. She attempted to scream. It came out a whisper. She felt herself slipping, sinking through the mattress. Something was wrong, dreadfully wrong. She tried to move her hand from beneath her and toward the nightstand. It inched at a horrifically slow pace.

A large white dog was in the hallway, teeth clenched on drapery. The head twisted on its thick muscular neck, ripping, tearing the fabric from the wall.

Julia was caught in her dream, in the hallway, trapped under the drapery, under her comforter, under her wings. There was the smell, but it wasn't coming from outside, but inside. Inside the mattress. 'Oh Christ,' she whispered, murmured. It was to her the smell of death.

Finally, fingertips touched the hard cool steel of the revolver. The gray vision receded, bringing her back into the darkness of her room.

The .32 was in her hand as she slipped off the bed. She could make out a form that was only slightly darker than the darkness in the hallway.

She could hear it breathing. She fired. The hall lit yellow, then white. She could see the golden, naked body with rivers of blood flowing from the face, shoulder and arms, crash against the wall. She waited. She could hear breathing. A heartbeat. The attacker's or her own? Her eyes scanned the darkness.

Though she doubted her perception, an amorphous form seemed to be moving toward her, she fired again. Another flash. The face was one she could almost recollect, but one she was sure wasn't the one. She wasn't sure how she knew that, but she knew. She sensed the form closer to her. She wasn't sure how she knew that either. Perhaps the breathing. She fired again. The light flashed, another single strobe flash that showed a body going down, face up, eyes open, looking toward her. Startled.

Julia stood in the dark, too scared to move. She understood that she might be in shock. She took a deep breath, moved back toward her room and flicked the hall switch. After the flash of the gun, the hall light seemed dim and muddied. What it revealed was the body of a naked man, sprawled on his belly, one arm reaching out toward her. Julia was surprised how the limp body seemed so relaxed, so much at peace. His youth didn't escape her notice. The attacker's body, at least from this angle, was beautiful . . . beautiful in the way wild animals are beautiful. Could be a freshly killed leopard robbed of its soul, leaving only its rich, sleek, elegantly formed body behind.

It was light by the time Gratelli arrived. The call from the local police he had advised earlier was a courtesy. The attack Gratelli suggested to the local police 'might' happen, did. Gratelli walked through the cop cars, ambulances, news trucks and the like up to the front porch. The front door was open. The window beside it was shattered. Jagged edges of glass had captured some blood. There was a small swarm of cops and cameras outside.

Inside, more cops and some guys who looked like medics bustled in the living room and the hall. There was no one to administer medicine to. According to the phone call, the intended victim was alive and physically unharmed. The attacker was dead. Julia Bateman was on the sofa near the front door, staring blankly at the broken window. Gratelli was glad she recognized him and had nodded. That meant she was in pretty decent shape. Considering.

'Everything is the way it was,' a local cop said. 'Gratelli?'

'Yeah.'

'What is this? Second time for the victim. This the strangler?'

Gratelli shrugged.

'She's a survivor, isn't she?' the cop continued. 'She got him back, the bastard. That don't happen often.'

Gratelli went toward the body. He dropped down on his haunches, bones creaking. He lifted one shoulder to get a better look at the face. It couldn't be; but it was. Earl Falwell. The boy's face and body was severely lacerated, but it was clearly Earl Falwell. Gratelli shook his head. How wrong could he have been?

'Crashed through the glass back there,' said the same cop who had followed Gratelli to the body, 'like a damned dumb animal or something. You know how those birds crash against the glass thinking it's sky or something? Weird shit.' The narrow hallway was crowded and the traffic was irritating to Gratelli, who wished he had his own people there. 'Car around the bend,' the cop continued, 'back in some trees. Stolen.'

'Thanks,' Gratelli said. He wanted the guy to go away. He wanted to think. How could he have been so wrong?

'You were up here before?'

'Yeah.' Gratelli answered, hoping the local officer would pick up on the impatience in his voice.

'Yeah, I thought so. With the other cop. I remember him clearly. Big fellow. Irish. Irish name, anyway.'

'Right.'

'How's he doin'?'

'Resting,' Gratelli said. 'You mind if I ask Ms Bateman some questions?'

'No, go ahead. This is the guy, right? This is really a better way, you know? Celebrity trial. Go on forever. Cost a fortune. He's dead. It's done. Over.'

'Could be.' Gratelli said, rising up slowly, his knees hurting, making that sound again. He looked down at the body again, thinking how fit the youth was. Strange who dies, who lives.

'Whaddya mean, "could be"? You don't think this guy is the strangler?'

'Oh, probably,' Gratelli said.

'Up here. There'll be a circus around here for months.'

'I'll be out of your way pretty soon.'

'Take your time, Inspector,' the cop said. 'Listen, the guy slipped by us. We had a car up here.'

'It's all right. It's all over now,' Gratelli said as he moved toward the sofa and its sole, lonely, frightened occupant.

'You OK?' Gratelli asked Julia Bateman.

'I don't know. I think so.'

'Did he say anything to you?'

'No.'

'You recognize him?'

'No. There's just something funny.'

'What?'

'I don't know how to explain it,' she said.

'Tell me. Doesn't matter what it is.'

'It's silly,' she said.

'Silly works for me,' he said.

'It's not who I expected.'

'Who did you expect?'

'I don't know.' She shook her head, gave Gratelli a feeble, hopeless kind of smile. 'I just thought I'd know who it was when I saw him.'

'You think the person who attacked you the first time was someone you knew?'

'No. I don't know. I half expected someone to come. I didn't know who it would be. But I kind of thought I'd know. Somehow, I'd have some form of recognition. I don't know this man,' she said emphatically.

'Funny you should think that,' Gratelli said. 'He's quite a surprise to me, too.'

Paul came in. Gratelli had called Paul when he was halfway to Forestville. They made good time.

Paul knelt in front of Julia. 'It's over now,' Paul said.

'Thanks for coming,' Julia said. 'Can I go back with you?'

'Of course.'

She walked toward the door. 'I think I'll just have the cabin burned.'

The protocol had been worked out. The Gurneville police chief would hold a news conference at nine a.m. in Gurneville. They would talk about that specific incident, not the broader implications. The San Francisco police chief would talk at ten a.m. in San Francisco and would address the serial angle. Julia Bateman would be in seclusion. 'Understandably, she is in need of a little peace and quiet,' would be the phrase they would use.

The *San Francisco Examiner* finally got some benefit being an afternoon paper. The headline: Bay Strangler Dead?

Police today confirmed that Earl Falwell, 22, was shot and killed early this morning in a cabin near Gurneville. Gurneville police believe Falwell broke into the cabin owned by San Francisco private investigator Julia Bateman in order to kill the woman whom he had attacked earlier this year.

San Francisco police did not deny the allegation that Bateman, left for dead in the earlier attack, had been marked in a manner consistent with at least eight victims of the so-called Bay Strangler. Police did not elaborate on the mark nor did police from either department confirm that Earl Falwell was responsible for the other killings.

However, Lt. James Thompson said that the serial killings had stopped during Earl Falwell's incarceration between March 2 and May 5. Bateman was attacked shortly after his release. Thompson also said that a witness could put an automobile similar to the brown Camaro owned by Falwell on Twin Peaks at the site and time of the killing of Sandra Ellington, one of the victims. Falwell had a record of deviant sexual behavior and violent crimes and had just been released on bail. He had been charged with brutally beating a co-worker.

Bateman reportedly fired three shots into the body of Earl Falwell who was found nude at the scene. Medical examiners on the scene said that there were other cuts and abrasions on Falwell's body. Police would not speculate why Falwell was naked, but indicated the cuts may have occurred during entry through a glass window. Falwell's clothing was found outside, neatly stacked. A stolen car was found a few hundred feet away. Bateman could not be reached for comment.

The story continued, reconstructing all previous related killings. It included discussions of the original psychological profile, quotes from medical examiners, family members of the victims and police. Investigators kept the secret of the rose tattoo from print, though the fact that the bodies had been 'tattooed' was now mentioned for the first time.

When the *Chronicle* came out the next morning, the media relations people from the police department were already suggesting that it was only a matter of time before Earl Falwell would be linked to all the other murders.

However, the quest for Julia Bateman had begun.

TV and radio ran features on Bateman, though none of them knew anything about her. They couldn't even come up with a picture. She was already being referred to as the 'tough P.I.'

'Thanks for being helpful,' Bradley said. 'You hate me?'

'No,' Paul said. He thought about adding, 'because I never really loved you.' It was true; but there was no point now. 'I packed your diary . . . your uh . . . chapbook. It's in with your leathers. And your other art is in the portfolio.'

'Thanks,' Bradley said.

There was something else on his mind, Paul thought. He didn't want to probe. He really wasn't interested.

'Have you decided? Are you going to continue modeling or become an artist?' Paul was escorting Bradley to the door with conversation. It was better than just asking him to leave. It was more like, here are your bags, Bradley, do you have to go? Let me get the door for you.

'I'll have to do something when my day in the sun is over.'

'Yeah,' Paul said.

TWENTY-EIGHT

Back at the office, Gratelli made three phone calls. First, he wanted a list of calls made to Earl Falwell in the last month. Second, he wanted to know who made bail for Falwell. Third, he set up a time with the perfumer the guy at Macy's recommended.

Number two was the first to yield some results. The bonding company was less than a block away.

'Cash,' said Toby Carbondale, the bondsman who handled Earl Falwell's release.

'Who from?'

'Messenger,' Carbondale said. He sensed Gratelli wouldn't be happy. 'A kid comes in with a box. I sign for it. Inside are cash and a note. Note says it's to free Earl Falwell. No signature. The money's right. Actually, it's a little better than right. A tip, I figure.'

'A messenger service?'

'Probably, one of those bicycle guys. I didn't pay any attention. Frankly, I was too busy worrying about whether some disgruntled son of a bitch was sending us a bomb.'

'You get a receipt?'

'Just signed a sheet.'

'You still have the box?'

'No. I'm sorry. Had no idea this kid was connected. We have no way of knowing.'

'Isn't it pretty unusual for someone to send you cash, to operate like this?'

'Real rare. It's happened before. Why isn't it my business? Like I said, I'm sorry. But the dude got caught, right? It's all over.'

'The note?'

'No. Nothing on it worth keeping. No return address, if that's what you mean. Typed.'

Gratelli shook his head.

'Wait a minute, trash hasn't gone out this week. Could have the box and the note.'

The box did reveal the messenger service. The note was printed by a laser printer. He took them both. Fingerprints? He doubted it. The messenger service wasn't much help. Earl Falwell's get-out-of-jail-free donor had left the box and a note with more than enough money to handle the delivery. They were left on the counter of the service. Whoever left the package and instructions had managed to come and go unseen.

'What?' Gratelli said. Most of the calls to Earl Falwell in the past thirty days came from public telephones. The selection was random. The sites were scattered about the Bay area, mostly around North Beach and Chinatown. One was from the Hall of Justice on Bryant. McClellan's direct line. One was from Tennessee. It hadn't been identified.

Gratelli dialed the number.

'Mildred O'Donnell, Valley Farms, how may I help you?'

'I'm not sure you can,' Gratelli said. 'I'm trying to get some information on Earl Falwell.'

'Earl?'

'Yes, do you know him?'

'My grandson. Why are you asking about him?'

'I was trying to locate him,' Gratelli lied. He hadn't prepared himself to deliver the news of Earl Falwell's death and the circumstances surrounding it.'

'He's in San Francisco. Is something wrong?'

'What kind of farm do you have there, ma'am?'

'It's not really a farm. We sell bulbs, flowering bulbs.'

'Like what kind?'

'Lilies, iris, daffodils.'

'Tulips?'

'Oh yes. Award winners. Our best sellers.'

'And roses?'

'No, no. Roses don't grow from bulbs, Mister . . .'

'Gratelli. Sorry to have bothered you.'

'It had to be Earl,' Paul said to Julia while he fixed coffee. It was his apartment. Paul sat at the small kitchen table. Julia moved into the other room. 'Had to be,' Paul repeated. Julia looked out the window. The second floor was high enough to see over the single story buildings across Hayes. She could see the wide expanse of the hills rolling south out of the city and the square stair-stepped houses that dotted them.

'I've always liked this view,' she said.

'You're not listening,' Paul said.

'I am.'

'You want this to keep going on? How else could it be? The guy was connected to the killings long before you. He comes back. How else would he know where you live? You want to think that the killer is out there. You want to live that way for the rest of your life?'

'Paul,' she said, urging him to understand. 'I can't help what I feel. You want it to be Earl so that it's all over.'

'Don't you?'

'Of course, I do. Maybe I don't. Maybe I'm crazy. Maybe I like all this. Who knows?'

'I'm sorry. Explain it to me.'

'I doubt if I can in a way that makes sense. I don't know that I know the killer. I just believe that I would know him if I were as close to him as I was to Earl-what's-his-name.'

'I'm still confused.'

'You're so cute when you're confused,' Julia said smiling.

'Being Chinese, I thought I was inscrutable.'

'Cute and inscrutable. Maybe inscrutably cute. Or cutely inscrutable.'

'You're so calm,' Paul said.

'Listen, I've spent months being a basket case. I'm not sure I have anything to lose.'

'Your life,' Paul said, 'if you're right.'

'You know,' she said, 'I'm not sure I mind so much the idea of dying. I just mind like hell the idea of this sonofabitch making the decision.'

'The top notes are your first experience,' said Daniel Alexander, a young black man who seemed to enjoy his task – to explain the nature of scent to a San Francisco homicide inspector. 'The middle note is the second experience, a second scent if you will.'

'So,' Gratelli said, trying to form a question while seated self-consciously in an ornate chair on the other side of an equally ornate table from Mr Alexander in what appeared to be some sort of parlor. 'If someone smelled butter . . .' Gratelli said, waiting for some sort of confusion to overtake the perfumer's calm, unlined face.

'Butter yes,' he said, smiling. 'Absolutely. Not at all odd. Was there another scent? Leather perhaps?'

Gratelli was stunned. 'Yes. Leather.'

Mr Alexander nodded. He rose from his seat, went to a large, wall cabinet and brought out some bottles and dabs of cotton. 'Here,' he said, letting the cotton absorb a tiny bit of clear liquid. 'Smell.'

'Something citrus,' Gratelli said.

'Take the scent in more slowly, for a longer duration. Do you smell butter, perhaps leather? It's subtle, but you can pick it up if you try to distinguish different qualities of the scent, allow yourself to discriminate. Maybe we can call it the levels.'

'Yes, butter.' Gratelli kept breathing it in. 'Yes, leather, for Christ sake.' Gratelli was amazed.

'Hmmm hmmmn,' Daniel Alexander said. 'It's quite like wine. If you pay attention, there's much more than just one level of taste.' He smiled at Gratelli's amazement. 'In scents, you see, there's a top note, a middle note and most probably a bass note, which lingers for quite some time. Even though scent is altered by the human pheromones through perspiration, there are characteristics of some colognes and perfumes that remain pretty consistent.'

'So is this the only cologne that has this leather and butter combination?'

'No. In fact this pairing of scents used to be quite common, but it is rare enough today. It is also quite costly.'

'Really?' Gratelli said.

'What you are picking up is ambre gris. It's only found in tropical seas. All of it is a bit morbid in a way. The sperm whale eats octopus, you see. The whale, however, is unable to digest the beaky matter of the octopus and therefore that particular matter results in intestinal calculi that is eventually ejected by the whale. It's found floating in the sea. It is soluble in alcohol and the essence is employed in the blend with other perfumes to give the scent a lasting property.'

'How lasting?'

'Centuries.'

'What?'

'Depending on the amount and the way it's blended. It clings to woven fabrics. It's been detected in material more than three hundred years old.'

'You're kidding.'

'No. Of course, the wearer adds his or her own special, very individual touch. Essentially perspiration. The very thing that people try their best to disguise. If George Washington had worn it, I suppose a good bloodhound could still determine which beds he really slept in.'

'What about washing? Can it be detected after the stuff has been washed or dry cleaned.'

'That's what they say. I haven't run any tests myself. It's part of the lore, though. I suspect it's true.'

'Which perfumes use this . . . substance?'

'Many of the expensive, fine scents.'

'Perfumes I can find at Macy's, Nordstrom?'

'A few. Certainly the custom-made perfumes and colognes.'

'Custom made?'

'Of course.'

'Like suits?'

'Yes. Custom scents. Designed for the desire or the need or the whatever of the individual. That's what I do. One gets

tailored clothing, handmade shoes, and made to order perfumes.
Why not?'

'I don't know why not,' Gratelli said.

'No way,' Lieutenant Thompson said. His gray eyes refused to
meet Gratelli's.

'I can't do my job,' Gratelli said.

'Too weird. You have to have more than that.'

'If I had enough to convict, I wouldn't need a search warrant
right now. I can't be sure without it.'

'He's the next D.A. for Christsakes,' Thompson said.

Gratelli knew what he was asking. And he knew who he was
asking, a cop who was successful by avoiding any and every
controversy and staying out of the way of those with political
power – any kind of power.

'I need it.'

'What have you got, Gratelli?'

'What I said. Motive? Julia Bateman frustrated him. They
dated. He wanted more. She gave him nothing. He wanted
something. She gave him nothing. Does he have the means?
He's fit enough. Knew enough about the case to make it look
like the others. Knew how to work the system. Who else knew
that?'

'You're assuming there was another murderer. And even if
that's true, that others did know the details. Knew about the
rose tattoo.'

'But it wasn't a rose after all. It was a tulip. Only Julia's
thigh had a rose and that's because her attacker got it wrong.
A copy cat who copied it wrong.'

'A small thorn? That's the difference? That's what you're
basing this on?'

'Opportunity? David Seidman knew where her cabin was.
Knew how to get there. And knew she was there. Both times.'

Thompson rubbed his eyes, let out a breath. Could have been
a sigh of defeat. Could have been the punctuation that would
end the discussion.

'No.' He said it with a shrug. 'I don't want you talking to
him. This is crazy. He didn't do it. Earl Rogers Falwell did it,
dammit. And he's dead. The case is over, Gratelli. We've got
other fish to fry. And we've got you a new partner. Get a life.
Get going!'

Thompson clapped his hands twice.

We have closure, Gratelli thought.

It made sense. Thompson and, perhaps his superiors, believed that Mickey McClellan might have had something to do with it. Now it didn't matter. Both Mickey and Earl were dead. Nothing could come back and bite them in the butt. The case was closed. The media was going silent. There weren't any trials to mess everything up again.

TWENTY-NINE

'I just want some oversight,' Gratelli said.

David Seidman sat on the sofa. It was a cool night. There was a fire in the fireplace. A Jack Russell terrier sat beside David, alert and looking at Gratelli with a friendly gaze.

'The guys from Quantico can help you better than I can. Tell you the truth, Inspector, I'd have had a helluva time prosecuting Earl Falwell with the evidence we have . . . I mean for all the murders. I'm sure he did them. But the only thing we really have to hang it on is the fact that he came back. That's pretty good, actually.'

'The mark?' Gratelli offered.

'The rose?'

'Yes. What do you make of it?'

'I don't know. I'm not the right person for this kind of thing. I'm flattered that you asked. I've not done any serial killers. Usually there's something. A mark is not uncommon. A trophy is not uncommon, but you haven't found any, right?'

'Not yet. How much do you know about the cases?'

'Why do I get this feeling you're not here in search of my prosecutorial wisdom and vast knowledge of the criminal mind?' He smiled warmly.

'I don't know,' Gratelli said. 'You mind if I use the bathroom?'

'One through there,' Seidman said. 'Can I fix you a drink, while you're freshening up?'

'Sure,' Gratelli said. 'Any old whiskey will do. Scotch. Irish. Italian.'

'Italian whiskey taste anything like Italian beer?' Seidman
asked. 'Is there such a thing as Italian whiskey?'

The bathroom yielded no bottles of anything. This was the guest
bathroom. If Seidman had colognes and aftershave, they would
be in the upstairs bath or dressing room or bedroom,
whatever.

Seidman's home was nice. Expensive. Anyone who owned
a single family dwelling had to have some money in this city.
Having a house slightly larger than modest in a neighborhood
slightly more than the usual still meant that the wealthy David
Seidman wasn't showing off his wealth. His clothing was probably off the rack too. Nice stuff. But off the rack. Would he
invest in an expensive, custom-made perfume?

'So,' Seidman said, giving Gratelli a glass a quarter filled with
caramel-colored liquid. 'I'm still a suspect.' Seidman smiled.
'Jilted boyfriend? That it?'

'Listen, this isn't formal . . .'

'I know, they want this case closed and all the bodies attrib-
uted to a crazy dead criminal. Good for the force. And they
need this one, don't they? They have other bodies in embarrassing places.'

'Yes.'

'This is good for you too. City cop, first on the scene. What's
eating you?'

'This one doesn't fit,' Gratelli said.

'This is the only one that *does* fit, Inspector. The others are
speculation. I mean we've got a classic return to the scene of
the crime.'

'You followed this closely?'

'Sure, after the attack on Julia, I sure did.'

'Why did you call it a "rose"?'

'That was what it was, wasn't it?'

'But why did you call it that? Did you see it?'

'No. Somebody told me.'

'Who?' Gratelli asked.

'I don't know. Paul Chang, maybe.'

'Are you sure?'

'No, I remember. It was your partner.'

'Mickey?'

'Yes.'

'He told you?' Gratelli was puzzled. 'When?'

'I stopped in Homicide. He was at the desk. Why?'

'Why?' Gratelli asked.

'I wanted to know. Wouldn't you? It was Julia. And I promised Paul I'd make sure the case didn't get lost.'

'Your friend, Paul?'

'I know what I've said about him. Sometimes I'm an ass. I know he cares about her and I didn't want him playing amateur detective in a murder. Anyway, your partner said something about it being a rose. He'd just talked to the medical examiner. He asked me some questions. Wanted to know about her habits. I told him. I think he was checking me out too. Actually, I think the case got to him.'

'He didn't tell me that. Didn't write it down.'

'I can't help you there.'

'Did he tell you how the girls died?'

'Strangled, right?'

'That's what he told you?'

'Yes.'

'I don't understand why you two met. He didn't tell me,' Gratelli said more to himself than to Seidman.

'I don't know what to tell you about that,' Seidman said. 'You're pretty good at the questions. The girls weren't strangled, were they? And obliquely, what you're telling me is that the mark isn't a rose. Am I right?' There was a pause. 'Inspector, I'm not an idiot when it comes to cross-examination. How did they die?'

'Do you happen to have an aspirin, Mr Seidman? This must be Italian whiskey.'

'Sure, I've got some upstairs.'

Gratelli followed him up, but was passed by the terrier. The three went into the bathroom.

'Nice house,' Gratelli said, watching as Seidman opened the wooden cabinet. There were bottles, but Gratelli – during his brief glance – was unable to confirm anything that looked like a cologne bottle or anything exotic.

'It's private. It's quiet. No cars.'

'Keep you in shape, being in the middle of this hill.'

'Yep. I work out a bit too. Otherwise I'd never make it. You see some of these older women up and down these steps

every day. At least once. It's good for them. They'll live to
ripe old ages. Here, some Excedrin. Good for headaches.
Advil?'

'Excedrin,' Gratelli said. The bath was pretty ordinary as
baths go. The upstairs was small. Two bedrooms up. A dressing
room wasn't likely.

'You live pretty modestly, Mr Seidman. A bachelor. I understand you're wealthy. You'd think you'd have Jacuzzis, walk-in
closets, one hundred pair of shoes and one hundred and twenty
dollar an ounce cologne.'

'You've got me confused with . . .'

'With who?'

Seidman smiled. 'With your caricature of the rich. Then
again, nothing innocent comes out of your mouth, does it? You
seem interested in my medicine cabinet at the moment. Why
don't you just tell me what you're looking for, Inspector. It'd
be easier.'

'I thought you'd never ask. Cologne, Mr Seidman.'

'Some here,' Seidman said, opening the cabinet again. 'Some
by the shower.'

Gratelli investigated.

'I'm not much for scents,' Seidman continued, bringing a
gold and silver container that bore the name Armani. 'Most of
the time I go without. I use this when I feel a little insecure.'
He smiled. 'It was a gift.'

Gratelli sniffed. The case held some Farenheit aftershave in
a spray bottle. The inspector found nothing similar to butter or
leather in either one. Then again, he wasn't an expert.

'So that's what they mean when they say the "police are
sniffing around"?'

'Yes. But it's only recently I learned to sniff properly.'

'Listen. Tell me what you're on to, here, Inspector. I'll help.
Tell me how I can help. If there's a killer out there, I want him
as badly as you do.'

'You knew she went up there when she did, didn't you?'

'Yes, I did. I wanted to go up with her. I was worried. I
practically begged. She took it as my just wanting to mend the
relationship. Probably was. What can I say? I loved her. Still
do. Why would I kill someone I love?'

'A lot of that going around though, isn't there?' Gratelli
asked.

'Yes. There is. I keep forgetting I'm talking to a policeman.'
'You haven't forgotten that for one minute, have you?'
'No,' David Seidman said. 'Not for a minute. If you are
waiting around for me to confess, it's not going to happen. I'm
serious. Let's work together. I can put some people on it. You're
probably officially off the case, aren't you?'
'Yes. You knew that too.'
'True. Word gets around.'
'You probably knew it before I did.'
'Don't fight me. Use me,' Seidman said.

Gratelli didn't have a chance to use Seidman. In less than a
week, the task force judged Earl Falwell to be the sole killer
of eight of the girls and Julia Bateman's attacker and everybody
who had to buy into it bought into it. Julia Bateman's file was
closed along with the others.

The serial killer had become old news. The police chief was
becoming big news because of the high society, big-time political connections to the body found in the car in St Francis
Woods. The body and the case were still in the deep freeze
waiting justice or, at the least, disposition.

The fall opera had opened. It was Gratelli's reprieve. He
missed opening night on purpose. He wasn't interested in the
minor spectacle of the first gala of the season. Gratelli went to
the opera as most people went to the movies. Often and without
fanfare, with the expectation that he'd be entertained, lifted
from reality for two hours or so. Pure escape. The difference
might be that he was destined to see the same operas over and
over again. There were very few new ones. And those few he
didn't like. At least he would see each old opera anew; different
sets, different talent, different interpretation. That gave him
comfort. Tonight, *Rigoletto*. He'd seen it a half dozen times.
Maybe more. Once in Milan at the *Teatro Alla Scalla*. The rest
here over the years.

At intermission, Gratelli was convinced of two things. One,
he had never been so hot. The city was suffering from one of
its occasional heat waves. Two, this was as good a *Rigoletto* as
he'd ever seen, including the one in Milan. This was an appropriate dark and brooding performance. It mirrored his mood.

Thaddeus Maldeaux was in the lobby. A young woman, girl
perhaps – someone who had the waifish charm of the young

Calvin Klein model reclining on a sofa – stood near Maldeaux's arm and seemed to be the sole object of his attention. The other two in the party looked more art than finance. A slightly bohemian man with a beard and a younger man with longish hair whose opera attire consisted of a white t-shirt and a pair of blue jeans.

In one swoop, Maldeaux pulled a cream-colored silk handkerchief from the side pocket of his dark suit coat and ran it across his forehead, back of his neck, and over his chin. He slipped it back in his jacket pocket.

The lights flickered and the crowd went to their seats. Gratelli's eyes followed Maldeaux. Maldeaux sat with the two men. The waif was down from them, third row center, apparently by herself.

Gratelli would listen to the opera now, but he was distracted. His eyes were on Maldeaux.

Gratelli had probably brushed against, bumped elbows with, or passed the sugar to any number of celebrities he didn't know. North Beach was and is a magnet for the rich and famous. And for the poor and famous as well. There were tourist traps here for the tourists. But there were legitimate landmarks that were little more than utilitarian for Gratelli. To him, City Lights was merely the neighborhood bookstore. Specs and Tosca and the two dozen or so legendary bars and espresso joints may be haunted by beat literary ghosts and current literary and film folks, but Gratelli saw them as neighborhood bars and coffee shops. Sure, he knew there were national and international celebrities who could be seen at Enrico's and had been for decades. Gratelli rarely recognized them and felt no different for having passed close to their orbit.

So there was another reason for the excitement in Gratelli's bones as he angled toward Thaddeus Maldeaux inside Tosca. More of a crowd had gathered around him.

What Gratelli had to do would be difficult, but not impossible.

'Mr Maldeaux,' Gratelli said, squeezing between the handsome young heir and a dark man with a beard. Fortunately, the androgynous model type was pressing against Maldeaux's left side.

'Inspector?' Maldeaux said surprised. 'The man who refused one of my great breakfasts. How are you?'

'Good. Excellent. Saw you at *Rigoletto*,' Gratelli said, the slightly arthritic fingers of his left hand lifting the right flap of Maldeaux's suit jacket.

'And you followed me here?' Maldeaux asked with humor. 'What did I do? Talk too loud during an aria?'

'I live just up this way.'

'Didn't know you fancied opera,' Maldeaux said. He introduced Gratelli to the bearded man and handsome but aloof young man – a director and actor. Gratelli thought the names familiar, but couldn't place them exactly. The young man in jeans and ponytail was at the bar. No one introduced the girl.

Only after Gratelli pocketed the pilfered handkerchief did he see her clearly. See the smart and hungry eyes of a woman much older than her face.

'Opera is one of the few things I fancy. A sad statement actually. Opera is my TV,' Gratelli said.

'We were talking about the great tenors,' Maldeaux said. 'I bet you've heard them all, then.'

'A few.' Gratelli smiled. He was so unused to social pleasantry, his own smile felt evil and twisted. 'I was young and heard Jussi Bjorling. Franco Corelli. And what's his name, now, the new one, Carreras.'

'The new one,' Maldeaux laughed. 'How about Tito Gobbi?'

'Baritone, I think.'

'Yes, he was. He was.' Maldeaux said. 'See how quickly I get out of my depth.'

'I'm going to move along now,' Gratelli said, offering a paler version of his earlier smile. He wondered if Maldeaux would notice he had left the bar without so much as a drink.

THIRTY

He saw her from the cab. It was daybreak. The heat broke about four a.m. Now it was gray, damp. Julia Bateman was on Thaddeus Maldeaux's front doorstep. There was a blue Miata parked in front. Behind it was a Taurus. Maldeaux thought he recognized Gratelli behind the wheel.

'Julia?' Thaddeus Maldeaux said, coming up to her. 'My God.' He looked past her toward the street. No one else.

'Hello Thaddeus. Another late night?' The tone was clear.
He seemed surprised by it. 'Come in,' he said opening the
door and stepping inside. She followed. 'Should we . . . Inspector
Gratelli?'

'No. I've asked him to wait outside.'

'How are you?' Before she could answer, he suggested they
go out to the back. 'Can I get you something?' he asked as
they traversed the hall and passed by the door to the kitchen.
'Coffee?'

'No. That's all right.' She was curt, cool.

Outside it was damp. Cool.

He offered her a seat at one of the marble-topped tables, one
next to the pot dripping with luscious leaves and purple flowers.
The purple flowers were everywhere, filling the ledge, which
was formed by the short wall that enclosed nearly the entire
balcony. The only opening was for the stone stairway that led
down on to the back lawn.

Julia didn't sit. She didn't say anything.

'I'm glad you're here, Julia. But I've got to confess I don't
know why you're here. You've been ignoring me. I
assumed . . . well . . . You don't look like you want to be here.
Is there some way I can help you?'

'No.'

'What?'

'Here,' she said, pulling out the handkerchief, letting it drop
on the table.

Maldeaux picked it up.

'What's this?'

'This is why I'm here. To return your handkerchief. See you
without your mask on. You needed to do it just once, didn't
you? One more experience in your search? To see what it was
like to kill someone while having sex? Afraid you'd miss some
life experience that you were no doubt entitled to because you
are you.'

'What are you talking about? Has something happened?'

'I will never forget that scent.'

Maldeaux took the handkerchief, brought it up to his nose.
He didn't answer.

'Well, you failed.'

Maldeaux shrugged. He had a little boy's sadness on his face.
'I've failed what?'

'I'm alive. You killed no one.' She wondered what was wrong with her. Every man . . . What did it matter now?

'You think . . .'

'I know. And I don't even have to ask why. The sad thing is you'll never be convicted of it. Your money, your power, your charm. Not to mention the fact that you were a pretty clever rapist. Left nothing behind but your scent. So lingering I could never, ever forget it. Yet so insubstantial no one would give it a thought.'

'Julia . . .'

'Shut up. And you sent a boy to finish your job. Did you make him an expendable member of your staff?'

'Listen.'

'Are you going to pick someone else out? So you won't be deprived of the experience of killing during sex? Or will you finish me off?'

'Julia!'

'Or have you done it to someone else already? You strike me as someone who usually realizes his goals. A true achiever.'

Maldeaux's face turned cold. His stare was ice. Slowly he put the handkerchief back down on the table.

Both were startled at the movement up the steps.

'I was fertilizing the bulbs down by the steps,' said Mrs Maldeaux. 'I didn't want to interfere.' Her graceless form slowly climbed the stone steps to the balcony. She carried a white bag and a small silver trowel. Her face was ashen. From the look she gave her son, it was clear she had heard more than she had wanted. Her hand shook as she set the bag and trowel on the table.

'The lilies, the iris, narcissus and the tulips need some bone meal through the winter to flower well in the spring.' She touched Julia Bateman's wrist with a shy tentativeness. 'I'm terribly sorry.'

Mrs Maldeaux went into the house.

Thaddeus Maldeaux seemed frozen for a moment.

'I'm not having much luck with women lately,' he said, shaking his head in disgust or frustration. He looked at Julia Bateman. Shrugged. Nothing else to do, the shrug said. Nothing could be done or said.

Her life changed. Before the attack, Julia had lived in the future.

Now she was tugged back to the past. Unfinished business. It would never be finished unless . . . Unless what? Until he finished the job? She wasn't frightened. But she was alert. And she was angry. All this thievery – of her time, of her mind, of her body, of her soul. Taken. He could never give it back. And he was never going to pay.

She was so close to falling in love with him. Perhaps she had. Boy, could she pick them. In the mirror, a sterner, tougher Julia Bateman looked back. She wondered, at times, if she could kill him. She'd played it out more than once.

But for the most part, she had settled in – back into her friends and activities. Movies with Paul on Monday nights. Aerobics with Sammie Cassidy on Tuesdays, Thursdays and Saturday mornings. That was as much physical therapy as fitness. She had gone with Gratelli to two operas. He had been appropriately fatherly, undemanding, informative and even funny. Dry, very dry humor. She had also reconnected to David. Just by phone, though. They had talked probably a dozen times. He'd lightened considerably. Said he was dating someone now. Someone he could get serious about. The old David was returning a lot faster than the old Julia.

Even so, she was surprised to see him. He had been waiting for her, in the landing, near the door to the exercise studio on Pine Street just off Fillmore. The light from the studio window flattened on the street in a small patch and a man stood at the edge of it.

'David?'

'Hi,' he said. His hair was mussed. He had a couple of day's growth of beard. Very unlike him. He looked forlorn. Maybe even a little down on his luck, judging by the clothes.

'What are you doing here?'

'I'm in need of a friend tonight,' he said.

'What's wrong?'

'I need advice about women,' he said, grinned. Shook his head.

'Women or a woman?'

'A woman. Yes,' he said. 'Can we go for a drive and talk?'

'Well . . .' She didn't have an excuse. Sammie hadn't shown up. Not totally unlike her. It was cold and dark and late. She had planned to walk back to her apartment. Still, she wasn't sure she wanted to be trapped into an evening with David. Buy some time, she thought. 'How did you know I was here?'

'Paul told me.'

'He did? Hmmmn. OK, for a little while. Maybe we could catch a drink or something. There are some places down on Hayes Street. I'd be nearly home.'

'I want to go somewhere quiet. Where we can talk. A little drive?'

'This isn't your car, is it?' Julia asked, as David opened the passenger door.

'Rental. Mine's in the shop.'

'You look different,' Julia said. 'You don't normally dress this way.' It started to seem odd to Julia. His happening there on the night Sammie didn't show up. A strange car. The slightly frayed outdoor look in clothing.

David Seidman laughed. 'I'm trying to relax a little. Enjoy life a little more. I'm trying not to be such an uptight asshole. And seeing what I look like in a beard. What do you think?'

'I don't know.'

'A little early yet. But I will probably shave it all off tomorrow morning.'

'So this girl is putting you through some changes?'

'Yes, you could say that.'

The car picked up the fog about the time they hit the Sunset district.

'Where are we going?'

'Ocean Beach. That OK? Just a few more miles. Quiet out there. Just the sound of the waves.' He patted her knee. 'And they don't make much noise anyway.'

'David, I'm just a little nervous. Could we go back.'

'Give me five minutes, OK. I really do need help.'

'OK,' she said hesitantly. 'Ummm . . . well, let's start. What's she like?'

'When we get there.'

'How's work?'

'Really good, Julia. The party's talked to me. There's no promises, but it could be prosecutor in two. Governor in six with some high visibility stuff in between.'

'Wonderful.' She tried to be enthusiastic, but fear made it increasingly difficult. She could talk with him. She'd get whatever weirdness was going on out in the open. By morning, she'd laugh about it. She was just being paranoid. That would be normal for someone who had gone through what she had gone through. Like the guy across Ivy Street. A moment of panic. She wasn't thinking rationally.

Visibility was nil. David had turned off the headlights, using only the parking lights. The windshield wipers kept a constant rhythm, brushing aside not drops, but a fine coat of mist.

'I don't like this,' Julia said.

'I'm not sure I do either,' David said. 'I was angry before. Even so, I didn't want you to see my face.' He could make out her face in the reflection of the dash lights. 'You're not surprised.'

'Too many already.'

He pulled a knife from his coat pocket, put it to her throat. 'Quiet now.' He reached down in the console and pulled out a telephone. He laid it on the dash and punched in the numbers.

There was a moment of quiet. Julia stared out into the gray nothingness that surrounded the car.

'Hello, Teddy?' There was a momentary pause. 'I need you out here. Ocean Beach, at the end of Balboa. To the right side. Be careful, it's foggy.' Another pause. 'It's the most important thing in my life. I need you. You'll see the tail lights.' He didn't wait for any more conversation. He disconnected.

'They will trace the call.'

'Not my phone. Not my call.'

'The scent. It's not yours.'

'No,' he said. He laughed. 'As many times as I screwed up on this one – you know, not killing you, getting the kid to try to finish you off. So fucking smart and so well planned and it didn't work either. And the thing that makes all of this work is that cologne. And that was an accident. Teddy had it in his locker that day. I tried it. I didn't pay any attention to it. That's what's so funny,' David said. 'I'm ten times smarter than Teddy. True. And he always gets it right. And I do all the right things. And it never turns out.' He laughs.

'David, you're destroying . . .'

'Oh shit, Julia. If I don't finish this and get it right, I will be destroyed.'

'So, you do me in and probably kill Ted . . .'

'Ted? Oh, that's nice. I didn't know you called him "Ted." Doesn't matter, Julia. Never mind. Yeah, I do you with the knife and shoot Teddy with your gun.'

'I don't have a gun.'

'Oh yes you do.' He pulled a gun from the pocket of the coat.

'It's not mine.'

David smiled. 'Of course it is. You ordered it. From Iowa. Came to you in Iowa.'

'What?'

'That's the part you don't know about. I had a gun sent to you – to a Post Office Box in Iowa – J. Bateman. I came there and picked it up.'

'You were in Iowa.'

'Oh yeah, Julia.'

'You were stalking me?'

'Doesn't seem all that serious compared to what's going to happen, does it? You know, you were going to kill yourself. Commit suicide in the cemetery. That fucking dog. Scared the shit out of me. Something weird going on there. So I was going to give it up. Just in case, though, I shipped the gun back to me here. Then you came back to San Francisco. I thought: What if you remember? What if Teddy, or Ted as you call him, remembers my using his cologne that day. It's fixed now. I've talked with Gratelli. He wanted to know the possibility of indicting Teddy with what little evidence you have. He believes Thaddeus is the murderer. He wants him. He came to me for help. This is going to be so easy.'

'David, you know this is deranged. Even you can understand how you're acting. Why don't we work on getting you well?'

'Oh Christ, Julia. You can do better than that. You kept me hanging for years. With you dead and with Teddy dead, I win. I win in so many ways.'

'David?'

'Be quiet.' He spoke softly, almost gently.

'You wouldn't let me go. Friendship, you kept saying. Right. You said that. You could handle it. We could be friends. Aside from Paul, I was the only close friend you had. I couldn't abandon you.'

'You know, Earl – the guy you killed – you know I probably was closer to him than anyone. Isn't that crazy?'

'It is. It is crazy,' Julia said. She was resigned.

'Yeah, well. I read his file. I read the police reports. His own parents wouldn't bail him out of jail. He had no friends. He lived in a little cave. Alone. You have no idea what world he could create for himself.'

'That wasn't your life, David. How could you compare yourself to him?'

'We're all just people. Some of us were just all by ourselves. I kept thinking . . .' He stopped and was quiet. 'You'd be surprised what worlds we can create for ourselves.'

'You sent him to his death,' Julia said.

'I gave him a fighting chance. I thought he'd do it. I would have put money on him.'

'You got him killed.'

'Yeah, I did that. After all, he wasn't innocent. I've done far worse.'

'What?'

'Court. Every day. The rich kids get off. Guilty or not. The poor ones, they do time. Guilty or not. And even if the system lets them slide out – and they do, they really do – they slide right back in a week or two later. They're dead men. They just don't know they're dead yet. Most of them. Ground up one way by their families or by the system. I sent one kid in, you know. Tried him as an adult. Raped, slaughtered. We were pretty sure he was dealin' drugs. Pretty sure, Julia. Enough to convict him. Didn't take much, of course. Who was going to defend him? We got him killed.'

'And you? Do you think you'll get off?'

'You've got a point, Julia.' He smiled. 'All these perfect plans. Every one of them got fucked up. They were good. Everybody thinks Teddy is so smart. Shit, he could never have come up with all of this. C'mon, let's get out. I don't want to be in the car when Teddy gets here.'

He left the car running, the lights on. Twenty feet on to the soggy sand, the wet, chilled air and the light was faint, dispersed. Just enough light for them to see each other. He had a knife in one hand, her forearm in the other.

'Limbo,' David said, looking around.

'David, maybe we can do something if you stop now. You've not killed anyone.'

'Yeah, is that right?'

'I'm not talking about what you've done as a prosecutor. You can't be held to that.'

'You're right about that. All perfectly legal.' In the silence, the waves seemed stronger. The air was wet and smelled of fish. 'You're so calm Julia. Around me, you're so calm. Teddy makes you nervous, doesn't he? He excites you.'

'David, listen before you take a step you cannot take back . . .'

'Your friend Sammie is dead. I killed her tonight. There's no going back. They'll think Thaddeus did it.' He shrugged. 'I'm surprisingly tidy. I've gotten better. I even left something of Teddy's there.'

'What?' Julia's mind was still on Sammie.

'She's dead.'

She tried to pull away. David pulled her back, the blade now at her throat, pulling in.

'Well, finally. I've upset you haven't I?'

She wasn't sure she'd ever feel that frightened again. The horror of that first night at the cabin. The horror of the second. Now, again. But fear gave way to numbness. Numbness gave way to an incredible, bottomless sadness. For herself. For her friend. For everyone. Even David Seidman, mad man.

She could see only a shadowed face. She barely recognized it. He was a stranger after all.

In between the black ocean out there lapping out the time of her existence and Ted's and the predators of the fog blind city in the other direction, she was right here, right now. Third time's a charm. A mad man determined to snuff out her life.

'It's sinking in, isn't it?' He took out a pair of handcuffs, slipped one cold, hard bracelet quickly and deftly around her wrist, then his. 'Don't want you slipping away.'

'David . . .'

'I want Teddy to see me kill you. Do you understand?'

'No.'

'Passion. You are dead to me. Have been for a while. But Teddy . . .' he said, pushing a handkerchief into her mouth.

They could have been standing at the end of the earth, at the end of time. Only cold grayness surrounded them.

'Waiting for Godot,' he said laughing. 'But unlike Godot, my god will come.'

Julia had no idea how much time had gone by. She had hoped someone would happen upon the beach. Not tonight. No sounds. Everything was lost and still and silent. Not even traffic on Highway One. She tried to find something to sense. Salt. She sensed salt; briny, fishy and now a hushing sound of the breakers somewhere out there. She wasn't even sure of the direction.

David Seidman was calm, patient. He seemed oblivious to the wait, to the cold.

At some point, the vague, formless light appeared. A car door slammed.

'David!'

'Over here, Teddy!' David put the point of the blade at her neck, under the chin. She felt the small hole as the blade went in, could feel the warm blood on her cool neck. She wasn't going to die yet. She thought maybe she could jerk David's arm. Jerk it at the right time to throw him off, give Ted a chance. But to move was to die. As long as she was alive, there was a chance for both of them.

'Where?'

'Follow my voice.'

'What is this?'

'You'll understand.'

'Too weird, David.'

'You'll understand, perhaps even appreciate it in a queer way.'

'David?'

'You're getting closer. Keep walking.' David moved behind Julia, brought the blade up to her neck with one hand, pushed the gun forward – in the direction of the voice. Footsteps in the damp sand made no sound.

An overcoat. A long, gray overcoat. A face. A damp face. Dark hair. Maldeaux.

'David? What is this?'

'Don't move, Teddy. Don't even raise an eyebrow.' There was a pause. Maldeaux said nothing. He didn't move. 'Very good. Very good, Teddy. Now, let me tell you a story. A short story. Very short. I am going to kill Julia, then you. Investigators will believe you killed her and then yourself . . . or if that gets too messy . . . that she got off a round before she died. You had come to finish the job. All done. About the happy ever after I don't know. Just "the end," you see?'

Seidman lifted the gun slightly, as if to make sure he was aiming correctly and the gun was moving down again, ready to settle in.

Julia felt the blade at her neck burrow in ever so slightly.

A flash of light, a flat loud crack.

For a moment, the three figures were frozen. Two in shock. One in death. David's knife fell to the sand. His body slumped down. The only sound was the crush of clothing as David

Seidman crumpled into the sand. Another blast of light and sound. David's gun, aimed out at the ocean, fired.

'I just didn't want to take a chance,' Gratelli said. He dropped down on one knee, his free hand steadying his body on the beach. 'My legs are like rubber.' He leaned over David Seidman, felt the neck for a pulse.

He acted like he didn't expect to find one.

'My God,' Julia said.

'I almost lost you twice in the fog out here,' Gratelli said to Maldeaux.

Julia looked puzzled.

'He's been following me for weeks,' Maldeaux said to her. 'Like you, he was sure it was me.'

Paul and a handsome blond fellow sat outside Cafe Claude's. The sun was out. The breeze was mild and held only a slight hint of a chill. They sipped coffee out of cups large enough to support a family of goldfish.

Gratelli had lunch at Brandy Ho's, a Chinese restaurant on the border between Chinatown and North Beach. He didn't know if he liked his new partner. That would take a while. But at least the new guy appreciated good food.

'Thank you for meeting me,' Maldeaux said to Julia. 'I felt as if we had some unfinished business.'

The maître d' took them through the dining room to the back, where the fenced courtyard held back the breeze, but allowed the immense spray of sunlight to warm the crowd of late lunchers and illuminate the bright red bougainvillea. There was a low tumble of conversations and the tinkling of wine glasses. Delicate sounds of violins and flutes filled the lulls of the human babble.

'How are you?' he asked as the waiter set the menus before them and disappeared.

'Doing OK,' she said. She knew her voice was flat. She was having trouble letting any feeling out. Not humor, not sadness, not anger. Julia actually felt all right . . . to the extent that she felt anything at all.

'You're remarkable,' he said.

She had absolutely no idea what to say to that.

Thaddeus paused for a moment. It was clear that he was giving something a lot of thought. Then he spoke. 'Are you getting any help?'

'Help?' she asked.

'With all this.'

'Paul is with me. We're getting the business going.'

'That's not what I mean.'

'I know. It will all work out.'

Thaddeus leaned over the table. 'You were attacked three times. You were terrorized. You killed a man. You saw another one shot in the head. I can't let you push all this aside like you sprained an ankle.'

'I know. I appreciate your saying it. That being said, I don't want to talk about it anymore. What's going on in your life?'

Thaddeus looked down at the table, then out over the crowd. The waiter came.

'White wine,' Thaddeus said to Julia. 'Something dry and light, you think?'

'That's fine,' Julia said.

'Pick out something,' Thaddeus said to the waiter, then to Julia with an obviously false smile. 'I like white wine before dark. Then red. How about you?'

'I never thought of it that way before.'

'The flowers are pretty, don't you think.'

'The flowers are pretty,' she said, a thin grin on her face.

'Really a nice day,' he said.

'Yes. Very nice.'

'I like the way you've done your hair,' he said.

'Thank you.'

'Did you hear anything about that new Monet exhibit?'

'No, I haven't. Where is it going to be?'

'I don't know. And don't care,' he said. 'I can't do this. I can't let you not live anymore. I don't want to be polite. I don't want us to be acquaintances.'

'We'll talk about it sometime,' Julia said. 'I promise.'

No need to talk. It was better not to. Words could betray her, make her vulnerable. She sensed her father inside her, the Bateman blood. So late to understand.

The waiter came by. They ordered. Both Julia and Thaddeus were quiet when he left. It wasn't awkward. Was this the end of it? Was this all it was ever meant to be? Meeting a bizarre intersection in each other's lives? Sharing such profound and frightening truths?

One day at a time. That's all it ever is, anyway. Life goes on.

A breeze swept across the tables. Awnings and umbrellas fluttered.